Fleur McDonald has lived and worked on farms for much of her life. After growing up in the small town of Orroroo in South Australia, she went jillarooing, eventually co-owning an 8000-acre property in regional Western Australia.

Fleur likes to write about strong women overcoming adversity, drawing inspiration from her own experiences in rural Australia. She has two children and an energetic kelpie.

Website: www.fleurmcdonald.com
Facebook: FleurMcDonaldAuthor
Instagram: fleurmcdonald
TikTok: Fleur McDonald (Author)

OTHER BOOKS
Red Dust
Blue Skies
Purple Roads
Silver Clouds
Crimson Dawn
Emerald Springs
Indigo Storm
Sapphire Falls
The Missing Pieces of Us
Suddenly One Summer
Where the River Runs
Starting From Now
The Shearer's Wife
Deception Creek
Broad River Station

DECTECTIVE DAVE BURROWS SERIES
Fool's Gold
Without a Doubt
Red Dirt Country
Something to Hide
Rising Dust
Into the Night

FLEUR McDONALD

Into the Night

ALLEN&UNWIN
SYDNEY · MELBOURNE · AUCKLAND · LONDON

First published in 2023

Copyright © Fleur McDonald 2023

Allen & Unwin
Cammeraygal Country
83 Alexander Street
Crows Nest NSW 2065
Australia
Phone: (61 2) 8425 0100
Email: info@allenandunwin.com
Web: www.allenandunwin.com

Allen & Unwin acknowledges the Traditional Owners of the Country on which we live and work. We pay our respects to all Aboriginal and Torres Strait Islander Elders, past and present.

 A catalogue record for this book is available from the National Library of Australia

ISBN 978 1 76106 647 4

Set in 12.4/18.2 pt Sabon LT Pro by Bookhouse, Sydney
Printed and bound in Australia by the Opus Group

10 9 8 7 6 5 4 3 2 1

To those who are precious and hold my heart

AUTHOR'S NOTE

Fool's Gold, Without a Doubt, Red Dirt Country, Something to Hide, Rising Dust and *Into the Night* are my novels that feature Detective Dave Burrows in the lead role. Eagle-eyed readers will know Dave from previous novels and it was in response to readers' enthusiasm for Dave that I wanted to write more about him.

In these novels, set in the late 1990s and early 2000s, Dave is at the beginning of his career. He's coming out of a rocky marriage with his first wife, Melinda, a paediatric nurse, as they've been having troubles balancing their careers and family life. No spoilers here because if you've read my contemporary rural novels you'll know that Dave and Melinda do separate, and Dave is currently very happily married to his second wife, Kim.

Dave is one of my favourite characters and I hope he will become one of yours, too.

PROLOGUE

2002

'Why do you have to be so bloody difficult?' Leo's hands shook as he tried to start the engine of the water pump. Pull out, yank, flick back in. It wound over once but didn't fire.

'Come on, you mongrel of a thing.'

This time the compression had built up inside the engine and the cord was tight. The starting rope was ripped from his hands as he pulled and the wooden handle hit him on the knuckles as it flew back inside the guard.

Leo wanted to swear, but instead, he stood up, wiped his brow and looked outside.

The pumphouse was set on the edge of a creek. White-painted corrugated iron for the sides and green for the roof, all dirty and peeling. A mirage shimmered across the hilly landscape, golden grass bent over in the heat, the air hot and oppressive, but still. Eerily still.

To the north, there was the normal build-up of huge white thunder clouds, accompanied by crickets chirping in anticipation of a cooler night.

Leo scoffed at the insects' hopefulness. The temperature hadn't dipped below twenty-five degrees during the hours of darkness in nearly two weeks and there was no reason why it would today.

Coffee, his kelpie, was laid out flat on the back of the ute, puffing under the sun. Coffee in colour, coffee in nature. Calming and enjoyable. When Leo let her off the chain in the morning, her large welcoming grin—the sort where her tongue lolled out the side of her mouth—always made the start of his day a good one.

The power was out for the third time this week. The energy company was all talk and no action! They promised to upgrade the lines, to stop pole-top fires by putting in underground cabling or perhaps generators on every farm. But as yet, zilch. Nothing ever seemed to change—the summer outages just kept on keeping on.

Leo's family farm was on the end of a spur line, sixty kilometres from Yorkenup township east of Perth. There were many days the electricity seemed to forget to run down those wires to spark up his house and sheds, as well as everything else that needed power to work.

On those days, the electric pump was as useless as tits on a bull. No power, no pump, and then the tanks that watered his sheep wouldn't keep filling.

Now, here he was, trying to make sure his stock had the essentials on a day that was forecast to reach thirty-five degrees.

Sighing, Leo thought about the brochures lying on the office desk. A solar pump would solve a lot of problems; the main one being he couldn't leave the farm for a moment during summer. If he wasn't checking the tanks, he was inspecting the troughs or flicking a light switch inside the house to make sure the electricity was still on.

Still, a solar pump was modern, and his father would have to approve the purchase, as he did with any decision Leo tried to make on the farm.

Grunting against the hushed landscape again, he saw himself on an endless treadmill of frustration and sheer hard work. There didn't seem to be any places where he could get off and take a breath.

Just a short while ago, Jill had snapped out that well-worn argument again.

'It's Saturday,' she told him, as if he had no idea of what day it was. 'Are you coming to tennis?'

The children's backpacks were on the bench, filled with toys, snacks and all the other paraphernalia young kids seemed to need.

Charlotte, the older of the two, ran into the kitchen tugging on her mother's short tennis skirt. 'Time to go?' she asked.

Jill put her hand on Charlotte's head and shushed her. Her eyes flicked over to Noah and back to Leo.

Noah was sitting on the carpet, staring bug-eyed at the TV, a piece of toast in his mouth.

'Carmel and Bruce are going to be there.' As she spoke, the lights flickered, before dying. His wife's mouth had formed a thin line. 'Guess that answers that question, doesn't it?'

'I don't do this on purpose,' Leo retorted.

'Sometimes I wonder.' Jill had grabbed her tennis bag and taken Charlotte's hand.

Leo had found his hat, jammed it on his head and stalked out of the house without saying goodbye.

With a heavy sigh, he had stared at the back of the LandCruiser wagon disappearing into town, his family on board, until it wasn't there anymore.

Leo took the fuel cap off the pump and checked inside the tank. Close enough to empty. Well, that would be why it wouldn't start.

Idiot, he thought. *Who forgets to put fuel in the tank? You've got too much on your mind.*

A sigh and a short walk to the back of the ute, where there were three plastic containers filled with petrol. Leo knew how dangerous it was to carry a flammable liquid, especially when one of the containers leaked a little from the plastic join. But other than putting a fuel tank next to the pumphouse, there was no other way of getting petrol to the water pump. His father wouldn't approve such luxuries.

'Take care of the pennies and the pounds will take care of themselves,' his dad always said.

Leo grunted again, his fist curled tight around the handle of the jerry can, the other resting on Coffee's head for a fleeting moment.

Within minutes the tank was full of petrol, and he pulled a rag out of his back pocket, swiping at the spill on the motor. He could see the vapour shimmering in the air as he did.

This time when he yanked the starter cord the engine kicked over. It almost died away but then chugged back to life. By the time it had hit full revs, the loud rumble reverberated around the shed, pushing out petrol fumes.

Leo heard the whoosh and gurgle of water through the pipe and reached out to touch it. The poly was cold and pulsing under his hand; there was water.

Good.

He turned back to the engine and frowned, not under-standing what he was seeing. Blue and orange flames, licking around the fuel tank.

Leo stood transfixed for far too long, then sprinted to his ute and his firefighting gear, pulling out his phone as he ran. He had to let someone know. Call for help!

Seeing that there was a line of flames following him outside sent shockwaves rolling over his body. The leaking jerry can that had been on the tray of the ute had left behind a trail of petrol and now the flames were skipping along the line and leaping towards him. The firefighting tank, full of water, was pushed up against the back window of the ute. Leo flicked the tank's switch on, before starting the pump and dragging the thick hose back to the shed.

'Come on, come on, answer,' he muttered into the phone, while with his other hand he took aim at the flames, which had doubled in size in a matter of minutes. 'John? Fire, my place. Pump shed on the creek!' he yelled into the phone as the fire captain finally answered.

He didn't have time to hear what John said, before a loud whoomph and then a shattering explosion came from the shed.

The jerry can! He'd left it half full inside.

Leo was thrown backwards, screaming at Coffee to 'Come behind!' The dog had jumped from the tray and was running at full tilt down towards the creek.

The roar almost deafened Leo and he threw his arm up in a futile attempt to block the heat that was thrown his way.

Heavy, hot air landed on his body and his skin seemed to shrivel and shrink, even though the flames didn't touch him. It was as if all the moisture inside had been sucked out. He smelled his own singed hair and he looked around again for Coffee, only to see flames quivering as they wrapped around the wooden beams and threw sparks into the dry grass. Spot fires flared, small at first, then galloping across the grass to meet as one, the ute in their path.

'No!' Leo scrambled back, watching in horror. He upended the hose above his head and let the water cascade over him.

Suddenly, Coffee was next to him, teeth nipping at his shirt. Leo pushed her away, trying to get to his feet.

Another explosion as the blaze found the second jerry can. More fire touching the sky, the surrounding area a matt of orange, blue and white flames, black burning grass and fierce heat.

So big and hot now, the fire was creating its own wind, jumping across the paddock with intent.

Coffee: more pulling at his shorts and shirt, and this time Leo stood up and ran, his dog at his heels.

CHAPTER 1

'I've organised for you to see Bec and Alice at a secure location,' Dave's lawyer, Grace, told him. 'The other party are requesting you take precautions to ensure that you aren't followed.'

'You're kidding?' Dave stood and started to pace the yard of the stock squad headquarters. He had been sitting astride his motorbike, ready to ride it onto the trailer when his phone had rung. Grace's name had caused a chain reaction of guilt, regret, sadness, resentment and anger, all in the same measure. 'Do I get to see my kids by myself, or do I have to be supervised?'

'Supervised.' The regret in Grace's voice was surprising. Dave was the emotional one when it came to his kids, while Grace usually kept a professional coolness, despite knowing her client was getting shafted.

Now, with one hand in his pocket and a scowl on his face, irritation was winning out. 'Guess Mark has got something to do with that?'

'I would imagine,' Grace said. 'There will be a car picking you up at one pm to drive you. The other party do not want you to know where the meeting place is in advance, in case your phone is bugged, okay? Any part of this you're not clear on?'

'I'm good.'

'Okay, let me know how it goes. Neither Melinda nor Mark should be present. If one of them is, leave straight-away. Even if you haven't seen the girls. You are not to speak nor get into an argument with either of them.'

'Got it.'

'The car will take you back to the stock squad office once you've finished. Talk to you later.'

The phone went dead.

This was Dave's third pass around the yard; he halted near the door into the shed, then started to walk again, almost before he'd stopped. The bubbling in his stomach made him want to move or jiggle in one spot or knock someone out. Mark preferably.

He should've been feeling excitement at the thought of seeing his girls in an hour's time, but instead he was edgy and annoyed. His former father-in-law always did this just before a visit: changed the rules, caught Dave off-guard. And he was always able to get away with it.

Apparently, the courts didn't like fathers who might be a risk to their children, even if said father is a cop. Mark had played that card throughout the whole custody proceeding, finally wining sole custody for Melinda, Dave's ex-wife. The woman who had wanted him to give up his career because it put those he loved and who loved him in danger.

Jamming his phone back into his shirt pocket, he threw a leg over the motorbike and turned the key. High-pitched revs sounded longer and louder than they needed to be as he drove up the ramp and onto the trailer. All the bikes had just been serviced, and Dave was repacking the trailer for whenever he and his partner, Detective Bob Holden, were called out for their next case.

Detective Sergeant Spencer Brown, Dave's previous partner in Barrabine, had always said: prior preparation prevents piss-poor performance.

After his phone call with Grace, Dave would have preferred to take the bike out onto some bush track, where it was just him and the wind, and let her rip so he could remember what freedom tasted like. Not this boxed-up, being-told-what-to-do-and-when feeling.

If you want to see your children, you *will* do as I say.

If you want to see your children, you *will* conform.

If you want to see your children, you *will* roll over and kiss my arse. Every time.

Fuck off.

Dave imagined Mark's smug face so close to his own that he could reach out and hit him with a closed fist. What pleasure that would bring!

Dave had done it once. Way back when he and Melinda lived in Barrabine, at his first posting as a detective. Mark had taunted him one too many times, and although Dave would never say that punching someone was a good idea, when his fist collided with Mark's chin, he'd known it had been the best notion he'd had that particular day.

Flicking down the motorbike's stand, Dave took the rough rope and quickly tied it to the rail of the trailer and tossed it over the seat, walking around to repeat the process, making sure the bike was bolted down safe.

The swag, tuckerbox and camp kitchen were already packed in the trailer, so Dave secured them as well, checking that nothing could fall off.

'Dave! Hurry!' Lorri, another detective, stood at the top of the office stairs and motioned to him urgently. 'Come here. Quick!' Then she disappeared back inside.

Dave raised his eyebrows, then, with one final wobble of the rope over the bike, he jogged up the steps and into the station.

'What's up?' he asked to no one in particular. Lorri's office was empty.

'Quick, Dave! Get the defib machine!' Lorri shouted from further inside.

Dave's head snapped around to the sound of her voice. Lorri was bent over a man on the floor in Bob's office. His legs were protruding from the side of the desk and Dave couldn't see his face, only his shoes.

'Call the ambos then get in here and help me.'

For a moment too long, Dave was frozen while Lorri's ponytail swung in time to the compressions she was counting out.

'Twenty, twenty-one, twenty-two . . .'

'Shit!' Dave ran back to the entrance and snatched the defib machine off the front wall. Moments later, he was inside Bob's office assessing the collapsed man, while talking into his phone.

'Police, fire or ambulance?'

'Ambulance.' The word came out of him like a bullet, as he opened the cover of the defib machine and pressed the 'on' button, listening to the voice prompts take him through what he had to do.

Lorri was breathing into the man's mouth now.

'Need to undo the shirt,' Dave told her.

With her fingers on the man's wrist, Lorri searched for a pulse. Her face held the trained professionalism of a copper, but her breathing was staccato-like, her hands shaking.

Dave kneeled now, grabbing either side of the man's shirt and giving one quick tug. Buttons skittered across the floor.

'Got a pulse,' gasped Lorri. She sagged slightly, her adrenalin released.

Dave heard the sirens wailing in the background.

The man groaned, then gave a hacking cough, before his eyes flicked open and his mouth formed an 'o'.

'Don't talk,' Dave instructed him. 'Stay still.'

Lorri kept her fingertips on his pulse and her eyes on her watch as Dave gave the man's leg a firm pat and went out to meet the ambulance crew.

'She got him back,' he said to the first paramedic who was jogging up the steps, gloves on and bag in hand.

The red-haired man nodded and kept going, while his partner, a small thin woman, also wearing gloves, ran up and followed him in.

Dave put his hands to his knees and took some deep breaths, listening to Lorri fill in the ambos.

For a stupid moment, when he'd seen the legs on the floor, he'd thought the man had been Bob, even though he knew his partner was away on holidays until tomorrow. His heart had doubled its rate in a split second. Surely, he wasn't going to lose another partner so soon after Spencer?

Instead, the man on the office floor was Parksey. Detective Senior Sergeant Parks, Lorri's partner. Another integral member of the stock squad. Dave knew he should still be upset, but all he felt was relief that it wasn't Bob.

He took a few shaky breaths and looked at the sky. Everything was the same as it had been half an hour before Parksey collapsed. But it didn't feel as if it should be. Something monumental should be happening outside to show that Parksey had nearly died. If Lorri hadn't got him back, a family's world would have been turned upside down. Dave swallowed hard and went back inside.

The ambos had now fixed the oxygen mask over Parksey's nose and mouth and were about to carry him down the steps on the stretcher.

Lorri was on the phone. 'What hospital?' she asked, holding the phone away from her ear. 'His wife wants to meet him there.'

The ginger-haired paramedic named the closest one, fifteen minutes away.

'What's the go?' Dave asked the female paramedic quietly.

'See what the doc says when he has all the scans, but you guys did good. He was in the right place, could have been much worse.'

Dave nodded. If Lorri hadn't been there when Parksey had collapsed, maybe he would have had to call the funeral directors rather than the ambulance service.

He walked to the head of the stretcher and leaned down to talk to his colleague. 'Mate, if we'd known you were going to lie down on the job, we wouldn't have given you the position as boss while Bob was away!'

From under the mask, Parksey gave a weak smile and held his hand out. Dave gripped it, gave a small shake then let him go. 'Be in to see you soon,' he said.

Back in the office, Lorri collapsed into a chair, her hand over her mouth.

Dave moved to stand beside her. 'He was lucky you were here,' he said.

Lorri didn't answer. Her face was pale and covered in beads of sweat that she brushed away unconsciously. 'God,' slipped out in a whisper.

Dave squatted down and looked her in the face. 'You were great. Did exactly as you were supposed to do.'

'This is Parksey,' Lorri gulped out. 'He's fit and skinny. What the hell?'

'The doc will be able to tell us more. I'm not going to promise everything will be okay, because we don't know. But he's going to the right place now and that's because you were here and knew what to do.' Dave stood up, patting her knee this time. 'Tell you what, why don't I lock up and you head over to the hospital. There's no point in you being here. Are you okay to drive or do you want me to call you a cab?'

He went to the water cooler and poured her a glass, then handed it to her.

'I . . . ah . . .' Lorri looked around as if she were seeing the office for the first time. She took a sip. 'Ah, no, I'm fine. Thanks. I'll head over there now.' Lorri didn't move, just kept staring at the ground.

Dave pulled out his phone again and dialled, ordering her a taxi.

'No, no, it's okay,' she told him again, as his words filtered through to her, but he held up his hand until he'd finished.

'You've had a huge shock,' Dave said. 'And we can't afford for you to have an accident on the way to the hospital, then we'd have two of you out of action.' His tone was gruff but there was a bit of a lump in his throat, so taking a practical approach was better. Lorri would probably be fine driving the short way down the highway from the hills of Perth, where the headquarters of the stock squad spread out over ten hectares, but he couldn't risk her or any of the public being injured. The hospital was on the outskirts of Perth and it would be peak-hour traffic soon. 'I'd take you but I'm going to see my kids . . .' He glanced at his watch.

The whole medical emergency had taken less than three quarters of an hour. The car Grace had organised would be there to pick him up in about twenty minutes.

Lorri stood up and went to her desk, searching for something. She tore a piece of paper from her notebook. Reaching under the desk, she grabbed her handbag. 'This came through this morning, from Arson. Parksey and I were going to . . .' Her voice trailed off, then she shook the paper at him. 'There was a fire about an hour and a half out of Perth, heading east. Near Yorkenup. The house and some sheds, plus about fifteen hundred hectares of land destroyed. Started by a petrol pump, but they don't think the fire was deliberately lit. More that Leo Perry, the owner, spilled the fuel when he was filling up the tank.' Her voice became steadier as she talked—work was a safe topic right now.

Dave took the page and started to read. 'But . . . ?'

'But they can't find the manager or his dog. Perry called the blaze in. Spoke to the fire control officer and requested help, and that's the last time anyone has spoken to him. There wasn't a body in the burnt-out wreckage of the ute, which was found near the pumphouse, nothing near or in the house or other sheds.' Lorri went back into Bob's office and came out with another file. 'SES are still searching. The area has been advised as safe in the last few hours.

'Locals have done a preliminary interview with the wife. Everything was fine between them, no money troubles, couple of young kids. No action on any of the bank accounts, phone, et cetera. I'm sorry, Dave, but there's a bit of urgency to get out there and find this bloke.'

'Right.' He flipped through the pages, only giving them a cursory glance.

In fifteen minutes he was due to leave to see his kids, and he needed to let Bob know what was going on.

'He was a manager for his own family farm,' Lorri said as she put her hand on the door. 'It's a weird set-up and Arson is recommending we take over from the locals.'

'Sure. You were headed up there today?'

There was a slight pause before she nodded. All the plans they'd made were now in disarray.

'Leave it with Bob and me, we'll sort it.' He tapped the file to his forehead in a salute.

A horn blasted from outside.

'That'll be you,' Dave said. 'Go on. Ring me if you need anything.'

Lorri nodded and turned to go. 'Thanks,' she said softly.

CHAPTER 2

'You're kidding? Shit, that should have been me not Parksey,' Bob said. His voice sounded husky, like he'd been at a Cold Chisel concert and spent four hours singing at the top of his voice. 'I'm the one who's out of shape.'

'Doesn't sound like you got the option,' Dave replied, holding the phone close to his ear. The bitumen road that the driver had taken him down had now given way to a gravel track winding through tall timber country. Enormous, skinny-trunked trees reached out their branches as if they were going to pluck a high-flying bird from the air.

Feeling uneasy, Dave leaned forward. 'We headed in the right direction?' he asked the driver.

There was only a nod.

'Where are you?' Bob asked.

'Going to see the girls. Same shit as last time. Secure location and supervised. Grace organised for a driver to take me.'

'You don't know where?' Bob's tone was steady.

'Nope.'

As he spoke, the trees thinned out to low scrubby native bush. In the distance there was a shed; further on, a lake.

'When are you due back?' Bob asked.

'Probably a couple of hours.'

'Check in as soon as you get back in the car.'

Dave's nervousness had rubbed off on Bob.

'Roger that.'

'I'll head to the hospital and let the rest of the hierarchy know about Parksey. Get his missus looked after and so on.'

'I've had a read through this file,' Dave said as the car came to a silent stop at the entrance to the shed. The smell of caffeine and baking came to him on the wind, and he could see there was a balcony over the water. 'We've got a fire that was an accident, a missing man and dog, and the SES are searching. No body so far. Fifteen hundred hectares burned. Not all of that land is Leo Perry's so I think there might be some insurance claims against Perry's insurance company.

'I finished packing the trailer ready for our next trip north. All we have to do is unhook it and take off in the troopy. Stay in the pub there or something.'

'Got a gut feeling?'

Dave opened the car door and could hear two high voices talking.

'No, Alice, it's mine. That's yours over there.'

'Not as yet. But we need to get up there today, see if we can get a feel for Leo Perry. Good thing it's closer to

Perth than where we usually work. Look, I gotta go. The girls are here. I can hear them.'

'Right. Make sure you call me when you get back. I'll start making the arrangements to drive out to Yorkenup.'

Dave closed the phone and reached for the two packages alongside him, both wrapped in pink paper. He thanked the driver, who nodded again.

His breath floated away on the breeze and he looked around. This was a cafe on a lake, but the car park was empty and there was not another person in sight. Had Mark hired this place because it was so far off the main road? God, the man must be paranoid.

There wasn't time to form an answer. A tall woman with fire-red hair and a strong step appeared in the open door. She assessed him for a moment, then held out her hand without smiling.

'I'm Olivia. Family support officer. Nice to meet you.'

Dave was impressed with her grip; strong and firm. After introducing himself, he indicated the surrounds.

'Off the beaten track.'

'Yes. There are cameras at the beginning of the road and alarms that will be triggered if someone else drives up here while you're visiting.'

Dave wasn't sure what to say to that, but wondered how Mark had pulled strings to get a business to shut down for a few hours for a custodial visit. Maybe he'd bought the cafe.

Olivia still didn't smile but indicated for Dave to go inside. 'I'm sure you understand that the well-being of these two young girls is of utmost importance to their family.'

'Of course, because I'm their father,' Dave reminded her.

Giving a thin smile, she inclined her head as if to agree but it was clear she didn't really want to.

'The girls are this way.'

Inside, the cafe was warm and smelled like a country kitchen—baking cakes and biscuits and brewing hot drinks. The tables were all empty, but still set with sugar bowls, salt and pepper shakers and identification numbers, as if waiting for the crowds to appear. A large blackboard hung over the counter, telling him a steak sandwich was five dollars fifteen, while a coffee was going to set him back a dollar fifty.

Large windows overlooked the lake. The water, dark and still.

Dave assessed the scene in about half a minute, then his eyes slid to the corner where a wooden climbing fort with two floors was set up, surrounded by cushions and toys. Bec was at the top of the slippery slide, poised to come hurtling down; Alice was at the base, standing up on unsteady feet, bouncing and looking up at her sister.

His heart felt like it was about to stop as he took in both girls. They'd grown taller and had rounder faces; Alice was standing and probably able to walk a few steps without falling over. She also looked like she wasn't wearing a nappy! Toilet-trained already? She was still so young.

Bec looked as if she'd been put on a traction table and stretched out. Her laugh bubbled out as she swung her legs down and kicked out. It only took a few seconds before her two feet landed in Alice's belly and she pushed her sister backwards, landing with a thud on the ground. Alice's mouth opened, as if she was ready to scream, but nothing came out for a moment. Then a shriek emerged that turned into tears. Bec got up and went to her sister, just as Olivia called out to them.

'Now, Bec, was there any need for that? Kicking your sister in the tummy isn't nice.' She went to Alice and picked her up, giving her a cuddle, then turned to Dave. 'Your dad's here, Bec.'

Bec's head swung around and she dived behind Olivia's legs. Two little hands snaked between Olivia's calves and pushed them apart slightly. Dave could see his daughter's eyes staring at him.

He took an involuntary breath through his nose, then squatted down, smiling.

'Hey there, Bec. And Alice, too.' He gave them a wave. 'Looks like there's fun to be had here.'

A woman appeared from the kitchen and put two milkshakes on the counter, then disappeared before bringing back two mugs of something and a couple of pieces of cake.

'We've got an hour,' Olivia told Dave. 'There's a coffee for you.' Her hand went to Bec's head. 'Want a choccy milkshake?'

The little girl nodded, her fingers in her mouth, while Alice stared straight at Dave, her hand jumping up and down, hitting Olivia's arm softly.

Dave went to the counter and picked up one of the plastic cups, then held it out to his older daughter. 'Looks yummy,' he said after he'd cleared his throat to make sure his words came out strongly, not wanting Olivia to know how much Bec's reaction was upsetting him.

The anger that was swirling around inside him shouldn't be obvious either, he told himself.

Fucking Mark. Fucking Melinda. It doesn't need to be like this.

Bec hesitated, then came out from behind Olivia and took a few tentative steps towards him.

'Daddy?' she said. Her eyes were wide and her face uncertain as her lips pursed into a rosebud shape.

'Yeah, honey, it's me. Daddy. Do I look different?'

A smile suddenly lit up the little girl's face and she ran towards him. 'Your voice sounded funny,' Bec told him as she snuggled her face into his neck and latched her arms around his neck.

'Oh, honey,' Dave said, this time not caring if he sounded wobbly. He hugged her back, committing the smell of her freshly washed hair and soap to memory, knowing there would be times he would need to revisit this moment.

'Daddy, guess what?' Bec asked, wriggling out of his arms.

Her little upturned face was a picture of innocence as she took his hand and led him over to her backpack, which had been slung by the fort.

Dave stopped to kiss Alice's cheek on the way over and motioned for Olivia to hand her to him, but Alice put her face into the crook of Olivia's neck, so he continued to follow Bec.

'You'll have to tell me,' he said, sitting down on the floor cross-legged, waiting.

His eldest daughter pulled something out and waved it at him. 'Look, this is Bonkers.'

'Bonkers?' Dave reached for the photo.

A black-and-white kitten sat in a pram, a pink bonnet tied around its head. The green eyes stared at the person taking the photo. *Probably willing them dead*, Dave thought.

'I've got a pet kitten,' she announced.

'Why did you call her Bonkers?' Dave asked, scanning the photo for anything that was familiar or would give him an indication of where they were living. The cat was too close for much else to show.

'He's an it, Mum says.' Bec lowered her voice. 'I heard her telling Livvy that he hasn't got any *balls*.' She grinned as if she knew the word was awfully naughty but was prepared to get into trouble anyway.

'Yep, well that would make him an it all right,' Dave said. 'You haven't told me why you called him Bonkers.'

'Coz he's crazy! He runs here and there and chases his tail and rolls over trying to catch the wool.' Her words were so quick, they almost ran together.

Laughing, Dave rolled over and put his hands and feet in the air, scratching them as if he were chasing a strand of wool. 'Like this?' he asked.

'Yes! You're so funny, Daddy.' She clapped her hands and watched him, her face alight.

Then all humour disappeared from her. 'Mummy says you're not going to live with us anymore.'

Her words stopped Dave in his tracks. He turned back and sat up next to her again, glancing at Olivia, who was holding the cup so Alice could sip the milkshake. She was listening, although pretending not to. Why did this awfulness have to play out in front of a stranger? Anger simmered throughout his body.

Gathering himself and turning so the family support officer was out of sight, he spoke quietly. 'No. No, I don't think I'm going to be able to.' He stopped short of saying 'for a while'. What was the point in giving her hope when there wasn't any?

'Is it because that man shot Gran?' Bec raised her little hand and pointed her finger and thumb like a gun. 'Bang! Bang!'

The words sounded so wrong, coming from a tiny child. 'Shot' shouldn't be a word a child Bec's age even knew.

Dave was having the same urge as earlier that day, to move and move and move. Instead, he sat still, reaching for Bec and pulling her onto his lap. She'd anchor him to the floor.

'Oh, Bec, you shouldn't make a sound like a gun. That's not very nice.'

'Why?'

'Because it'll upset people.'

'But is it because of that?' she persisted.

'I guess it's a part of the reason,' he said. 'But there's a bit more to it. Your mum and I, well, sometimes people are better not living together.' What words did he use to explain divorce to a child? 'We still want to be friends and we both love you and Alice very much, but we are those people who are better off not being together.' Was his explanation too adult-like for his small daughter?

Bec snuggled in closer and put her chubby hand on his cheek. 'I miss you though, Daddy. Can't you come and stay sometimes?'

For a moment, the pain in his chest was so intense, he wondered if it was his turn to have a heart attack.

'No, honey. Not at your mum's place. Maybe one day you can come to my house and have a sleep-over. Would you like that? In time,' he added quickly as Olivia made to say something.

'And Alice?'

'Alice, too.'

'Pa and Jonno don't tell stories the way you do.'

The unfamiliar name, Jonno, took a second to register and, out of the corner of his eye, he could see Olivia moving closer again, so Dave chose not to comment on it yet. Still, he wasn't surprised. The first time Melinda had left, it had only been a couple of months before another man's name had started to come into conversation.

'Would you like me to read you a story now?' he asked.

Bec nodded and got out of his lap. 'I brought my favourite book,' she told him, getting it from her bag.

'Great. Let me talk to Alice and then I'll read it to you, okay?' Dave got up from the floor, feeling pins and needles in his toes. He picked up one of the packages wrapped in pink from where he'd dropped them on the nearby table and handed it to Bec. She squealed in delight and started tearing at the paper.

Alice watched, her eyes interested. She clapped her hands happily.

'Hey, Alice, you want to come to Daddy?' he asked, holding out his hands, the other package tucked under his arm.

His youngest daughter hesitated then reached out.

Holding a breath, Dave put her on his hip and handed her the package. 'Shall we open it? Look, if you tug here . . .' He showed her where the sticky tape was and mimicked where to put her finger.

Alice's pale blue eyes looked up at him again. They were the same colour as his. Her face was round like his and her chin a little pointy, like his.

Dave had never said anything to anyone, but there had always been a question as to whether Alice was really his child. The one night he and Mel had been together in the space of, well, a long time and she'd become pregnant.

Back then, there were too many other issues for him to want to create one more by querying something so sensitive.

Looking at Alice now, there was no doubt that she was her father's child, and his heart squeezed extra tightly, a small smile playing around his mouth.

Back on the floor, and bending his head close to Alice's, he watched while she unwrapped the soft toy.

When Dave had left, his present to Bec had been a black-and-tan kelpie stuffed toy, and he told her if she ever needed him and he wasn't there, the kelpie would take care of her, because that's what kelpies did. Now there was the same for Alice. Not that she would understand his explanation, but he'd tell her now and the next time and the next time, so one day she would cuddle that dog at night and think of her daddy.

'Livvy, look at this!' Bec's high pitch told Dave that his outdoor bubble-blower was a hit and he grinned, getting out a small camera he'd brought to take a photo.

'Bec, smile for Daddy?' He lined her up in the frame.

'No photos,' Olivia said softly.

'Sorry?'

'Don't make a scene. One of the rules. No photos.'

Dave's nostrils flared open, and he pressed his lips tightly together.

Olivia gave a small shrug and bent down in front of Bec, so Dave didn't have a clear view. Seething, he put the camera away. Grace would be hearing about this and fixing it for next time. Photos were a father's right.

'We need to pack up,' Olivia said. 'There's only ten minutes left.'

What? No! He'd only just arrived. They were finally beginning to gel as Dad and daughters. Dave wanted to beg for more time. He'd hardly started talking to Alice and certainly hadn't finished talking about Bonkers with Bec. How could nearly an hour go so fast? He was used to them dragging by when he was at home by himself.

Instead, he pressed a kiss to Alice's head and held up the stuffed toy to her nose, wiggling it. She giggled and flapped her hands to get him to stop. Dave laughed and did it again, all the while telling Alice the story about the loyal kelpie.

'You gave me one of those!' Bec said, looking up from her bag, which she was stuffing the bubble-blower into. 'I called him Daddy because you told me he'd always be there.'

'That's right.' Dave tried to smile, but it was getting harder with each passing second.

'Daddy sleeps on my pillow every night,' Bec told him.

'That's one lucky dog.'

Outside a horn blasted through the still atmosphere and Olivia resumed her stiffened stance.

Dave wanted to make it difficult for her; he could refuse to leave. After all, what was an hour with his kids in five months? Fight rose in him. He'd stay longer. No one could stop him. The court order didn't say only one hour!

But then Bec put out her arms. What was the point in making the visit finish badly? Especially in front of his kids. They didn't need to know about the arguments between the adults. In the end, he was the only one who'd be hurt, because Mark would see to it.

Mark seemed to know when Dave was on his knees and acted on it.

CHAPTER 3

'Parksey looked like shit, didn't he?' Bob said quietly.

From the driver's seat, Dave glanced over. His partner hadn't said much since he'd climbed into the passenger's seat at the hospital car park. His fingers continually tugged at the collar of his shirt as if he needed more air.

'I've seen him look a whole lot better,' Dave agreed.

'All those bloody noisy monitors and the like. Oh, I know he's got to have them on, but they'd have to remind him that he's been pulled back from the brink.'

'You've been there.'

Six months ago, Bob had been admitted to hospital after an incident with some drug runners in the north of Western Australia. The only good thing to come out of his head injury was his very new and tentative relationship with Betty, one of the nurses who'd looked after him.

'Don't I know it! I lay there in the hospital and went over and over what had happened in my mind and I damn well bet Parksey is doing the same.' He paused. 'Still, I did meet Betty during the hospital visit. She was the best nurse a man could have asked for.'

Dave smirked. Bob had been knocked off his feet by the pretty, petite blonde nurse. Betty was only slightly younger than Bob and had moved to Perth to live with him. The transformation in Dave's partner had been as big as the deep laugh he had.

Dave changed the subject, aware that he was feeling a bit testy and lonely. 'Has Parksey got any results yet?'

'Ah, you don't know then?'

Dave felt his heart sink a little and held the steering wheel tight as a road train carting sheep rattled past the troopy. The stench of sheep shit hung in the air after the truck had disappeared, wafting in through the air-conditioning vents.

'No.'

'Going to have a stent put in later tonight, son. They're waiting for the specialist to get there.'

'Shit. Still, he's in the right place, by the sound of it.'

'Only spot for him.' Bob turned to the window. 'Been a while since I've been out this way. Looking like they've had a good season.'

The hills were covered in golden grasses. Harvest was finished and now the stock were spread out across the thick barley and wheat stubbles, or camped under the gum trees in the heat of the day.

The river that wound its way from the Swan River all the way down to the middle of the wheat belt alternated between large and wide, needing a bridge to cross it, to tiny streams a child could jump over. But in summer it was mostly dry and if there was water in a pool, it would be rank and covered with algae. Somehow the native animals and birds knew not to drink from the edges when the water smelled of decay and was stagnant.

Dave checked the odometer. One hundred and twelve kilometres since they'd left Perth.

'Can't remember a time I was here at all,' Dave said. 'Pretty different from the places we usually go.'

'Boss wants to put out an urgent All Points Bulletin.' Bob brushed at his clean and freshly ironed stock squad uniform. Since Betty had come on the scene, his usually crumpled uniform and food-splattered tie had become neat and starched.

The other big change had been Bob's usual lunch at the local around the corner from the stock squad headquarters. Apparently, Betty didn't like him going home smelling of beer. What was even more surprising was that Bob was happy to oblige.

'Why only an APB? They only go to police stations. Don't we want the public to get involved?'

'I think so, son. It's over twenty-four hours since Leo Perry was last seen, but let's wait until we get more information from the locals. I'll clear it one way or the other.'

Bob turned a few pages of the file that was sitting on his lap, then gave a soft snort. '*Leo was a loving husband and great dad. Very popular around town,*' he read. 'Wife's statement, so to be taken with a pinch of salt.'

It was Dave's turn to grunt. 'That's cynical of you.'

'My oath. After our last case at Corbett Station Stay, I'll find it hard to take a woman on face value ever again.' His voice lowered in wonder. 'I still can't work out how Jane deceived all of us. She was so convincing.'

'She was certainly that.'

Bob turned his attention back to the file. 'No vehicles missing from the farm, according to the wife, so allegedly he hasn't absconded with the family car.' Bob took his notebook out of his pocket and scratched something in it. 'We'll need to get Licensing to run a report of what was registered to each family member and the business, so we can verify that statement.

'And the dog, Coffee. She's missing, too.' Bob looked up and out the window vaguely, while he tapped his pen on the paper. 'That's an interesting point. I've been to suicide scenes where the victim has shot his dog first, then turned the gun on himself. Or the victim hasn't been able to bring himself to shoot his best mate, done himself in, and the dog hasn't left the body until they were found.'

'Remember that one Spencer told me about?' Dave asked, referring to his previous partner from Barrabine Police Station. 'The body was hanging from a tree out in the middle of the scrub, and the only way they found the fella was because his dog was lying underneath howling like a dingo. Sent shivers down my spine for months every time I thought about it.'

'Yeah, stuff that.'

'SES hasn't found a body yet. Why did you mention suicide?'

Bob adjusted his glasses and turned a few pages. 'This morning after the area was declared safe, SES and the local vollies started to conduct a search under the guidance of the local boys. They examined the surrounding paddocks and roads. So far, they've come up with nothing. At last report, they've searched thirty, maybe forty per cent of the property, so there's still a chance they might find a body. The Arson squad have been through the burnt-out house and any sheds that were untouched, and other areas where he might have been caught out by flames. Again, there's nothing. Not even a dog collar. This fella he's, what, thirty-one years old. A farmer with two little kids. Probably on the young side to fit a suicide profile, but got to look at all possibilities.'

'I would have thought if he'd suicided, someone would have found his body by now.'

'Not necessarily. Perhaps he didn't want anyone to find him. To avoid bringing shame on the family, that sort of thing.'

'Yeah, good point. Who knows what goes through people's minds when they're teetering on the brink.'

'How'd you go with your kids?'

'Yeah, all fine. Wasn't long enough.' Dave wasn't pleased with the shift in conversation.

'No shit from anyone?'

Dave shook his head. He told Bob about Olivia. 'I didn't get to ask what her role was, but she seems to be some type of security cum babysitter, passing as a family support officer. Knows everything that's going on, and if I did something that wasn't in the rules, she called me on it. Tried to take a photo of the girls and she put a stop to that quick smart.'

'Bit over the top.'

'Couldn't see the point in arguing. Anyway, she must work for Mark in some capacity.' Dave sighed as another truck rumbled past on the way to the abattoirs. 'You know, sometimes I wonder if the visits are worth it. There's so much angst leading up to them and then I've got to reconnect and get the kids to remember me again. It's harder with Alice, because she's never really known me . . . Guess she never will, hey? Anyway, an hour isn't long enough.' He paused. 'I miss them a bloody lot afterwards.' Dave's voice was low. 'A bloody lot' wasn't even close to describing how he felt after he had hugged his two daughters at the end of their visit. There weren't words.

'That Mark is a mongrel,' Bob said. 'I haven't finished with him yet.'

Dave gave a little scoff. 'Oh yeah, and what are you going to do to him?'

'Haven't decided yet, but when I do, he'll know it's me and why.'

Dave looked over at his partner, trying to work out if Bob was serious or not. He decided he wasn't. 'You and whose army?'

Bob turned in his seat a little and looked at Dave over the top of his glasses. 'Now, son, if I told you that, it wouldn't be a surprise, would it?' Settling back in his seat, he ran his hand over his chin, brow furrowed.

Dave got the feeling Bob's thoughts had gone back to Parksey, but Dave hadn't finished telling him about the visit yet.

'Mark must be really paranoid,' Dave said, bringing Bob's head back to look at him. When his partner didn't say anything, he continued. 'I had to meet them way out in some isolated cafe.' He shook his head. 'Took a heap of time to get there and back again, just for an hour. All the organisation that's gone into it! Crazy. And the stupidest thing is that Bulldust is in jail. We're all safe while he's there!'

'Bulldust,' Bob muttered in disgust. 'You know it's a sign of a weak man when they take women hostage and use them in negotiations,' he said. 'That's what that idiot did, more's the pity about your mother-in-law, especially when it was you who he was wanting, not your family. Anyway, we've been over this hundreds of times, haven't we? Ellen dying wasn't your fault, Mark is a bully and Bulldust is a vile human being. Good thing we've got something different to focus on now.' He folded his arms across his chest.

'Yeah, yeah, I know, it's just that Mark's paranoia seems over the top. If anything did happen out there, it would be harder to get help. I noticed there wasn't any mobile range. Do you reckon he could be delusional? Grief does that to people.'

'Who knows. Wouldn't have thought so though—he's always been a fuckwit. Still, from what you're telling me, everything was monitored and there weren't going to be any unforeseen issues.' Bob's mobile gave a chirp. He looked at the phone as if it were a piece of dog shit, then opened it and read the message. 'You want to come to tea when we get back? Betty's asking.'

'Ah, domesticated bliss,' Dave teased.

'Yes or no, son.' Bob didn't seem to be in the playing mood today. He was probably shellshocked from Parksey's heart attack. Feeling his own mortality.

'That would be great, thanks,' Dave said.

Bob laboured over the small keypad, pressing the keys once, twice or three times to get the letters he wanted then leaning back to read the words, before pressing send.

'Bec mentioned a new name. A Jonno,' Dave said quietly.

'Oh?' Bob looked over at him as he put the phone back into his pocket. 'Guess that was always on the cards. Now he'll have to deal with Mark, not you. I'd be enjoying that, son.'

'God, I wouldn't wish that on my worst enemy!' He paused. 'You haven't said anything about your holiday.'

Bob stretched out his arms towards the windshield. 'Real good, real good. Never been to Rottnest Island before, but it was nice enough. People everywhere, though. Kids running amok. Have to say—' He stopped and cast a glance towards Dave. 'Now, don't you mention anything, but I didn't like the boat trip out. Not that I told Betty, but there's better ways to travel than bobbing up and down like a cork on the sea.'

Dave grinned. On Christmas Day, Betty had been so proud of the gift she'd bought Bob.

'Four days overseas just sitting on the beach and relaxing,' she'd told Dave in the kitchen, while Bob was at the barbecue.

'Overseas? For only four days? Where are you going?'

'A trip to Rotto. Never been there and neither has Bob, but I love sailing so I thought it would be something different.'

Different all right, Dave had thought. Bob hadn't taken any holidays in the whole time they'd worked together and Bob hated moving water.

'Give me good solid ground any day. Can't fall off the side,' Bob always said.

Still, his partner had applied for five days' leave— factoring in an extra day to get his land legs back—but now he was back on his last day of leave and they were on a job.

A road sign told them to slow down to eighty, then to sixty and Dave changed back a gear as they drove into Yorkenup.

The main road through the centre of town was wide, although the footpaths were so narrow that there was no room for trees, which would have shaded the cement path. A few shops had pots of flowers blooming at their entrances to help soften the harshness of the paving.

The colonial architecture gave York an English feel as they followed the road towards the town's centre. Churches, town hall, and the hospital featured prominently. As they hit the town's centre, the shops became closer together. They were painted yellow and dull pink; some with bullnose verandahs and green or brown windowsills. There were small shopfronts with faded, peeling iron bars behind.

'God, this looks like the wild west, even though we're still in cooee of Perth,' Bob said.

'There's a bakery—let's grab a coffee and some peace offerings for the local coppers,' Dave said. 'See if we can stave off any animosity that might be coming our way.'

'Dave, this could be a missing persons case and it's nearly three o'clock. We need to go straight to HQ.' Bob looked over at him, incredulous.

'I know, but I haven't eaten and I need a coffee if I'm going to operate at my best.' Dave flicked on the blinker and parked parallel to the kerb. 'God, I hate this type of parking.' He pulled the key from the ignition, swinging open his door at the same time.

'Let's make it quick,' Bob said.

A couple walked past, staring openly at the unmarked troop carrier, while a middle-aged man, with glasses pressed close to the window of a bookshop, took them in.

'Welcome to stare town,' Bob said, hitching up his shorts and tightening his belt. 'G'day there.' He nodded to a woman walking to her car, holding a bag of groceries. She dropped her head and didn't look at him as she walked past.

Under tilting verandahs, they made their way to the bakery and went in. The aroma of hot coffee and cakes made their stomachs rumble. The line-up was almost out the door, so Dave was sure the food was going to taste as good as it smelled.

A few people turned around and looked at the two men as they took their positions at the end of the queue.

The store was narrow, with a high roof and decorative pressed tin lining the ceiling. A glass cabinet was filled with lamingtons, cupcakes, large chocolate and sponge cakes and vanilla slices. The next one had pies, pastries, sausage rolls, bite-sized pizzas and more.

Dave felt his mouth watering. He hadn't had any breakfast, only what Spencer would've called a dingo's breakfast—a drink of water, a piss and a look around. And lunch had been even less.

Bob got out the police credit card and looked expectantly at Dave. Then his face changed and he nodded towards the noticeboard.

Aging notices of lost dogs and firewood sales were attached to the small pinboard, but on top of all of the previous notices was a fresh one.

Have you seen Leo Perry? There was a photo and a phone number underneath.

CHAPTER 4

'Have you seen these posters?' Bob waved the missing notice in front of the young man who was manning the desk at the Yorkenup Police Station. 'How did this happen?'

'Um . . .' The young constable's eyes slid towards the back of the office, making Dave aware there was a senior copper around who was yet to make an appearance. Constant radio chatter and a phone ringing were all signs there was something out of the ordinary going on in this police station.

'Do you know anything about who has put these up? Must be the family.' Bob's voice was frustrated.

'No, sir,' the young man looked confused and shocked. His badge said he was Constable Mulligan. 'Um, who are y—'

'Do you know if there are any more? We're going to have to get them taken down.'

Mulligan shook his head. 'Why do we need . . . I haven't even seen that one before, how could I? Can you tell me your name . . .'

'We need to find out whose number this is.' Bob tapped the bottom of the sheet of paper.

'Holden, what the fuck do you think you're doing to my young connie?' The slow, lazy voice flowed like a slow stream out into the reception area, followed by the plodding footsteps of a large, beefy man.

Bob jerked around, the smile already on his face. 'Ah, Red, you old bastard! I should've checked to see who was in charge here.' He held out his hand, walking towards the senior sergeant, who towered over him by a good foot.

'It's been too long, Holden, too long. See you haven't lost any of your fire or bluster.' Red shook Bob's hand hard.

'Ah, you'd be surprised. I leave the bluster up to young Dave here these days.' He nodded towards Dave. 'This is Senior Sergeant Barry Redford.' His eyes slid back. 'And I guess you're still moving so slowly they've gotta poke you to see if you're alive?'

'I've found the poking is intrusive. I prefer a question now.'

Bob snorted, his eyes crinkling.

Red looked over at Mulligan. 'This whirlwind is Bob Holden. Worked at Major Crimes together, didn't we?'

Mulligan seemed to have regained his composure.

'Nice to meet you.' His glance moved to Dave, who didn't wait to be introduced.

'I'm Detective Dave Burrows,' he told the young constable.

Mulligan nodded, then realisation spread over his face. 'You're the fella who went undercover in Queensland? Got shot in the process?'

Dave shifted uncomfortably. If he knew that much, then Mulligan knew the rest of his story.

'Tell me, Mulligan,' Bob interjected, 'been here long?'

'Couple of years—' he wavered as if he wasn't sure how to address Bob '—Detective,' he added.

'Like the town?'

'Um, yeah. Nice enough.'

'And this old bugger treats you okay, does he?'

'What do you reckon?' Red interrupted as he turned to Mulligan. 'Can you run down to the bakery and grab some food and coffees for everyone, please? These guys look famished. Stick it on the tab, yeah? Then we'll get stuck in and tell them everything we've got. They're going to need it.' He rubbed his brow then looked at Bob and Dave. 'Just over twenty-four hours since the fire and we're no more in front than when we first started. It's a worry.' He motioned to the back, where the radio was alive again. 'They're all still out there.' Then he spoke to his constable. 'Don't mind this old bastard,' he told Mulligan, indicating Bob. 'His bark has always been worse than his bite.' His eyes went back to Bob. 'Mulligan here is a good cop, so go easy.'

'Yeah, sorry 'bout that. Didn't expect to see a wanted poster. Guess the family have done that?'

Ground rules set down, Red invited them back into his office.

'I don't know,' Red admitted, pulling in an extra chair from the reception area as Mulligan collected his hat and headed to the bakery. 'I haven't seen the posters either, but

I can understand why the family put them up, if it was them. It's not going to hurt the cause. There's no sign of Leo anywhere. It's like he's disappeared into thin air. No body, no dog, no reports from the public they've sighted him. Anyway,' his tone was resigned, 'we'll wait until Mulligan gets back before we start. He was the first on the scene after the firies.'

'Sure. Small team?' Bob asked.

'Yup, me and Mulligan. Town's only fifteen hundred people, and even though we get a lot of grain trucks during harvest, we're on the way to nowhere, so we don't need anything more than what we've got.'

'Mulligan go all right then?' The chair groaned under his weight as Bob finally sat down.

Red let out a laugh. 'You'd better think about taking a few kilos off. You'll never be able to sprint after a suspect and catch them.'

'Mate, I'm at the wrong stage of life to be doing that sort of shit. That's why I've got Dave here and you've got . . . What's his first name?'

'Robbie.'

'Right you are, that's why you've got Robbie.'

Red smiled and shook his head. 'You always had the answers, didn't you?' He turned to Dave who was watching the exchange with a reasonable amount of amusement. 'This fella give you a hard time?'

'Me? No, never.' He winked.

'I'll bet,' Red said dryly. 'What about you, Bob? We haven't caught up in ages. What's new for you?'

'Not a lot,' Bob said. 'Still chasing cattle in the mulga and crooks out in the bush. Like my life simple like that. And you? How's Annie?'

'She's fine. Enjoys life here. It's quieter than the city and she doesn't have to worry as much. I'm glad I made the move.'

'That's great to hear. Sometimes it works and sometimes it doesn't. She never was a city girl, though, was she, your Annie?'

'Not her thing.' Red put his hands over his stomach and watched Bob. 'Anyone managed to tame you yet?'

'I don't want to be tamed. Like being wild, like the life I live.'

'So wild,' Dave agreed dryly, a half grin on his face.

Red laughed.

'But,' Bob continued, ignoring the banter, 'as it happens, I've met a nice lady who came to my aid in the last case we were working up north. Early days, though.'

'Well, well, I'll be, the great Bob Holden in domesticated bliss, huh?'

'Now, now, Red, don't you be talking like that! You'll ruin my reputation.' Bob grinned as he put his ankle over his knee.

A cluster of noises reached their ears as Robbie hip and shouldered the door open, carrying coffees and food in both hands.

'Good work,' Bob said, as Dave stood up to help.

The smell of coffee and warm pastries filled the office and, despite the warm breeze, Dave couldn't wait to have something to eat.

'So, Arson put the call out for you to head this up? I know we need some experts on this case, but I thought they would have called in Missing Persons rather than you boys. Haven't heard any reports of stolen sheep.' Red took the coffee Robbie held out and nodded for him to pull up another chair.

'We're more than stock theft, Red.' Bob's voice rose a note in disbelief. 'You know that. Any crime in rural areas is for us. They've changed our name now, you know. Rural Crime Squad. But I still think of it as the stock squad. Too old to go with that change.'

'But if you guys are supposed to solve all the rural crimes,' Robbie asked, in between blowing on his coffee, 'what are we meant to do? We're stationed out here in the country for that exact reason.'

Although the question was asked with sincerity, Dave got the feeling there was an undertone to the words. He reassessed Constable Robbie Mulligan.

Young, maybe twenty-five or twenty-six. Well-built and obviously worked out. Blond hair. The absence of a wedding ring on his left hand didn't mean anything, but Dave didn't think he'd tied the knot yet. He was sitting, casual and relaxed, foot resting on his opposite knee, leaning back, watching the two ring-ins carefully.

Dave refocused on Bob and how he was going to answer.

'Son, you've got a lot of work to do out here. Us fellas, we're around to help out when we can; bringing more honed skills towards farms and the like. Dave here, he rides motorbikes and drives a truck when we're doing a muster, checking stock numbers. And me? I'm pretty adept at trawling through invoices and paperwork, talking to blokes in the stockyards and the like. Understanding ferti-liser rates and DSEs.' He leaned forward and gave Robbie's foot a consolatory pat. 'Do you know what DSEs are?'

Robbie's eyes narrowed, unsure if this was a test or a casual question.

'No,' he answered.

'Dry Sheep Equivalent. Got to do with the amount of sheep you can run in a certain area. Look, don't worry about us. We're not here to take over. We're just here to help.'

Robbie's face didn't give the impression he was convinced about that last sentence. In fact, he hadn't rolled out the welcome mat since they'd arrived, but Dave decided to give the young constable the benefit of the doubt. Bob's heavy-handedness first up, and perhaps comments that could be classed as condescending, might have had something to do with Robbie's attitude.

Bob spread his hands out and gave a smile. 'Now, I hear you were first on the scene. What can you tell me?'

'Lots of smouldering logs and burnt grass. I didn't see or smell any dead stock, but I didn't get much further than the house, which there was really nothing left of. Weatherboard and tin so it went up easily.' He referred to his notebook. 'I've got photos if you want them. Conditions on the day were average. There was an FDI of—' Robbie stopped himself. 'FDI means Fire Danger Index, in case you're unsure.' He threw Bob a look as if to say, *I know the farming language, too.*

Dave laughed inwardly. Robbie was going to be able to give back as good as he got.

Bob smiled. 'Yeah, of course. How high was it?'

'Severe. Fifty-three.'

'And how is the FDI worked out?' Bob asked.

Dave snuck a glance at Bob. They had their own weather meter as part of the kit, in the troopy. Bob was clearly going tit for tat here, and if Dave knew anything about Bob, he was the one who would come out on top.

'Measurements of wind speed, temperature and humidity. Fuel, such as dry grass or stubble, also play a part. They put them all together and come up with a figure in a category of low, moderate, high, all the way up to catastrophic. The wind came up late morning and it was strong, but the temperature, even though there had been forecasts of above thirty-five degrees, hadn't got above the high twenties. Unusual for this time of the year and there had been a fog the day before, so humidity was higher than normal, which kept the rating down. Still, with the wind, the fire got away fast and it took time for the brigade to get out there. Leo called to alert the fire control officer. A John Guthrie. Everyone downed tools to come and help, but a lot were off the farms and they had to get back from town before they could get to their fire units.'

'Mostly volunteers?'

'Yeah, farmers with fire trucks or small units, and the town crew came as well. The first ones there were about forty minutes from seeing the smoke—that was the farmer three farms away.'

'Got a name?'

'Travis Patton.'

Dave wrote it down.

'Tell me about the family,' he said, looking at Robbie. 'Did you interview the wife?'

'Yeah, she's distraught. Can't understand what's happened. Jill . . .' He reached for the file sitting on Red's desk. 'She left yesterday morning to go and play tennis. Said she'd asked Leo to come with them.'

'Them?' Bob glanced up from his notebook and over the top of his glasses.

'Two kids—Charlotte is seven and Noah is five. Anyway, he didn't want to, so she finished getting ready and left in the family car.' Robbie stopped so the information dump could be absorbed. 'In saying Leo didn't want to go to tennis, I need to clarify. If the power is out, Leo won't leave the farm, and it had tripped as they were deciding whether he was going to go to tennis. As soon as the power went off they both knew he wouldn't be going with Jill and the kids.

'On Jill's way out, she saw Leo's ute driving towards the shed where the pump for watering all the stock is located, but she can't tell us anything else. She was in town; verified by about thirty other people. The next thing Jill knows is there's a fire at their property. One of her friends raced in to tell her, so she left the kids with some friends and tried to get back out there, but we stopped her where we'd shut the road. There was too much smoke and fire to allow anyone onto the farm. Wasn't safe.'

'Take long for the power to come back on?' Bob asked.

'Was out all day. About eight o'clock that night the other neighbours told us it came back on, which cross-checks with the power company.'

'Okay. Does Mrs Perry work off-farm?' Dave asked.

'No, but she's busy with community work. Secretary of the P and C, president of the tennis club, helps out at the pool, all that sort of thing. Nothing paid.'

'Right, good community lady, by the sounds. And the rest of the family?' Bob asked.

'The family is pretty well-known within the community. Farm has been within the Perry family for three generations; Leo being the third.'

Bob referred to the file that Dave had given him when they'd left Perth. 'It was mentioned that Leo was managing the farm for his family.'

Red cleared his throat. 'Stephen and Jan Perry are retired and living in Margaret River. They've got three adult children, Leo's the youngest. The other two siblings aren't involved on the family farm and neither live here in Yorkenup.'

Now that's an interesting point, Dave thought. *Usually, it's the eldest who comes home.* His stomach dropped a little as he thought of his own situation. At Wind Valley Farm, his father had kept his two older brothers home . . . and told Dave to find his own way.

'Bit of a sad story, really,' Red continued. 'Stephen had a farming accident about twelve-odd years ago. He was out fencing and some wire snapped and ended up in his eye. Lost the whole eye, not just the sight. Then, about nine years ago, Jan had a stroke and couldn't use her left arm and really couldn't be on her own. The family decided they needed to leave the farm, but no one wanted to sell.

'Elliot, he's the oldest, was flying commercial jets for Qantas at that point and hadn't any plans on coming home, while Sally, the sister, is a lawyer in Sydney so . . .'

'No chance of her returning home either,' Bob finished. 'Family of highflyers. Pun intended.'

No one laughed.

'Yeah, and Leo, he'd always been at home on the farm, but never given the reins. Stephen paid the bills and made the decisions, while Jan did the books.'

'Normal old-style family set-up. Let me guess, no succession plan in place.'

Robbie shook his head and took up the story. 'Very grudgingly, Stephen agreed that Leo would get paid for managing the farm, and once the profit was known, it would be distributed to the rest of the family.'

Dave leaned forward. 'So, let me get this straight. Leo did the work and was paid to do it?'

'Yep.'

'Then the profit was divided between the parents and the other two kids, not him?'

'That's right.'

'And none of the others were helping in any real way now?'

'Not that we know of. They're still all living in other parts of Australia so they couldn't do much really.'

'Then Leo was getting shafted,' Dave said. A feeling of resentment started to build in his chest. Why did families think it was okay to treat their sons and daughters like paid labour, or cast them off without another thought? He felt for Leo, suspecting the farmer might have been feeling like he had the short end of the stick. After the way he'd been treated by his own father, Dave hated the thought of anyone else experiencing the same.

'How so?' Red asked.

'Well, the others are getting money for nothing. Profits from the farm. They're still employed and being paid, just as Leo is, but they're getting extra from the farm on top of their incomes, whereas Leo is working, receiving his wages and nothing else. Seem fair to you?' He turned to Robbie. 'Will the money being distributed to Sally and Elliot come off the final figure Leo would have to pay for the farm, when the parents die, and the farm goes to him? Actually, the first question should be, is the plan for Leo to inherit the farm once his parents die?'

The two local coppers looked at each other.

'Can't say I asked that question,' Red said.

'Ah well, not to worry,' Bob said, getting up and holding his hand out for the file. 'All good. We can find that out.'

'Wait,' Robbie said. 'I don't understand what the problem is.'

Bob gave a small smile. 'Yeah, I can see how this would be confusing. Succession planning in farming families is important. Especially if there's only one child at home, but others who aren't working on the farm. Land is worth a lot of money, and everything must be fair. Well, that's the way I see it,' Bob said. 'Not always the way it happens.

'Leo is running the place on the ground, making the decisions all the time and the other two are getting money from the farm without helping out. When the time comes for Leo to take over or the farm has to be sold, Leo hasn't had any income apart from his wages. No free rides, like the others have been getting, see?'

Robbie nodded slowly. 'Yeah, I think so. A cause for resentment.'

'Could be.'

'Woah,' Robbie said, blinking. 'A motive if the investigation was focused in a different direction such as murder.'

Bob nodded. 'Motive only on Leo's behalf.' He looked across at Robbie. 'Without being rude, I guess that's part of where our expertise comes in. We understand the agricultural industry.'

CHAPTER 5

'Hello, Mrs Perry. I'm Detective Bob Holden and this is Detective Dave Burrows. Sorry to barge in on you so late in the day, but we need to ask you some questions about your husband.'

The slight woman with glossy brown hair had a small boy clinging around her legs. His nose was runny and her eyes were red, with dark circles under them. If she'd slept since the fire, it wasn't apparent.

She clutched at the young boy as if frightened to let him go, and the lost look on her face tugged at Dave's heart.

Bob peered behind her and saw that the table of the motel room was piled high with food containers and games for the kids. 'Would you mind if we came in?' He indicated for her to move from the door.

'Uh, sorry, yes. I . . .' Her voice trailed off and she stepped away, leaving the entrance free for them to walk through.

'G'day there, young fella.' Bob ruffled the boy's hair on the way past and stepped over a trainset, engines and carriages hooked up to follow the rails.

'We're sorry we have to bother you, Mrs Perry,' Dave said, following in behind. 'We'd really like to build a bit of a picture about Leo, if that's okay with you. I know it's a really hard time.'

'Sorry. I'm just so . . .' She glanced around as if seeing the room for the first time, then she managed to unhook her son from her leg. He screwed up his face, but she shushed him. 'Can I get you a cup of tea? I'm sorry about the mess. There's not a lot of space in motel rooms, is there? Not after a big farmhouse.' Her voice matched the bewildered confusion that radiated from her body.

Dave had seen the same look many times before. A person trying to comprehend the incomprehensible. But Jill was small and thin; she seemed like a tiny broken bird that needed someone to care for her.

She looked, Dave thought, as if her world had ended.

'Please, don't worry about any of that.' Bob glanced around, looking to see if there was a courtyard. 'Would we be able to have a word outside, do you think, Mrs Perry? Away from . . .' He looked pointedly at Noah.

Jill bent to turn on the TV. 'Of course. Stay here, Noah. I won't be long. Oh look, High Five is on, you like them.' She tried to keep her voice bright, but there was a waver as the dancers dressed in brightly coloured clothes moved on the screen.

The boy climbed onto the couch and looked up at his mother. 'Is Daddy coming soon?' he asked.

She leaned forward and pressed her lips to the boy's forehead, her shoulders shaking momentarily, before straightening up. 'He'll be home before long, darling,' Jill whispered, then put her hand over her mouth as she turned to go outside with the detectives.

'Is your daughter here?' Dave asked, opening the sliding door to let her walk outside first.

The late afternoon summer air was scorching. Dave felt the wind move over his bare arms and calves, and sweat broke out on his forehead. Sometimes, the southern heat seemed fiercer than the north, he thought.

'No.' Jill picked her way around the fallen gum leaves that were covering the paved patio area. 'She's with friends for the afternoon. Just to give me a break.' She moved to the shade of a tree overhanging the tall brick wall at the back of the tiny courtyard and crossed her arms. 'Have you found him? Found Leo?' Tears were in her voice, her arms wrapped around her body as if she were desperately trying to hold everything in. 'Please tell me you have.'

'We're very sorry for what you're going through,' Bob told her, dabbing his face with his hankie. 'But no, we haven't had any breakthroughs. There are, however, a few things we need to follow up on after Re—um, Senior Sergeant Redford's and Constable Mulligan's questioning.'

Jill didn't move, only closed her eyes. 'I don't know how this has happened to us,' she whispered.

'When did you speak to Leo last, Jill?'

'Just as I was leaving to go into the tennis club on Saturday morning. I tried to ring once I heard about the fire, but he didn't answer the phone.'

'Were you surprised that he didn't answer?'

'Not really. Leo didn't always take calls, especially if he was busy, and he would have been trying to fight the fire. But he does always call back.'

'And when did you start to get concerned that you hadn't heard from him?'

'When the fire was safe. Once a fire has been contained, usually the guys are put on a rotation system. I tried to call a couple of times and didn't get him, then I rang some of the blokes asking if they'd seen him.' She swallowed and pinched her fingers over the bridge of her nose. 'They hadn't realised he wasn't around either. Everyone was consumed by trying to get the fire under control and no one had grasped that Leo wasn't there. He hadn't signed off from the fire ground.'

'I see.' Bob made a note then looked back at Jill. 'And Leo has fought fires before?'

'Oh, yeah. Everyone has out here. All the farmers are volunteers; it's not like we have a professional brigade here. Leo used to be the fire control officer but he decided not to take the job on again after Noah was born. He was happy to help out, all farmers are, but he felt he'd shouldered the responsibility for long enough and wanted someone else to take over. Takes time, you know, keeping up with the training and so on. Then there's a lot of paperwork afterwards.'

'Seems to be the way of the world,' Bob lamented. 'Paperwork and more paperwork. I can understand why he'd like a break.'

'Gotta share these positions around when you're all vollies, don't you?' Dave added.

She nodded and glanced back inside to check on Noah. He was lying on the couch, glued to the TV.

'To clarify, you've had no word from Leo?'

Jill paused, her throat working as she tried to control her emotions before finding the word: 'No.'

'Okay.' Bob was gentle. 'And now we're getting into the stage where it's unusual he hasn't contacted you, yeah?'

'Yeah. Leo would have always rung to tell me he was safe by now. And if he couldn't ring, he'd text or at least get a message to me through someone else. It's unlike him to leave me wondering. He knew fires scared me because I know how unpredictable they can be. Fire is second nature to people who have grown up in the country, but I wasn't raised out here so to me it's a frightening force. I don't understand the way it can move, so he always, *always*, gets in contact. Leo is a . . . good communicator.'

'Tell me about Leo,' Bob said as he leaned against the wall.

Dave checked the little boy inside again, but nothing had changed there. He kept his notebook in hand, ready to write down any tiny thing that might make a differ-ence to the investigation.

Jill let out a sigh and gave a shrug. 'What do you want to know? He is a great father, even though he works all the time. All his mates say he is a successful farmer; I assume that's right because, again, not having grown up on a farm, I couldn't be sure. But my understanding is that Leo is respected as a good farmer around the community.'

Dave thought about those terms: 'Good farmer', 'Good man'. These words were always bandied about in rural areas.

'Ah, he was a good bloke,' they'd lament in the pub as they talked about the death of a grazier. 'A hard worker.' People were judged on their ability of being 'good' at what they did and whether they'd been a workaholic, rather than the actual person they were.

'Is he involved with any farming groups?' Dave asked.

'Yeah, when he and I first got together he was the president of the Young Farmers but as we got busier, he gave it up. He used to love playing sport, but again, the farm took precedence. I'd try to get him away over the weekend for a day or so, just to spend some time with us. Leo found it really hard to leave the farm during summer, with the threat of fire and so on.' She paused. 'And he's always trying to prove to his father he's capable.'

'That must have been upsetting for you? Leo putting the business before your family?'

Jill gave a wry smile. 'All farmers do that, don't they?'

Bob gave a soft smile and nodded slightly. 'You and Leo are happy?' he asked.

Twisting her lips, Jill looked at him. 'Yes. If you can disregard the fact I did get annoyed that he didn't seem to make time for us. The kids are missing out when he's not there watching them play sport or at a school assembly.

Still, it's not only Leo. Heaps of other dads around here are constantly busy. Not just farmers, people who own their own business and can't get away because of the pressure or the fact their business doesn't operate if they aren't there. It's a long, well-worn argument that many self-employed families have. I've talked to Nicola and Andrew about it before and it's just how it is.'

'Nicola and Andrew?' Bob asked.

'The Pearces. Friends of ours. Andrew has known Leo since school.'

'What about Leo's other friends?'

'Chris Barry and Bruce Cameron were his closest friends, along with Andrew. They all went through school together, played sport. I can give you their contact details if you like?'

'Yeah, we're going to need to talk to them as well. Have you checked his bank accounts? Has there been any withdrawals of large amounts? Since the fire?'

'No, Leo hasn't taken any money out or accessed the accounts. I gave the other police officers all the details and they said they were going to be checking.'

'Yeah, there is an alert on your joint bank accounts and his phone number. Look, I know it might seem as if we're repeating questions and going over and over the same things the other police officers have already asked you, but it's important for us to get a clear picture and not to miss any small detail. That's why we like hearing the information for ourselves. I'm sorry that we might seem to be a nuisance,' Bob repeated his earlier apology.

Dave referred to his notebook. 'Jill, you said there weren't any vehicles missing from the farm. That's correct, is it?'

'None that I know of, but if a tractor or big piece of machinery was gone, I couldn't be sure. They're so large, those machines, and they kind of scare me, so I've never driven one. I don't really know what's there. I don't help out on the farm. The outside work has always been Leo's domain. He loves it. My strength is looking after the kids and being part of all their activities. Leo understands that and doesn't mind that I don't work outside like some other wives.'

Like some other wives. Who were the 'some'? Dave wondered. That sounded like it was a well-worn argument. Dave scratched a note to follow up later.

'Okay, we've got ways to check the equipment. What type of phone did he have?' Bob was asking the questions now.

'Mobile? Yeah, a Nokia. The type everyone has out here because it's got the best range.' She leaned up against the high brick wall, seeming oblivious to the heat. The wind grabbed at her hair, like invisible fingers were playing with the strands.

Bob took a step closer to her. 'And you've kept ringing his phone?' he asked softly.

Jill let out a little sob, turning away. Her shoulders and skirt moved in time with her sobs. 'So often. Hundreds of times,' she whispered again. 'First, I left messages. Angry ones, then pleading ones, then I just hung up when the message bank answered. Now I just ring to hear his voice.'

'He never answered?'

'Not once. Wherever his phone is, it must've run out of battery because it doesn't connect anymore. Just goes straight through to the message bank.' She rounded on them both now. Tears still wet on her cheeks but eyes flashing. 'Where is Leo? There's nothing to say he's dead, so he must be somewhere. And why won't he come home? Even if he doesn't want to come home for me—' she threw a grief-stricken look through the sliding door, to where Noah was still sitting on the couch staring at the TV '—he should come home for the kids.'

'Why do you think he doesn't want to come home for you?' Bob asked.

'What? I don't, but even if he didn't want to . . . the kids keep asking for him.'

'We're working on finding your husband, Jill,' Dave said. 'Now, what we're about to propose is going to be confronting, but we believe it's the only way forward. We'd like to involve the media. Put a request out for people to help us. Maybe Leo has been hurt or got a bump on the head and can't remember who he is. That happens in traumatic situations. There is a possibility that someone has seen him wandering down a road, or something similar.'

Jill's eyes widened. 'That must be it! He's lost his memory.' She reached out and grasped Bob's hand, since he was the closest. 'You need to find Leo! What if he's hurt? God!' When Jill let go Dave saw the white marks on Bob's hand, where she had squeezed hard.

Bob gently stopped her as she fished in her pocket for her phone.

'All of those things might be the case, Jill, but we don't know. So, let's wait before you start calling people. Do you have a photo of Leo we can use for the media?'

Jill stared at him uncomprehending for a second then shook her head. 'The house burned down! There's nothing left.'

'What photo was used for the posters in the bakery? Can we use that one?'

'Posters?'

'Yes, we saw posters asking for information about Leo.'

Slowly, Jill shook her head. 'I don't know anything about them. Must've been done by his parents. Or our friends.'

'Do you recognise this phone number?' He held up the poster.

'Ah, yes. That's Stephen's. Leo's father.'

'His parents must have a copy of this photo then?'

'Oh.' Jill linked her fingers together as if they were cold. 'Yeah, they will. I'll ask them.'

'Okay. This is what we're going to do. First off, we're going to put out a press release saying we are calling a media conference, then Dave and I are going to speak to the media, asking for any information the public might have.

'When people ring, there are going to be cops in Perth answering the calls and feeding information through to us here. Cops from the same squad as we're from so they will know what kind of questions to ask country people, okay?'

Crumpling into a chair next to her, Jill stared at the ground, not speaking. A moment later she looked up and asked, 'What squad are you from?'

'The Rural Crime Squad.' We're experts in rural areas.'
It was not quite the normal explanation, but enough to get
Jill to relax again.

Blowing out a breath, she nodded. 'I don't . . .'

'That's okay. You don't have to be involved at this stage.'

Jill clutched her hands to each upper arm, as if giving
herself a hug. 'I loved him,' she said. 'I don't know why he
isn't coming home.'

'We're doing as much as we can,' Dave told her gently,
at the same time noting the use of *loved*.

'Have your in-laws arrived in town yet? I was told they
were coming.'

Jill tipped her head to the side. 'They're next door. They
came the moment they heard about the fire.' Her voice was
weary, as if she couldn't say another word.

Everything about her body language was familiar to
Dave—it was how he'd felt after his mother-in-law, Ellen,
had died from that godawful gunshot of Bulldust's; when
he'd known Mark and Melinda weren't ever going to let
his children live with him again.

To Dave it was clear that all Jill wanted to do now was
go back to bed and curl up in a ball and never, ever think
about this again. To wake and have everything back to
normal, even though that could never be.

Dave had felt exactly the same. Except he'd raged against
the unfairness of it all as well.

Jill seemed too lost and bewildered to be angry yet,
although Dave suspected the ire would come soon enough.

'Okay, we'll have a chat to them now while we're here.' Bob fixed Jill with a look of concern. 'Can we help with anything? I can get a family liaison officer to come here to give you some support.'

Jill was shaking her head. 'No, that's . . .' She seemed to gather herself and remember her manners. 'Thank you for the offer. But we'll be okay. I've got plenty of friends and people who'll help me here. I don't want the kids to be around strangers.'

'That's fine. We understand. It's only an offer,' Dave said quickly. The Major Crime Squad had also tried to call in family liaison officers for Melinda and the kids, but they'd refused. Children—or anyone who'd gone through a tragedy—needed the ones they loved around them; if they were still able to be.

Bob fished out a card from his pocket and handed it to Jill. 'Now you call Dave or me anytime, doesn't matter whether it's day or night. If you need us, we will be here. If you have any questions about the investigations, we'll answer them. Anything at all. If we can't take your call, we'll ring you back as quickly as we can. Okay?'

'Thank you,' Jill whispered as she took his card and then the one Dave held out. 'Thank you.'

'Can you answer a couple more questions?' Dave asked just as there was a loud knock at the front door.

Noah jumped up from the couch. 'Daddy?'

Through the window they saw the door, which was chocked ajar with a yellow toy truck, open gently, the head

66

of a young woman peeking through the gap. When Noah saw it wasn't his father, he started to cry.

'Hello? It's only me,' the woman called out.

Dave judged her to be in her mid-twenties, with a long dark ponytail swinging behind her. She entered the room, holding the hand of a blonde child in a pink tutu, but quickly dropped it and swept up Noah, kissing his face and wiping his tears away.

'That's Carmel. Bruce's wife. We play tennis together. She's the one who's been looking after Charlotte for me.'

'I'll just say hello,' Bob said. 'After you answer Dave's questions, we'll be out of your hair.'

Bob opened the sliding door and walked back in. Dave heard him introducing himself to Carmel and talking to Charlotte.

'I hate to ask this question, Jill, but I have to. Do you know of anyone who was upset or angry with Leo?'

'As in someone who would want to hurt him?' A smile played around her lips; her eyes dewy as she thought about her husband. 'No. He's always kind to everyone. Leo, ah, you'd have to meet him to understand, but he's got this like, um—' her hands fluttered around in front of her, as she tried to find the words '—charm? No, that's not really right. Charisma? Anyway, something that draws people to him. I don't know anyone who doesn't like Leo.' Her gaze became dreamy. 'It's going to sound stupid but his smile always lights up a room. And he makes everyone feel like they're the only person in the world when he's talking to them. He's always keeping eye contact and listening intently.' She paused. 'That was one of the reasons I fell in love with him.'

Dave paused and let the words and emotion settle around them before he asked the next question. 'I know you've said you were both happy inside the marriage, Jill. There wasn't any talk of a separation or divorce?'

'No. Never. We had fun together. I guess we have our spats like all married couples do. I get annoyed because he works so much and doesn't always come with us to community events and sport and so on, but it's minor stuff.'

'Family? Everyone gets along okay?'

Jill crossed her arms. 'They do.'

There was something about her tone that made Dave ask another question. 'Do you get on with all of Leo's family?'

'Not always.'

CHAPTER 6

'Leo Perry is thirty-one, with red hair and blue eyes. He has a four-centimetre scar across his chin on the left-hand side. He was last seen wearing denim shorts and a navy blue Hard Yakka work shirt, Blundstone boots and a wide-brimmed hat,' the anchor of Seven News told her viewers.

'His constant companion is a tan kelpie called Coffee.' Another photo of a smiling Leo, leaning against the tray of his ute, his hand on Coffee's head was now on the screen. The dog looked as if she were smiling, too, tongue lolling out and her yellow eyes staring at Leo with such love that Dave's heart gave a bit of an extra hard thump.

The TV in the police station flashed back to the news anchor, her face concerned, the photo of Leo in the corner of the screen.

This then cut to footage of Bob standing at the front of the Yorkenup Police Station, Dave in the background, his

69

hands clasped in front of his body. Bob's face was serious as he spoke directly into the camera.

'Leo may be suffering memory loss or be injured. He is not dangerous, but instead of approaching him, we're asking for the public to contact Crime Stoppers if you see him.

'Again, we're appealing to everyone travelling on any of the roads in and around the Yorkenup Shire to be on alert and watch out for Leo.'

Bob disappeared and the news anchor was back. 'If you have seen Leo Perry, please call the number displayed on your screen.'

The last picture of Leo filled the TV, the Crime Stoppers number large at the bottom. Jill had told them the photo had been taken at his brother's thirtieth, where he'd been wearing a suit with a grey shirt and tie, his hair brushed and gelled down. His smile broad, but his mouth dropped a little at the right corner and showed a row of teeth an orthodontist would have been proud of. The thin white scar, which he got when he was twelve from a wire scratch, was clear at the bottom of his chin, but Leo didn't appear to be self-conscious of it. His whole face and body were open and friendly.

Dave had decided he liked what he knew about this young man; a farmer who seemed to be stuck in a hard situation.

Bob leaned back in his chair and looked across the room at Dave. 'See what information that brings, I guess,' he said. 'Hopefully the crew back at headquarters will have something for us soon.'

Robbie stuck his head into the small room that Red had told Bob and Dave they could use. It hadn't taken long to set up their computers and a printer, to clean the whiteboard down, ready for timelines, suspects and information.

A pile of witness statements was sitting in front of Dave. He'd run a cursory eye over the top one or two and noted the names of two firefighters who had made the original report that they believed Leo Perry was missing. Someone would head down and talk to them shortly. He and Bob had already had a quick chat with Leo's parents, Stephen and Jan, but that hadn't shed any new light on the situation except that it had been them who had put up the posters in desperation to find their missing son.

'I'm heading off. You blokes okay?' Robbie asked. 'The search crews are winding down for the night. No sign of him or the dog.' His voice was solemn.

'Thanks for letting us know, Robbie,' Dave said. 'If anything comes up during the night, we'll ring you.' He paused. 'Can you give me a quick rundown on the topography of Leo's farm and surrounding areas?'

Robbie leaned against the wall. 'Like most places around here, it's a pretty flat landscape. There are a few creeks that run through farms, but none are deep. Maybe a metre or so, and perhaps three metres wide. I guess there could be some tree trunks a body could get caught around if there were a flood, but at this time of year, the beds are dry.' A thoughtful look settled on his face. 'If Leo was trying to outrun a fire and look for a safe place, the creek isn't going to be it. He could've got trapped in around roots or tangled up in a log.'

'If he was looking for shelter, where would he've headed to?'

'The sheds or house I would reckon. But the house, well, that's gone. Arson have searched and there's no sign of him in there. Most of the sheds are still standing. The guys got the graders around them and put a wide firebreak in. Saved the lot . . .' His voice trailed off and Dave could see he was imagining finding a charred body, huddled in the house or near a tree.

'Any other type of protection he could have used to get out of the way of the fire?'

'Not really. If anything, you'd get caught out in the open and the flames would overrun you.' Robbie paused. 'A body would be easy to find then. There's not really any rocks or caves that would have given him any protection.'

'Right.' Bob tapped the desk, thinking. 'So not a lot of shelter to be had in those areas?'

'Nah. Flat ground, a few large-trunked trees and that's about it really.' Robbie rubbed his hand along the back of his neck. 'You fellas right then? Got the keys to your motel rooms?'

'Yeah, we're all good, thanks. Which is the best pub for a feed?' Bob asked.

'Top one. On the way out to Perth.'

'Cheers, son.'

The constable withdrew and Dave picked up the keys for the troopy. 'Too late for a visit to the farm?'

'Thought you'd never ask,' Bob said, checking his watch: six pm. 'We've got about an hour's worth of daylight.' He picked up a couple of books and went outside.

Dave locked the door behind them.

'Leo's father organised the last few years' financial records for us,' Bob told him, holding up three ring-bound booklets. 'I've pulled all the licence records for the vehicles and farm machinery, and the insurance agent has emailed the list of what is insured with him.'

'We can check off the machinery against the lists?'

Bob nodded. 'You know, considering how hot the fire was, the vollies did a great job at stopping it before it got to the shed. I know it's pretty awful to lose the house and memories—photographs and such—but imagine losing millions of dollars' worth of machines.'

'All insured, I guess. You can't get photos back. I talked to John Guthrie briefly. He's the fire control officer for this area. He had two graders and a dozer cutting fire breaks where he could. They were there within a few hours of the fire starting. They put a wide break in around all of the machinery sheds, just like Robbie mentioned.'

'That'd do it,' Bob said.

The dirt road was wide and well used; small, rolling hills on either side. Summer colours of gold and brown covered the land. This was farming country. Expansive paddocks. The only obstacles in the way of huge boom sprays and seeders were a few clusters of trees, and mounds of granite. Out here the runs were long and the sky a large vastness of blue or grey, depending on the time of the year.

Copper-coloured dust rose in front of them, indicating another car was on the road, and it wasn't long before a white Nissan Patrol passed, keeping far to the left to avoid stone chips in the windscreen and dust. The driver, sunglasses covering her eyes and bare-tanned shoulders, raised a finger to wave.

'Check out that tower over there.' Bob pointed to a metal construction rising high on the top of a hill, thick steel cables fastening it hard to the earth. On the top, repeaters and satellite dishes. 'Bloody eyesores, aren't they?'

'Helpful when you need a fire truck, though.'

'True enough. What'd you make of Jill Perry?'

'Shattered.'

'I agree.' Bob looked out of the window, while Dave kept his hands steady on the steering wheel, watching the road. 'Look, here it is.'

The gateway into Leo and Jill Perry's farm was wide and planted with flowering geraniums and agapanthus. The mailbox was a forty-four-gallon drum painted white, with a lovely covering of brown dust over it.

'Roadside mail delivery out here. Wonder how often the mail is brought out,' Dave said. 'Perhaps the mailman might have seen him.'

'Not on a Saturday, I wouldn't have thought, but we can check.'

They followed the gravel road past the machinery sheds.

Bob gave a low whistle. 'This place would be worth a small fortune,' he said. 'Fences are top notch and it's in a real safe grain-growing belt. Enough rain, but I guess they might get a few frosts out here, which could tune up the crops at the wrong time. Not far from Perth. Might be worth four or five mill, bit more even. Even if you didn't want to be a farmer, there wouldn't be too many better positions than the ones in this area.'

'Money is always such a good motivation,' Dave said. 'Any talk about selling?'

'Not that I've heard.'

A wide scar across the land encircled the sheds: the fire break.

Another three kilometres on, the telltale signs of blackened earth and burnt grass came into view. Tongues of fire had chased under fences and down into the small stone-covered creeks. Some areas had nothing to burn, and the fire had come to a standstill. In other places, the flames seemed to have skipped over rocks and thick tree roots and started to burn the grass on the other side.

Further on they came to the burnt-out ruins of the house and shearing shed. Yellow and black tape warned that caution was needed.

Dave pulled up at the edge and stopped the car.

They both looked at the devastation in front of them. Blackened, twisted tin, shattered glass from where the windows had exploded, and a crumpled chimney.

Slowly opening their doors, they each got out. In the silent evening, just as the sun had hit the horizon, the smell of old smoke and burnt belongings rose to meet them. Goosebumps spread over Dave's skin as he imagined the house in flames.

'Thank god no one was home,' he said, starting to walk around and take notes. Something glinted on the ground, and he squatted, using his pen to turn the object over.

Beer top. He smiled. Something normal. Then his smile dropped away as he saw the swing set, warped and almost melted inside a sandpit.

Opening the file, he checked the photos the Arson squad had taken. *There is nothing to prove this is more than an unfortunate accident,* had been the official line from them.

Only the fact that Leo Perry was missing indicated there could be more to this fire than met the eye.

Dave stood up and looked towards the shearing shed. He heard his name being called so he followed Bob's voice to a pen about twenty metres from the house.

'Chook pen?' he asked, seeing the collapsed structure.

'I'd reckon. No mention of any chooks though.'

'Mightn't have had any. What have you got?'

'Probably nothing, but there's a burnt shoe here.' Bob was bending over, a pair of gloves on his thick hands. 'Could be a bloke's, could be a woman's if she has big feet.'

'Work boot of some description,' Dave agreed. 'This has all been searched, though, hasn't it?'

'That's my understanding.' Bob pulled a bag from his pocket, swishing at the flies that were clustering around his face.

Dave went over to the crumpled heap, pulling a couple of sheets away and looked underneath. Plastic drums, which would have been used as nests, were a pile of melted white on the ground, while a few rocks were charred against the wall. Dave supposed they were there to discourage foxes from trying to dig under. He shifted another piece of tin, this time seeing only dirt.

'Nothing,' he called back to Bob.

'Didn't think there would be. Those boys are good.'

'Let's go and check out the machinery shed, get a list of the machines that are still there.' Dave headed for the troopy as Bob's mobile rang.

Bob let out a surprised gasp and stopped, midstride, then cursed.

'Bloody phones! You'd think I'd get used to them.' Bob held the phone to his ear, sooty fingertips marking his cheek. ''Ello? Holden here. That right? Well, that's a good job.' Closing the phone, Bob looked pleased. 'Parksey's come through the op all okay. That's such a relief.' He stopped for a moment and looked out across the land.

'Best news I've heard in ages,' Dave told Bob.

The sun was slowly sinking in the west, the golden glow spread out before them. Galahs and crows were strutting around the ground, looking for seeds and grain. The silence seemed to rise towards the deepening blue sky, and Bob nodded as if he were thanking someone or something in that great expanse of sky. 'What a bloody relief.' He breathed deeply and, as if a weight had lifted from his shoulders, his body relaxed. 'Well now, let's check out those sheds.'

Inside the tin walls, Dave made a list: three tractors, two headers, a boom spray, a truck, plus numerous utes.

There were other smaller machines: a square hay baler and dipping crate.

'Got the monopoly on crappy utes. Looks like he hit up every clearing sale in the district. What is there? Eight? Why did he need eight? Only one of him to drive them and, according to the report, he had a Nissan Patrol that was only a couple of years old.'

'Jill said he kept them for seeding and harvest time when he had more staff and needed them to be able to get around. Some are still registered.'

Dave stopped. 'Really? What's it cost to register a ute these days? Five hundred bucks? Lot of waste sitting here for three months of the year.'

'Well, son, let's look into it, shall we?'

Dave went around to the first ute and peered inside. He fiddled with the handle and the door opened with a loud screech.

'Oil needed,' Bob said.

Opening the glove box, Dave had a quick rifle through, then flipped down both visors. Nothing of interest. Under the seat didn't show anything except spider webs, dust and alfoil that had been chewed by the mice that obviously inhabited the vehicle. A scrap of paper in the footwell had a phone number and business name scribbled next to it. Dave took a wet evidence paper bag from his pocket and picked it up, writing the date, place and time he found it.

'Probably nothing, but who knows,' Dave said as he tucked it in his pocket.

Bob, who was looking through a different ute, slammed the door and moved on to the next one. 'Too early to have any idea,' he said.

Grabbing the torch from his waist, Dave flashed it towards the darkening edges of the shed. Galahs were screeching overhead as the sun dipped below the horizon; complete darkness was approaching. The smell of burnt grass and charred wood was on the breeze. He paced the perimeter, making sure that all the tin fitted flush with the frame. The utes had been wedged and parked towards the back and were fitted together like a jigsaw puzzle, with very little room between any of them. They almost looked as if they were characters in a children's story; ready for visitors to come and look at their headlights, or run their hands over the cracked vinyl seating; sit in the old seats and reminisce over tall tales, true or otherwise.

Dave had never seen anything like it before.

With a crash, Bob had opened the header door and accidentally tripped over the oil drums close by, sending them tumbling to the ground. He swore and reached up to grab a guard on the side of the header to steady himself. Instead, the guard wobbled and tumbled to the ground, opening up the side of the machine.

'You okay there?' Dave asked, peering over the roof of another ute.

'What the hell?' Bob muttered, dragging his bulky frame off the ground and dusting off his hands. 'Well, well, lookie here. Dave, see what you think about this, son.'

At the sound of Bob's tone, Dave frowned and squinted in Bob's direction before closing the door and winding his way through the machinery and vehicles to where Bob was inspecting the side of the header.

'What have you got?'

'Have a squiz up in there.' Bob pointed upwards as he backed out.

Wriggling his way underneath, Dave flashed the light inside and saw thick black belts, pulleys and a lot of chaff and dirt.

'Hasn't been cleaned since harvest,' he called back. 'What am I looking . . . Oh.' Dave looked around for something to stand on and dragged over a twenty-litre container of oil. 'That looks like something has been hung from the top pulley and has been blowing in the wind, by the marks.'

'Make a detective out of you yet,' Bob said. 'Now why would there be something hanging from a pulley? To my way of thinking, whatever was there would cause damage when the header was started and put into gear.'

'Pass me the camera.'

While Bob was gone, Dave inspected the rest of the machine. Then the next one. If it had been something like mouse baits, hanging from a tin or tucked into little pouches, to keep the mice out of the header, then there should be similar markings on every machine. But, no, this one seemed special.

The u-shaped marks had rubbed through every speck of dust, leaving the paint underneath clean and shiny.

'Here you go, son.' Bob handed him the camera and he climbed back up onto the drum, clicking eight or nine photos, then voiced his thoughts about baits, before leaning his heavy frame against the large wheel. 'If Leo didn't want mice or rats in his machine, you'd clean the bloody thing down and make sure there wasn't any grain around. That box at the back has about three bags' worth of seed in it. Dunno why people don't look after their gear.' Bob's voice held pure bemusement.

'Reeks of fermentation so, at some stage, the grain has got wet, too. Recently, I'd say.'

'I could smell it when we first walked in.'

Dave stood back now and surveyed the whole scene from a distance. 'So, what was here?' he asked, tracing the marks without his fingers touching the area.

'We've got no idea if there is anything missing from the house, do we? It was burned down before Jill got back to the farm.'

'That's right.'

Dave moved away and leaned against the bench, looking at the eight worn-out utes lined up and the large machinery, uncared for, despite everyone saying that Leo was a good farmer.

A whisper of Dave's spider senses slid across his skin and he glanced towards the darkness. 'Something isn't right here,' he said.

CHAPTER 7

The Top Hotel had people spilling out from the front bar onto the street when Dave and Bob pulled up for dinner. Their unmarked troopy drew a few curious glances from the patrons leaning against the rails and sitting at tables under the verandah.

'Ring-ins,' Dave heard someone say through the open passenger's side window.

'Saw that vehicle at the motel on my way here. I heard they called in outta town coppers. Reckon they could be them?'

True enough. Dave grinned at the comment. Such was the bush telegraph in a small town.

They'd checked into the same motel that Jill and her in-laws were staying at. There hadn't been many other options, although both Bob and Dave would have preferred to be somewhere away from the family. Sometimes there needed to be a boundary between them and the victims of crimes.

Heat shimmered just above the cement footpath and sweat lined many of the faces drinking outside. Dave and Bob were regarded with a curious openness as they walked through the doorway, into the cool. They nodded and said g'day to a few of the blokes who were happy to look them in the face.

Without asking, Dave pushed his way to the bar and ordered two beers, while Bob elbowed through the crowd to the dining room. They had their routine down pat these days. Dave looked after the drinks and Bob the food. If they camped out, it was the other way around.

'Last table,' Bob said when Dave found him in the corner of the dining room.

Dave handed him his beer and they clinked glasses. 'Wonder what's going on tonight to get so many people through the door? Looks like the whole shire is here,' Dave said.

As if in answer to his question there was the loud screech of a microphone, a tapping noise, followed by heavy breathing.

A smart-arse from the bar let out a loud whistle. 'Get on with it, Mac!'

'Hello, can you hear me out there?' More tapping as a few claps started across the room and then morphed into a cacophony of whistling, stamping and clapping.

Dave swivelled in his chair and looked around, his elbow hanging over the back of the chair. In front of the microphone was a man with a slightly bemused expression on his face, patting down his work shirt over his protruding stomach. The black hat he wore was like the ones that Dave had seen country music stars wear on stage, while a moustache dropped down over his top lip and ran all the way to his jawline. He could easily be a farmer, stock agent or country singer, although he didn't seem to be comfortable in the limelight.

'Ah, good evening, everyone,' he said. 'Thanks all for showing up. For those who don't know I'm Mac. Darts grand final night is always a big one, but now we're raising money for the Perry family, it's got even bigger. We're going to run the darts final after the auction, so stay around and watch Team Bullseye and Team Ace go head to head in grand final action.' Mac seemed to have settled into his role by the time he'd finished talking about darts.

At the mention of the Perry name, the room fell silent, save a few clinking glasses.

Dave flicked a look at Bob, but the older man was leaning forward, listening with intent.

'As we know there's been a fire over at the Perry place and we need to make sure Jill and those littlies are looked after. We're still all a bit gobsmacked that Leo hasn't shown up.' Mac ran a hand over his hair and shook his head. 'It's a bit of a bloody mess, isn't it?' He sounded as baffled as Jill had earlier that day. 'Leo is such a good bloke and the fact he's not here? Well, there's got to be some sorta reason for that. Not sure what it could be . . .' His voice trailed off, but when he spoke again, it was strong. 'The Perry family have been around Yorkenup for a long while. Leo, his dad before him and his grandad before that. They've always been good community members, watching out for our families and loved ones. Stephen was a vollie ambo. First one on site in the accident of my girl, Carla.' Mac cleared his throat. 'And now something's gone amiss, it's our job to return the favour. Jill does a lot for the P and C and tennis club, helps out in the school canteen and generally around town.

'Now, for those of you who haven't caught up, Leo's immediate family are staying at the motel on the main street. The house at the farm has been incinerated and we'll be having a working bee out there in the next few weeks to clear up the site so rebuilding can begin as quickly as possible.'

Mac glanced down at his notes. 'Stephen and Jan, Leo's folks, are also staying at the motel. And Elliot has arrived now, too. Sally is trying to get back from Sydney as quick as she can. If you haven't caught up with them, call in and say g'day. They'll be happy to see you.

'Both families have enough food and the like, so what we're raising money for here tonight is their accommodation and any other, um, extras that might come up. You know, for when we find Leo, and what that might entail. The bank will probably freeze all the assets until they know what's going on, so basically just a bit of help for them all, you know what I mean?'

Mac's voice was drowned out by more clapping, even with the indirect comment that a funeral might be in order at some stage.

'Good-oh, then. Hands deep in your pockets, everyone, and we'll start the auction with a donation from the butchers. A meat pack worth one hundred and fifty bucks. Lookee here at it.' Mac's voice changed to the auctioneer's quick-speak. 'We got porterhouse and loin chops, few snaggers there, good for the barbie. Especially during these summer nights. What have you got? I say one sixty, one sixty.'

There was a yell from another man who had climbed onto the stage and pointed to someone deep in the crowd, who had their hand in the air.

'One seventy, one seventy. Thank you, sir! How about one eighty, good cause and all, one eighty!'

'Yep!' Another loud yell, indicating the price had risen another ten dollars.

Bob leaned forward to Dave. 'He's got a point. Not knowing where Leo is, the bank will freeze the assets for sure. I reckon the insurance company will baulk at paying anything until things are resolved. That'll mean the house won't be being rebuilt anytime soon, and without a body there won't be any life insurance, either. Be interesting to see the family's reaction once they find that out.'

Dave nodded and scanned the crowd, wondering who everyone was and how they fitted in to the community. They'd find out soon enough, once they started asking questions. He waved the menu at Bob and held his beer up, wanting to know if his partner wanted another one.

A quick nod and Bob took the menu while Dave went back to the bar.

'You one of the coppers they've brought in from outta town?'

The voice was at Dave's elbow, just as he ordered the drinks. Then he felt a body push alongside him and he turned.

'Sure am. Dave Burrows,' he introduced himself. 'And you are?'

Another farmer, for sure. Weathered, tanned skin and clear blue eyes set in a lined face.

'Andrew Pearce. Mate of Leo's.' As he said the words, a heaviness came over his face. 'This is a bad, bad business.'

Dave got his wallet out to pay for the drinks. He slipped his business card out at the same time and handed it to Andrew. 'You wouldn't happen to know where he is, would you?'

Shock flashed across Andrew's face. 'What? Not on your life! Why would you ask that?'

In the background Mac had moved on to offer a gift voucher from the local nursery and a month's weekly house maintenance from a cleaning company.

'Just a normal question in this type of inquiry, I'm afraid,' Dave said. 'Good mates, were you?'

'Known each other since we were kids. Played footy together right from year one, all the way up to vets now.' He gave a wry grin. 'Who would've thought being over thirty constituted playing vets?'

Dave laughed. 'You're better than me. Can't remember the last time I pulled on a footy jumper. Listen, you got a few minutes? My partner and I are in the dining room waiting for dinner. We would've tracked you down to ask questions anyway. Do you want to come and answer some now?'

Andrew nodded. 'I'll get a refill and be over.'

Dave made his way back to the table and noticed Bob had brought back a couple of bread rolls and butter when he'd ordered. He told Bob about Andrew and pulled his notebook out, laying it on the table.

'Fast work.'

'Might as well make the most of it.'

His words were drowned out by a ruckus as Mac knocked down a thousand-dollar fuel voucher to a young man wearing a shearing singlet and a pair of moccasins, which Dave found odd because shearers always took their shearing shoes off before they left the shed and put on boots or sandshoes.

A chair pulled out from the table alongside of them, and Andrew swung it around to face theirs, sitting down. He held out his hand to Bob.

'Thanks for giving up your time at the pub,' Bob said warmly as they shook. 'Dave here tells me you and Leo were good mates.'

'Yeah, long-time friends. Just saying that we played footy from primary school until we hit vets. Then Leo bowed out, but I kept going. Like to keep fit.'

'Why'd Leo pull the pin?'

'Not really sure. He said it was because his knees were giving him the shits, but I think it was more. Been a while since he's been involved in too much outside of the farm.'

'As in months or years?'

Andrew took a long drink, seeming to think on the question. 'You know, now you mention it, I think it's years. I've been playing vets for five years. I think it's been since about then.'

Bob nodded. 'What did he used to be involved in?'

'Everything. Cricket, footy, he was the treasurer for the show and liked to go along to the Rotary Club meetings occasionally. Not that he was a member, just enjoyed the social aspect of the dinners, so he'd go along as a guest.'

'Did something happen to make him take a step back?' Dave asked.

Slowly, Andrew shook his head. 'I can't think of anything. Oh, well, I guess the kids came along. But other than that . . .' His voice trailed off. 'What type of thing are you meaning?'

'Anything really. Money troubles? Depression, maybe even having a falling out with someone. We hear that his family had a few problems health-wise.'

'His olds have done in the past for sure, but Leo has worked on the farm since he finished school and he was happy to keep going. His siblings, Elliot and Sally, were never going to come home, and if Leo hadn't stayed then they would've put the property on the market. He's happiest when he's mucking around in his paddocks and putting a crop in.'

'What's Leo like?'

'Oh, great bloke. Loves a good time, a beer. We knocked around being idiots when we were teenagers, then he was best man at my wedding and I was at his. Kids came along then we started to get these grey hairs! Dunno where the time has gone, really.' He gave a smile that faded as quickly as it had arrived. 'But yeah, Leo is a great mate and we've got a lot of history together.'

'Leo never struggled with any mental health issues?'

'Nah. Us blokes, we had an agreement that we would always talk if anything was upsetting. Lost a mate to suicide when we were nearly at the end of high school. Rocked us all so bad that one night, after Dougo's funeral, we'd drunk about five bottles of Stone's Green Ginger Wine out on the footy oval. We swore on each other's life that we'd always talk. And we do.

'Leo's a good communicator and would let us blokes know if there was any trouble at home, with the kids or on the farm. Just as we all knew if Bruce or Chris or I were struggling.'

It was Dave's turn to ask the questions. 'Do you know if Leo and Jill had any marital problems?'

Andrew leaned back in his chair and regarded both men. 'Do you guys have kids?'

Dave nodded.

'Well then, you'd know what it's like when they come along, and I think Leo and Jill were the same as every couple I know. Kids wear you down and you don't get any time alone. They were solid, but life tended to test them. Jill told my wife, Nicola, heaps of times that she would've liked Leo to go to the kids' sport events a bit more, get back involved with the community, but I can understand why he didn't always make it along. I farm as well, and it's all-consuming. You could work twenty-four seven if you wanted to. There's always something to do. Leo is a perfectionist so if there is something to be done, he stays home and takes care of it.'

The word perfectionist rang in Dave's ears. That wasn't what the machinery at the farm had portrayed.

'I used to be a farmer as well, so I understand,' Dave said. His father had never ventured too far from the boundary fence, and certainly never watched any of his children play sport. That was women's work. 'They don't have to be the big jobs like shearing or seeding, but maintenance or something of the like.'

'Yeah, that's right.'

Bob leaned back in his chair to let the waitress put down the chicken parmi he'd ordered. She unceremoniously dumped a knife and fork wrapped in a napkin next to the plate and hurried off again, probably to get Dave's.

'Thanks, love,' Bob called after her.

Andrew grinned. 'That's Hannah. Worked here for a long time, and never discovered how to smile. Jacinta, she's another barmaid, is the complete opposite. Want to watch out for her, she's always looking for fresh prey.' His glance slid across to Dave and he winked.

'Good to know.' Bob chuckled.

'Anything else I can help you with?' Andrew asked. 'I should leave you to your dinner.'

'I understand there was a bit of tension between Jill and Leo's parents,' Dave said, leaning back in his chair. 'Do you know anything about that?'

Andrew nodded slowly. 'Yeah, I do. But I think that information should come from Jill, rather than second-hand. I'm happy to tell you if needs be, though. Don't want to be seen as . . . what do you call it? Obstructing?'

'Sure, no worries, but perhaps you could tell us whether the tension damaged the relationship between Jill and her in-laws?'

'Without a doubt,' Andrew said. 'In fact, if they had been my parents, speaking about my wife, there would have been a lot more feathers flying.'

'Leo didn't stand up for Jill?'

Again, another pause. 'Not as much as he should have. But that's only my opinion.'

'Did that cause any friction between them?'

'You'll have to ask Jill. I can't speak for her. Although Nicola would probably know.' Andrew crossed his arms. 'Look, Leo talked about it with us blokes, too. Once you've found out from Jill what happened, I'm more than happy to have this conversation again. That be all right?'

'Have you got a phone number we can contact you on, Andrew?' Dave asked, making a note of Andrew's name in his ever-present notebook.

Andrew recited his mobile number.

'One more thing,' Dave said, after he'd repeated the numbers back. 'Did Leo ever talk to you about succession planning?'

'Oh yeah.' Andrew groaned at the memories. 'Leo was really caught between a rock and a hard place. He loved farming, like I said, but his family were taking him for granted, for sure. His parents, as well as Elliot and Sally, I mean, not Jill. Never any help coming his way, and his father always questioned his decisions, right down to how much fertiliser he was putting on the crop.'

'And that was still happening?'

'Not as much as when his dad first retired to Margaret River, but enough to piss Leo off.' Andrew leaned forward. 'And I'll tell you something else for nothing. Leo wasn't getting paid anywhere near what a manager should be. He was running that place for mate's rates.'

CHAPTER 8

'Handy that Leo's old man wanted copies of every invoice and payment slip,' Dave said as he surveyed the paperwork spread across the table in the police station. A hot coffee was close to his hand and he wanted to stretch out his back after sleeping the night in a bed that had a dip in the middle and lumpy pillows.

Folders from the last five years containing everything needed for the tax office were piled in the middle, and Bob and Dave were checking each one, slowly, pulling out any piece of information that warranted further investigation. 'Reckon old man Perry has killed a few trees in his time.'

Bob snorted. 'Sure has, son. He wouldn't trust a computer to save his life. That's part of the problem with these old-timers who won't let go. They need everything done the way it has been for years. I bet my last dollar that Stephen would use a physical cashbook for his accounts, not a computer.'

'How many times have we seen that?' Dave replied.

'Yeah. And I reckon this poor bastard is really under the thumb, which gives him a great motive to disappear. What do you think, son?'

Sighing, Dave picked up a hire purchase invoice, indicating that a new John Deere tractor had been bought five years ago. Scanning the page, the information told him that there were four quarterly payments of over thirty thousand dollars each left on it.

'Not sure, but I'm finding it hard to reconcile that he'd disappear when he has two young kids. If it were me and I had two kids out there who I couldn't have anything to do with, well, I'd think long and hard about vanishing and starting a new life.'

'He mightn't have had a choice.'

Dave paused. 'Good point. If you're going into witness protection, you can't have anything to do with family or friends once you leave.'

Bob scratched a note on the whiteboard. *Witness Protection. Ask if there were any incidents/accidents/ request to testify.*

Dave went to speak again, but Bob held up his finger. 'Still won't get anything out of the Wit Protection department.' He looked over his glasses at Dave. 'As you know, the only person who knows about this type of disappearance is the handler. No family, and no other coppers.

'Let's look at everything we have so far. It's an unusual case for a disappearance, like I said earlier. First, Leo doesn't fit the profile for suicide. And we haven't found a reason for him to do anything so drastic.' He ticked one finger off. 'Second,' he touched his middle finger, 'he has a young family and a seemingly happy marriage. Third, where's he going to get money from to disappear? I've been through the bank statements, and everything has to be double-checked by Stephen, so there has been no opportunity to skim anything from the farm, which by the bank accounts is doing very well.

'Looking at his personal joint accounts with Jill, they've got extraordinarily little excess cash. I can understand why the town wanted to raise money for them.'

'Have either of them got accounts by themselves? Any chance of Jill hiding any money on their behalf?'

'I didn't put a rush on information for her accounts, so they're still waiting in the system to be accessed, but they need checking, for sure.'

Looking down at the invoice again, Dave noted the tractor's numberplate and pulled the list of registrations towards him.

'By the sounds of what you're saying, you believe he's alive?'

'The SES finished searching today and they've found nothing. We found a hiding place for something—whatever that was, under the header's guard. He's being controlled and is unhappy with his present situation, wife and kids excluded. That's enough for me to think he is still alive, and not coming home. Better option than pushing up daisies.'

'Hmm.' Dave frowned. 'Do you think we should go back out to the sheds and see what else we can find?'

'We've been through all the glove boxes and hidey-holes. I don't think there's anything else to be discovered. We're going to have to look further afield.'

'I still don't understand why he'd set a fire and burn his house down. Don't forget he called for help.'

'Yes, I agree, son, but I don't think he meant for the house to burn. Arson don't think he expected the fire at all. That was something fortuitous that happened, and maybe he just took advantage of it.'

Dave shook his head. 'I don't buy it.'

Bob shrugged. 'What's the next option? I'm all ears.' He scratched at his upper arm, causing a pimple to bleed. 'Bugger it.' Getting out his hankie, he held it over the wound, stemming the flow.

'I don't know right now,' Dave said. 'If I go back to the things we do know: there isn't a body and his dog is missing. That would all indicate he could be alive, like you've said. *But* there's no movement on his bank accounts, his phone is dead, and we haven't found anything in these accounts to show there was a problem. Moderately happy wife, kids.' Dave held up his hands. 'No transactions on the bank accounts doesn't really tell us anything. There're plenty of ways still to live, like cash and so on . . . if he had access to that.'

Checking his arm wasn't bleeding anymore, Bob tapped on the files. 'But where would he have got cash from? Stephen Perry reigned with an iron fist. Everything I've looked at crosschecks to no money problems within the farm. In fact, there would be many farmers who'd like this balance sheet!'

Dave stood up and stretched. 'I'm going for another coffee. Want one?'

Bob shook his head. 'Later.'

Wandering outside, Dave felt the heat hit his skin. For early morning, the sun had a fierce bite, and he pulled his hat down to cover his nose. This case was bothering him more than most other investigations.

Why would a father walk away from his children?

He did have to agree with Bob in one way; it did appear as if Leo was still alive. But what possible motivation did he have for leaving? And if he was living off cash, where did he get it from?

Changing direction, Dave headed for the motel, hoping to catch Jill.

The sound of an engine slowing behind him made Dave glance over his shoulder. Red was winding down the window in the patrol car, Robbie in the passenger's seat.

'Morning, boys.' Dave leaned his forearm on the roof of the car. 'Busy day?'

'Quiet as a church mouse,' Red told him. 'No word on Leo, SES has been stood down and there's nothing new anywhere.'

'Yeah, frustrating. What do you boys think has happened?'

Robbie leaned forward and looked up at Dave. 'Wish I knew, but I don't have a feel.'

'You don't have a feel?' Dave was surprised. As a copper, you had to rely on gut instinct. Spider senses.

'Nah. Seems to me that he's dead, but . . .' Robbie gave a shrug. 'Who knows?'

'I knew him, but not well,' Red said. 'He never struck me as the sort of guy who needed to leave. From a distance, he had everything. Pretty wife, couple of cute kids. The farm. He was successful, you know? So, I reckon he's dead, too. Maybe he sheltered in a log or something and burned. We just haven't found him yet.'

'All options,' Dave agreed.

'We're going to get coffee. Want one?' Red asked.

'Yeah, I'd love one, and a pie too, please.' He reached into his pocket.

Red waved him away. 'We've got a tab. All good. Divvy it up before you leave.'

'Cheers. Right-oh, better get on. Going to see Jill with a few more questions.'

They said their goodbyes and Dave continued towards the motel.

Bec and Alice came to mind—their smiles and sparkling eyes as he gave them their presents. God, he knew what it was like to have kids he couldn't spend time with. Why would anyone deliberately choose to put themselves in a situation where they weren't going to be able to be a part of their lives? Still, perhaps he was oversensitive at the thought of leaving the kids, since he couldn't see his own.

In the motel car park, Jill was loading the children into her car, while a man stood alongside her. Dave recognised Leo's brother, Elliot, from the photo his parents had supplied.

When Elliot saw Dave, his body stiffened. 'Is there any news?'

Dave approached him and introduced himself, and they shook hands.

Elliot didn't smile. Instead, he looked pained at the yelling Noah was doing.

'Where's Daddy? I don't want to go, I want Dad!' Fat tears ran down Noah's red cheeks and he leaned forward trying to avoid Jill clipping in the seatbelt around him.

Dave clocked Elliot as not having any children himself by how uncomfortable he looked, as if he were waiting for instructions. 'Hard for the little ones who don't know what's happening,' Dave said, nodding towards Noah.

'Certainly seems that way,' Elliot replied. 'Do you have any news?' he repeated.

Dave waved at Charlotte who was already belted in, waiting patiently, but frowning at her brother's tears. She picked up a doll and held it to her ear, then spotted Dave. Charlotte waved back, a wide grin showing off the gap in her front teeth.

'Have you found my daddy?' she asked, innocently, straining against her seatbelt, to get closer to Dave.

Dave ignored both questions and focused on Noah. 'Hey there, Noah,' he said and flashed a smile to Jill. 'Whatchya getting yourself all worked up over? Can you take a breath for me?'

'Oh my god, what a day and it's only nine o'clock,' Jill said, as Dave gently pushed his way in and took the seatbelt in his hand. With a couple of swift movements, the belt was clicked in and the boy secured. Noah was so shocked he stopped yelling.

'Can you tell me anything yet?' Jill reached out and put her hand on his arm.

Dave turned to her. 'No, sorry, Jill. I don't have any more information for you, but I have more questions.'

'Do we need to do this now?' Elliot asked, impatiently. He looked like he was desperate to get out of the parking lot while Noah was still quiet. 'We have a few things to do.'

Jill's face flushed red and her eyes filled with tears. 'God,' she whispered, 'if I knew something, anything, maybe this wouldn't hurt so much.' She spread out her hands as Noah started crying. 'I don't have a body to bury, or even know if he is d—' Her voice choked at the word 'dead'. Noah let out an extra noisy cry and she turned to the child and banged her hand on the roof. 'Stop it!' she yelled. 'Just stop it!'

Elliot stared at his sister-in-law, his mouth pursed in disapproval, yet he made no move to help. From the motel a door opened, and Jan stepped out.

'Jill?' she called, her speech slurring over the name.

Stunned into silence at the noise, Noah stopped crying, but it was Charlotte's turn to start.

'I want Daddy,' she whimpered.

'What a circus,' Elliot muttered to himself, then to Dave said, 'Detective, I understand you need to ask your questions, but could we do this another time? We were heading to the insurance company so we could lodge a claim for the house. And obviously this isn't a good time with the children.' His body hadn't lost the tightness it had displayed on first seeing Dave and his words were as uncompromising as his stance.

'This won't take too long,' Dave said. 'And I would like to talk to you as well, Elliot.'

Dave drew Jill away from the car. 'I know this is tough, and we're trying our best to get you some answers. Can I ring your friends and get them to come over and help you? I think a bit of time to yourself would be a good thing.'

'Jill?' Jan repeated her call. 'Are you okay?'

When he'd spoken to Jan Perry yesterday, Dave had noticed her slightly slurred speech from the stroke she'd had nine years ago. It seemed more pronounced today.

'We're fine,' Jill called to her mother-in-law. 'Everything is fine.'

Jan looked uncertainly towards the car until her husband pushed past her.

'For god's sake, what's that bloody noise. Charlotte, what's wrong?' Stephen Perry stomped out to the car and pulled the door open, bending down and looking inside. 'Noah?'

Elliot was still standing woodenly by, not knowing what to do.

Jill made to go back, but Dave gently put his hand on her arm. 'Let me ring your friends.'

She shook her head. 'No . . .'

An engine roared down the street and a moment later a white Nissan Patrol wagon pulled into the car park. Dave saw the driver was the woman from the day before. He wouldn't need to call anyone now.

The driver hopped out and took in the scene, before moving to the car and speaking quietly to Stephen, then to each child. She put her hand on Elliot's arm and relief flooded through his face. Leo's brother tried to smile, but suddenly there were tears on his cheeks. He swiped them away, while the woman looked at him gently, rubbing his shoulder.

Dave could see her mouth the words, 'It's okay. It's okay.' Elliot's body language changed at her words and for a moment his grief seemed to escape.

He refocused on Jill. 'I need to ask you about the morning of the fire. Can you tell me what happened?'

Jill put her hand to her forehead as if she had a very bad headache. 'The kids and I were getting ready to go to tennis, and I asked Leo if he was going to come with us. Then the power went out, and every time that bloody power goes out, the electric pumps don't work, so he won't go anywhere. Leo went down to refuel the petrol pump in the shed and I left to go to town. That's all.'

'And what sort of mood was your husband in?'

'A little grumpy, but that's typical when I ask him to come with us. He doesn't like it when I put pressure on him to come to town and socialise.'

'Why's that?'

Letting out a heavy breath, Jill raised one shoulder. 'I have no idea. Especially when his mates are going to be there. Us girls, we've made sure the kids are playing the same sport so all the blokes can catch up once a week, but still Leo didn't want to come. Not even with the lure of beer at lunchtime.'

'Okay, so Leo didn't seem upset or worried? Agitated maybe?'

Jill was watching her friend get Charlotte out of the car, while Stephen was trying to unbuckle Noah.

'No more than normal.'

'Normal?' Dave picked up on her words.

'There's always a bit of stress during summer. Water for stock, feed, fires, thunderstorms, all that type of thing.'

'Of course. And when he said goodbye to you, he seemed okay?'

'We didn't really get to say goodbye. The power went off and I left, and so did he. We didn't have words as such, but he knew I was annoyed and I knew he was pissed off.'

'He was pissed off with you?'

'Probably more with the electricity company.'

'Okay. Was Leo a record-keeper?'

'Record-keeper? What do you mean, we had to keep all the farm records.'

'Like a daily diary recording what he'd done for the day.'

'Oh yeah, Leo's compulsive like that. He's got a black diary, one of those one page per day types sitting on the kitchen table and he'll fill it in after dinner, every night. Right down to what bills he paid and if I'd refuelled the car.' She broke off as she glanced over at Jan and Stephen, who were busy entertaining the kids now playing in the parking lot. Noah was smiling as Stephen threw him a ball and he caught it awkwardly against his chest.

The woman and Elliot were in deep conversation, although it seemed to Dave that the emotion had gone from Leo's brother now and there was just a deep sense of exhaustion.

'Did your husband keep a diary in his ute, too?'

'No, he has a little notebook that fits in his breast pocket. Leo makes shopping lists in it and keeps an inventory of things he doesn't want to forget.'

Dave wrote that down. 'And one last thing. Did Leo ever store anything like clothes, or something of the like, in the sheds where the machinery was kept? You know in case he spilled chemicals and needed to change.'

'I hardly ever went down there, but I wouldn't have thought so. He keeps his fire brigade uniform behind the seat in his ute, so he had it in case he ever got a call out. If he got covered in sheep shit or spilled chemical or fuel, he'd come home, have a shower and change his clothes, so there wasn't any reason for him to keep anything elsewhere. But he's careful. You have to be around chemicals.' As she finished talking realisation came into her eyes. 'Have you found something?'

'All my questions are routine, Jill.' Dave avoided answering her. There was still a lot more to find out before mentioning the header. 'Thanks, Jill. I'll be back in contact as soon as I know more.' Dave started to walk away then remembered he had another question. 'Did Leo have any identifying features? You know like a birthmark or tattoo?'

From the look on her face, she knew why he was asking that question.

'The scar on his chin,' she whispered. 'And a raised mole right here.' She pointed in between her breasts. 'Why has the SES search finished, if they haven't found him?' Tears were in her voice again.

'They've exhausted the search area and haven't found, ah, any sign of Leo, so we're looking at other possibilities, like we talked to you about before—being injured with a lack of memory and so on.'

Jill blinked and her mouth opened in a quiet 'o'.

'Unfortunately, nothing has come through from the news report, but that only went out last night. There's still time.'

'I think I'd know if he was dead,' Jill whispered miserably. 'I'm sure I'd feel it. He's not dead.'

Dave gave her arm a squeeze, waved to the other adults and started walking back to the station. His mobile phone rang. 'Have you got something?' he asked Bob, when he saw the name on the screen.

'Maybe. There's a report of a man matching Leo's description in the Northton Hospital. Came through a phone-in.'

'I'm on my way back now.'

'Thought you were getting coffee?'

'I was, but we hadn't asked Jill what Leo had been like the morning of the fire. I wondered if he had been extra affectionate with the kids, saying goodbye or the like. But that was a dead end. It all sounded as if he expected to see them that evening.'

'Right. Okay, I'll pick you up and we'll head over to Northton.'

'Hang on, let me come back to the office. I need to check something before we go.'

Bob was quiet. 'Want to tell me what?'

CHAPTER 9

'I realised on the way over I hadn't finished checking off the vehicles against the list that the licensing department gave us,' Dave said, shifting papers around the desk.

Bob stood near the whiteboard, with his arms crossed. 'Don't you think it might be more important to get over to the hospital?'

'It'll take me a couple of minutes. Does the troopy need refuelling?' Dave knew something was niggling at him about the tractors and he wanted time to look at the paperwork again, but he understood Bob's urgency, too.

'Good point. I'll go and do that while you finish up here, but be quick, all right, son? We've got important things to do.'

'Jill tells me that Leo has two identifying features,' he told Bob and explained where they were.

'Good to know.'

Pulling out his chair, Dave sat down and quickly crosschecked another five regos to the list of machinery, then found the invoices of the two tractors and one header that had loans against their names.

John Deere 6530 with a front-end loader. Payments of $65,000 per year, which worked out to $16,250 per quarter. He ticked off the tractor against the registration number, then found the bank statements that correlated with the outgoing payments. They all matched.

Case IH 2366 Header, payments of $14,000 per quarter. Again, everything matched against registration records and payments from the bank.

The second tractor wasn't mentioned on the registration list.

No numberplate and yet the invoice included a numberplate. Had Leo deregistered it? Looking for the insurance file, Dave read through the documents, but the tractor wasn't listed there either. There was no way a farmer could have a tractor on which money was owed without insuring it. The finance company would have kittens!

Dave tapped the pen against his lips, thinking. He pulled his laptop over then brought up the licensing department and typed in the plate number.

No result.

Outside, the horn tooted. Bob was back and he was raring to go.

Knowing he couldn't hold his partner off any longer, Dave grabbed his wallet and slipped it into his pocket, scooping up the file to take with him. With any luck, they'd find Leo knocked around a bit in the hospital, but alive and well so he could explain what was going on.

'Find what you were looking for?' Bob asked when he climbed in.

'Nothing is sticking out, except the John Deere 6920 tractor isn't on the registration list and it's not insured either. It's financed so the company would have asked for an insurance certificate of currency. Did we see that tractor in the shed?' Dave adjusted the air-conditioning vent, so it blew on his face. The vinyl of the troopy seats was hot, and Dave shifted his weight from one bum cheek to the other as he tried to settle in without being burned.

'Don't remember,' Bob said, putting the car into gear and taking off with a jerk. 'Let's see what we find at the hospital. If it's not Leo, we can call in at the farm on the way back and check.'

'How's Betty?' Dave asked as they slipped out of town onto a one-lane bitumen road. Either side was lined with gum trees, planted by the council; underneath was a carpet of yellowing grass, and purple and white flowers. Statice grew just about everywhere and flowered in the middle of summer. Whenever Dave saw the tiny paper-like blooms, he thought of his mum, who had loved these wildflowers. She'd always picked large bunches from the side of the road, bringing them home to decorate the kitchen or lounge room.

'Fine and dandy,' Bob answered.

Glancing over at his partner's tone, he saw that there was a frown set on Bob's face.

'Trouble in paradise?'

'Not really. She's just having difficulty adjusting to the city. Once Betty finds a job and meets a few more people, I'm sure she'll be more settled. Big shift all the way from Carnarvon to Perth, and of course it's harder when I'm away.'

'Haven't we been through that before?' Dave replied wryly.

Bob gave a small sigh. 'This is the whole reason I should stay single. Betty is understanding of what we do, and she knew that there would be times I'd be gone for weeks on end, but until she's experienced it, well . . .' His voice trailed off. 'Anyway, she's got an interview today at a small private hospital, so let's hope she gets the job.'

Dave still heard all the unsaid things; yeah, he was away, and yeah, Betty was lonely. She didn't know many people in Perth, all her friends were in Carnarvon. Had she made the right move? Had Bob? Would Betty be able to cope? Would Bob? What if Betty left and Bob was alone once again? All questions, guilt and thoughts that every copper wrestled with most days.

He looked for a subject change. 'What's going on with your arm?'

'What?' Bob glanced down and swore again. 'Got a pimple on the back of my arm that's itchy. Keep scratching the top off it and then it bleeds like a bastard. Remind me to get a bandaid when I get to the hospital.' He rubbed at the blood on his shirt as if he hoped it would disappear. 'Have you heard from Shannon?'

Dave closed his eyes at the sound of Shannon's name. He could feel Bob's gaze on him when he didn't answer straightaway.

'Son, what the hell? You guys are perfect for each other. Why are you making this so hard?'

'I don't think this all falls on me,' Dave said fervently.

'Are you sure? Last I heard, you were calling it quits because *you* weren't sure. That sounds to me as if it does fall on you.'

Dave could feel the heat of Bob's stare and the warmth that rose from his face.

'It's complicated,' he said.

'You don't say?' Bob retorted. 'Given any thought to how Shannon might be feeling in all of this? One minute you're shagging her while you're on a case together, then the next you're avoiding her, telling her you're not sure if you're ready for another relationship after Melinda. Seriously, son, it's a wonder she hasn't given up on you completely. I would've.'

'If it makes you feel any better, I spoke to her last night, after we got back from tea.'

'And how did that go?'

'Fine. She's got three autopsies lined up today and a court date tomorrow.'

'And?'

'And there's nothing more to say. We're going out for dinner when I get back.'

'Music to my ears.'

For a moment, Dave was lost in his memories of Shannon's warm, soft skin. Her lips on his and her long dark hair trailing over his stomach. The soft laughter as they skinny-dipped in the sea at Corbett Station Stay. He wouldn't admit to anyone how much he wanted her to be part of his life, but he was almost too gun-shy to try. Melinda had seen to that.

'Don't you think?'

Bob's voice brought Dave back to the present. 'Sorry?'

'I said,' Bob sounded long suffering, 'we should check this fella at the hospital out together, don't you think?'

'Yeah, absolutely. I've got the photo used in the media to do a comparison. What was the deal with him?'

'Walked in covered in dirt and not talking. That's all.'

'Sounds promising.'

Bob shook his head. 'Could be anything. He might've been involved in a car accident, which no one has reported, or taken a beating. Who knows.'

'Let's hope he's our guy.'

Dave fell silent and they rode in companionable silence until Bob nodded to the file sitting on the seat between them.

'Bit strange that tractor isn't mentioned in either the regos or the insurance docs. It's the insurance that's more telling, isn't it? Everyone is going to cover their machinery in case of fire or some other damage. So why hasn't Leo covered that one? Is there any paperwork to say it's been sold?'

Picking up the file, Dave opened it, all the while shaking his head. 'No, I looked for that specifically, but the loan documents say that it's not due to be paid out for another three years, so it wouldn't have been sold. I checked out the licensing department and it's not mentioned there either.'

'Okay.' Bob cocked his head to one side, thinking. 'When did he buy it?'

Running his finger down the page, Dave tapped at a date. 'Five years ago and the purchase price was . . .' He cited an eye-watering figure, then paused. 'That can't be right. Even if there wasn't a trade-in on the machine, that's too expensive.'

'Which machinery dealer did he buy it from?'

'The invoice is from Great Northern John Deere.'

'Why don't you give 'em a call and see if there's any information about the tractor they can give you. Have you got any range here?'

Dave pulled his phone out of his pocket and flipped it open. 'Two bars. Let's see how we go.' He flicked over the pages until he found the invoice and number in the top right-hand corner. The details also told him the salesman had been Greg Shaw.

When the phone was answered, he introduced himself and asked to speak to Greg, just as the eighty-kay sign came into view. They were on the edge of Northton now, and Bob was looking for information that would direct him to the hospital.

Dave searched for the speaker button and pushed it hard, so Bob could hear the conversation, too.

'Greg Shaw here, how can I help?' The voice was deep and gruff; the sort who wouldn't suffer fools.

'Detective Dave Burrows,' he said, 'from the stock . . . ah, Rural Crime Squad. I'd like to ask you a few questions about a customer of yours, Leo Perry.'

'Do you need a warrant for that?' Suspicion filtered through the line. 'How do I know you are who you say you are over the phone.'

'We're part of an investigation into Mr Perry's disappearance. I guess you've heard about it on the news.'

'Yeah, I have. Not good news.'

'As investigating officers we're able to interview you without a warrant. I can give you my badge number if you want to ring Perth and have it verified.'

'I see.' There was a pause. 'What do you need to know?'

'Five years ago, Mr Perry bought a new John Deere tractor from you. A 6920 model.'

'No, he didn't.' The words were spoken without hesitation.

'Sorry?'

'No, he didn't. The previous year he bought a 6530 model, but Leo never owned a 6920. I wouldn't have sold him one. That model was a lemon.'

'I have an invoice here from your dealership.' Dave read out the date and trading name.

'Well, if you do, it's a fake. I know every piece of machinery I've sold since I've been here in the last eight years and to whom. If Leo has a 6920 sitting in his machinery shed, then it's come from another dealer.'

Bob turned the corner and headed up the hill, flicking on his right-hand indicator and entering the car park at the hospital.

'Did Leo ever buy machinery from another business?'

'Not that I'm aware of.'

'Are you going to be in your office in thirty minutes?' Dave asked.

'I can be.'

'Yes, please. My partner and I will be in to see you.'

They hung up and Dave pulled out the statements then crosschecked the payments to the bank statement. 'Well, it's the amount that's on the invoice,' he said, holding the pages up to show Bob.

'Get Fraud to check which bank account that money was going into,' Bob said. 'Perhaps our Mr Perry had worked out a way to even up the score with the rest of his family.'

CHAPTER 10

The sterile smell of the hospital made Dave's stomach contract the minute he walked in through the quiet sliding doors.

He was thrust back to when Bulldust had shot two of his family members. The nurses jogging alongside the trolley, taking Bec into surgery, the quietly spoken doctors with their heads together, bent over his lifeless mother-in-law. The sobbing from Melinda, and the furious, white-hot anger and grief from Mark when they told him there was nothing they could do.

Dave swallowed hard and reached deep inside himself to gather up the façade that all coppers had to have.

The nurse at the front desk smiled, then a look of recognition came into her eyes. 'Ah, you're the detectives come to see our Mr Mute.'

'Mr Mute? I didn't think . . . Oh I see, "mute" as in not talking,' Dave said, wanting to kick himself.

'I'm Sadie,' she said, frowning. 'This is all a bit of a concern, not knowing who he is. We're really hoping he's your guy. I'll take you down there.'

'Can you first tell us how he was brought in?' Bob asked, leaning against the counter and depositing a dollar coin into the Lions fundraising container before picking up a roll of mints.

'Sure, he came in the other day. Just walked in dazed and confused. He hasn't told us anything, not his name or address, or next of kin. There aren't any bad injuries, although he has a pretty horrible gravel rash down his back consistent with having been dragged down a dirt road. But there's nothing else to suggest that's the case. No bruising or grazing around the wrists or under his arms. We don't have any reason to keep him here except he won't talk or tell us who he is or where he's come from, and he seems frightened. If I had someone to release him to then he could go, but . . .' She spread her hands out and shook her head.

'How old do you think he is?'

'Late twenties, early thirties, I'd say. Quite a good-looking young man. Red hair and he has a mole there.' She pointed to beneath her breasts. 'We're hoping he might be your guy so we can get some answers.'

'And who brought him in?'

'No one. He wandered in through the door and collapsed right where you're standing. Fainted, rather than anything untoward. We got him to ED and checked him all out. That's when we found he couldn't speak.' She frowned.

'I've never seen anything like this before and neither has the doctor who examined him.'

'Okey doke. Anything else we need to know?'

'I don't think so,' Sadie said.

'Does he have any tattoos?'

'Not that I've seen.'

'Scar on his chin?' Dave asked, holding his breath.

Sadie thought. 'Not that's obvious.'

Bob nodded. 'Well then, let's go and see our mystery man. With any luck he'll be our missing person.'

They followed the nurse down the quiet hallway, her rubber-soled shoes not making a sound.

A couple of the doors were closed, and had names in flowery writing on them, in stark contrast to the impersonal hospital ward. Bob indicated to them. 'Is there a nursing home in Northton or is that the hospital's job, too?'

'We've got a couple of people who are full-time residents here, yes. We battle to get people to come out to the country and care for our oldies, so we're happy enough to do it, especially if they have private health insurance because they pay us. Gives the hospital the opportunity to invest in some niceties that we'd never get the funding for.'

'Like so many other country hospitals around the state.'

Sadie stopped in front of a doorway and indicated they had arrived. A curtain was pulled across the entrance, hiding the occupant.

'Okay?' she asked, then without waiting for an answer, entered the room and pulled the curtain out of the way.

'Hello there. I've got a couple of police officers who'd like to have a chat with you. This is Bob and Dave.'

Both men put their hand up when she mentioned their names and gave a little wave.

'Now could you talk to them for me?' Sadie asked. 'If you need me, I'll be right outside.' She left the room without a sound.

Dave stood back and let Bob pull up a chair next to the bed. The man was alert and watched them carefully.

There wasn't a scar on his chin. His hair was a lighter shade of red and his eyes a different colour from those of their missing person.

This was not Leo Perry.

Dave felt his heart sink a little as he looked at the name-less patient. There was a mixture of curiosity and fear in the man's eyes, and his hands trembled a little.

Bob explained who they both were and then asked if the man was in any trouble.

He shook his head.

'Is there any way we can help you? If you don't want your family to know where you are, that's fine. We won't tell them, but they might like to know you're safe.'

Tears filled the young man's eyes, and he held his hands up helplessly, before making the sign for a pen.

Dave grabbed his out of his pocket and then tore a page out of his notebook, before handing them both over.

The man scribbled down two words. *Gray* and *Land*s.

Bob exchanged a glance with Dave then nodded.

Graylands Hospital provided help for people with mental illnesses through inpatient care. This man needed to get back there quickly.

'Ah, okay. No worries, mate. We'll make some calls and get you back to Graylands. Is that what you want?'

Confusion crossed the young man's face.

'You,' Bob pointed at his chest, 'want to go here?' He tapped the words.

The man took back the paper and wrote a Y.

'Are you on any medication we need to know about?'

He didn't seem to understand the question, so Dave tried a different tack.

'Do you know your doctor's name?' He made the sign for a stethoscope hoping the man would understand.

Barr. The man pushed the paper towards Dave this time.

'Dr Barr?'

Another nod.

'Right-oh, mate. Leave it with us and we'll get you back there. You okay here for the moment?' He readjusted his words and gave the thumbs up, then made the sign for the phone. 'We'll ring them.'

The man leaned back against the pillows and closed his eyes, as if shutting out the world, so they quietly left his room, pulling the curtain back around, blocking him from view.

Bob let out his breath. 'Hope he's not off any medication he shouldn't be,' he said quietly. 'How the hell could he have got up here and why isn't someone screaming from the rooftops looking for him?'

'Maybe he checked himself out,' Dave said as they headed back to the reception area.

'Can people who need mental health care do that?'

'I don't know. Just thinking aloud. Or maybe he needs to go there but hasn't been for a while.'

'Ah well, there you go, that could be the case,' Bob said. 'I just assumed he was a patient.'

'Anyway, he's not our man.'

'No, he is not. Ah, Sadie, you've got a young man there who needs to get back to Graylands.'

Drawing in a breath, Sadie looked at them, startled. 'Graylands?'

Dave handed over the piece of paper. 'He doesn't seem to understand all the questions, but we got through by miming actions and him writing down some of the answers. Looks like Dr Barr is who you need to get in contact with.'

'Thanks. I'll get on it.' Sadness crossed her face. 'I wonder where that young man's family is,' she said softly. Then she seemed to put her own thoughts aside. 'He's not your bloke, then?'

'Nope, not who we're looking for.'

'Okay, well, thanks for helping us with our Mr Mute.' She stopped and frowned. 'That seems a little unkind now. Do you think he is mute?'

'I wouldn't like to say,' Bob said, then he tapped the desk. 'But he doesn't understand full sentences. Perhaps he has an intellectual disability to boot. We'd better get going. Thanks again.'

Sadie said goodbye, but she was already preoccupied with finding the number for Graylands and picking up the phone.

'Bugger,' Dave said when they got outside.

The wind had picked up, a furious hot wind that tossed the branches and leaves around like confetti flying through the air. The temperature had risen, too, and Dave judged it to be above forty degrees. He checked the horizon for smoke; an old habit from his farming days.

Cereal stubble was starting to break down and the soil in paddocks that had been cropped was beginning to shift, throwing dirt and dust up into the air. The ochre-coloured cloud was now hovering above the town.

'Bugger of a day. Glad everyone has finished harvest.'

'Yeah, hope no one is out in the paddocks, that's for sure. Guess they've probably put a movement ban on.' That would mean that, other than making sure that livestock had water, no farmer would be able to drive around their paddocks, lessening the chances of a vehicle starting a fire.

The sky above the dust was a deep blue and stretched out until it merged with the golden horizon, the landscape flat and uninteresting. Birds were drinking from the fountain at the front of the hospital garden.

'Best get around to Greg Shaw to find out what the hell is going on with this tractor.'

In the troopy, Dave checked the address on the invoice and made for the industrial area of the town. They passed electricians, plumbers and two other machinery dealerships before seeing the green and yellow sign with the outline of a deer in the middle.

'That'll be us,' Dave said. As the words came out, he wondered why he said such obvious things.

The street was devoid of trees, and high fences ran down either side, with gates open to let the customers in.

Wishing there was some shade to park under, Dave swung the steering wheel around and bumped through the gate. They both cracked their windows slightly and got out, Bob holding the invoice and hire purchase agreement.

'Hope they've got air-con,' Dave said as he grabbed a hat and pulled it on.

'Me too.'

They pushed open the door and a blast of cold air hit their faces. Bob mopped at his brow. 'By god, that's a nice feeling,' he said, enjoying the cold air.

The showroom had a cement floor and was lined with shelves displaying John Deere toys, with two large counters featuring a sign indicating they were in the 'spare parts' section. Behind were three desks and, further back, glass-walled offices, where two men sat, wearing green shirts, and jeans.

'Can I help you?' A woman with tightly curled hair came around from behind one of the desks. Her hands were worn and dry as if she'd just spilled petrol on herself and it had sucked the moisture from her skin.

'G'day there, Sandy,' Bob said, reading the name embroidered on her shirt. 'We're Detectives Holden and

Burrows to see Greg Shaw, if you wouldn't mind.' He put one elbow on the counter and leaned against it with a grin.

Dave saw the reaction on the woman's face that Bob always received. Part curiosity, part nervousness, but everybody always smiled back at the jovial detective.

'Sure,' Sandy said and turned to find a solid man standing next to her, also dressed in a green shirt and a pair of denim shorts. He thanked her, then he indicated that they should follow him into a back office.

Once there, he held out his hand and Dave was impressed with the tight grip he had. Greg would be a favourite among farmers, he was sure. He had an open face with laugh lines around his eyes; a few broken capillaries across his nose, indicating his fondness for a beer.

Today, however, he was serious.

Greg didn't wait to be asked any questions, he got in first. 'Have you got the paperwork there?'

Dave handed it over. 'These are the originals, so we'll need them back. The house was lost in the fire, but Leo was required to send paperwork to his parents in Margaret River and keep copies at the farm. Everything I have is from his father's records.'

Greg took a glance at the papers and frowned, then tapped on his computer keyboard. The screen lit up and he typed in a few letters and reached for the mouse.

He shook his head. 'This doesn't make any sense. This is certainly our letterhead and paperwork, but it hasn't been issued from this office. If I didn't know any better, I'd say someone has taken some stationery out of our cupboard, because,' he turned the screen around and pointed at the records, 'Leo didn't buy a 6920 from us. You can see all the other machines he purchased.'

Bob and Dave leaned closer and then Bob fished his glasses out of his pocket.

'Blind as a bat,' he said to no one in particular.

'Can we get a printout of this?' Dave asked. 'Along with the tax invoices, please. And you would have pointed him in the direction of finance if he'd needed it? Anything to do with that, too, if you don't mind.'

'No problems.' Greg tapped a few keys and a printer under the desk whirred to life.

Straightening up, Bob rubbed his eyes. 'Well, that's interesting.'

Dave took the piece of paper Greg held out and scanned the writing again. Definitely no mention of a 6920 John Deere tractor.

'What was Leo like?' Bob asked.

'Real nice bloke, the little I knew of him. Spade was a spade, but he wasn't difficult to deal with, if you know what I mean. If I said I needed this much money, he never tried to bargain with me, it was either yes or no.' Greg leaned back in his chair. 'Well, he'd test me once every couple of purchases, but I'd know that's what he was going to do. I always make sure I give the client the best price I can, right from the start. Saves a lot of time and energy that way.'

'Course it does. You'd have a reputation for that, I'd think?' Bob said. 'Farmers like knowing they haven't been ripped off.'

Greg grinned. 'Just easier for everyone that way.' His smile faded as he talked about Leo. 'Even though we live in different towns, I did see him in our pub here occasionally and he was always up for a yarn. He'd tell me about what was going on with the farm, his kids. That sort of thing. And he always had Coffee with him. Even at the pub. We had to sit outside because of that bloody dog.' There was no malice in his voice.

'Can you remember when you saw him last?'

Greg thought for a moment, then shook his head. 'Not exactly. But it would have to be around the time of the local show. I always put show specials on, and he usually takes advantage of stocking up on filters and spare parts, so he comes over to pick them all up.'

'And the show is on when?'

'Reckon the dates change every year, but early part of October.' Greg leaned forward in his chair. 'Can I ask something?'

'Sure?'

'What do you think has happened to Leo?'

'We're investigating a few different lines of inquiry. His disappearance isn't clear-cut.'

'He loved his kids,' Greg said suddenly. 'I remember he had a photo of them he showed me last time. Unusual for any bloke to bring out pictures of their kids. The only photos I get sent are of compliance plates or belt numbers so we post out the right part!' He gave a grin and the detectives laughed, too. No more taking home the wrong parts thanks to modern technology.

'But this day he had a pic of his little girl dressed in a tennis uniform. Said she was going to play her first game that day.'

Dave jotted down more notes, then looked up. 'Have you got access to the bank accounts here?'

'Yeah, this is my business so I can access whatever you need.'

'Really appreciate that. We'd like your statements for the months these payments were supposed to go into your account, if you wouldn't mind.'

'Sure. I'll get Cathy, my wife, to do that now.' He picked up the invoices and contracts lying in between them. 'But they wouldn't be going into my account, the money would be deposited into the finance company's account.'

'Yeah, we understand, but we'd like to make sure there's no mix-up.'

Greg nodded and disappeared into the main office.

'What do you think?' Bob asked.

'That there'll be none of Leo's money going into Greg's bank account, nor will it be in the finance company's account.'

'Yeah, I agree. Where does that leave us?'

'Leo had a secret stash. He's mocked up these invoices and contract to make everything look legit and handed them across to the family. Then he's made the payments as indicated to the payment schedule, but he's been paying himself. If these contracts are the real deal, in as much as from this dealership, I wonder how he got access to them?'

'Mmm. I agree with that, too. And that question is a good one.'

The door opened and Greg came back in carrying a sheaf of papers, which he handed to Dave.

He tucked them into the manila file and kept them sitting on his lap.

'Thanks very much, Greg. Got a question. Do you have any idea how Leo could have accessed your letterheads? Would he have ever been left alone in any of the offices?'

'Our contracts are written out in triple carbon copies: one for me, one for the buyer and one for the finance company. I have a contract book, then my wife issues the invoices through the computer. For Leo to be able to access any of these areas, he would have had to have passwords. There's just no way—' The man broke off thinking hard.

Silence filled the room.

'Unless . . .' He reached for the paperwork again, and Dave handed it over. 'Yeah, I think he's managed to get a letterhead and create an invoice that looks the same. And yes, I guess if he'd been left alone in my office, he could have snitched one, for sure. They're kept in that cupboard there.'

All three looked to where a floor-to-ceiling cupboard stood next to shelves that held trophies proclaiming Great Northern John Deere was the best dealership for 1998, 1999, 2000 and 2001.

'You don't have the handwritten copy of the contract, do you?'

'No, we don't,' Bob confirmed.

Greg went to the cupboard and pulled out a lever-arch folder, opening it, then placing it on the desk. 'It's pretty hard to pick the difference in the invoices, isn't it? But these are legit ones. Ones that Cathy has raised.'

There was hardly any difference that Dave could see. Perhaps the date was a couple of lines further down on the page in Leo's copy.

'Leo's drawn this up with a word-processing program like Microsoft Word,' Greg said, lining up the pages next to each other.

'Could we take a legitimate invoice for comparison in our records?' Bob asked.

'Sure. I'll get a dummy one printed.'

'One more question? Would Leo ever have kept anything up behind the header guards, like spare belts or parts?'

'What do you mean?' Greg looked puzzled.

'On the underside of the header, where the pulleys that drive everything are situated, would he ever have kept any spare parts there?'

Greg shook his head. 'When the machines are in operation, the pulleys and belts are all moving real quick. Everything has to be synchronised otherwise part of the machine would fly to pieces. If there was something there that shouldn't be, it'd get pulled in and that would destroy not only what was there, but the pulleys and belts, too. It would be the most ridiculous—not to mention dangerous—place to store anything.'

CHAPTER 11

'The BSB and account number are . . .' Dave paused as he heard Detective Jamie Patterson from the Fraud Squad writing down the numbers. The Yorkenup Police Station was quiet as Dave repeated the numbers for clarity.

'Looks like a BSB number for one of those small rural banks,' Jamie said. 'I'll get an order to produce raised and we'll be onto it. See what I can find out for you. You want the signatories, too?'

'Anything you can give us. If there are transactions of the same amount going into the same bank account numbers that would be handy. Dates, times, places.'

'Sure thing.'

'We'd appreciate that, mate. Any chance of fast-tracking it? I've got a missing—'

'Yeah, yeah, all you blokes want everything yesterday. We know. On it.'

The dial tone was humming in Dave's ear. 'Such a friendly lot in Fraud,' Dave said.

Bob snorted, his eyes still on the paperwork in front of him. 'Can't blame them. They're not let out in the sunlight too often. Spend all their time staring at computer screens. They don't know how to be friendly except to figures.'

'Would have been nice if they could've given me an idea of when we'd hear back from them.'

'Give 'em a day or two, son. With any luck, they've got nothing on their desks and they're running the numbers right now.' Bob stuck a pen in between his teeth and slid a ruler under a line of figures, then slowly ran it down the page, checking each line.

'We know the likelihood of that is zero and none.'

Around the pen, Bob said, 'Why dom't you go and imterview shum of hish matechs. Go talk to that Chrich and Brusch.'

'Chris Barry and Bruce Cameron?'

Bob took the pen away and marked the page with a red line. 'Yeah. They said they'd be available any time when I rang to let them know we'd need to speak with them. Chris is the local mechanic, so he might have something interesting to say, and Bruce, what was Bruce?' he muttered to himself, shifting a few pages around. 'He was the . . . Yeah, he owns the local snack bar. Opens early in the morning to cook stroke and heart attack food for the shearers and truck drivers and then anyone else who happens to call in.' Bob glanced at his watch. 'It's late in the day for him. You might get him as he's closing. Then we need to talk to the family.'

Dave stood up and gathered his notebook and sunglasses. 'Sure, boss,' he said with a grin. 'Anything you say.'

Bob looked up and above the rims of his glasses. 'Good to know you understand how things work around here, son.'

A few moments later and Dave was out the door, into the suffocating heat and flies, making a beeline for the troopy. The less time he had to spend out in the summer sun, the happier he was.

As he ripped back the reflecting windscreen cover he'd bought in hope of keeping some of the warmth out, Dave wondered why the northern summer didn't bother him as much as the southern one did. The atmosphere always seemed a bit more humid down here than it did out in the centre of Western Australia, but on the coast in the north, well, the humidity would be off the charts if there had been a bit of rain around.

He shrugged slightly and shifted his attention to the hot steering wheel, vinyl seat and whining that seemed to be coming from under the bonnet. Dave frowned and leaned forward to turn on the air-conditioner, listening to what turned into a screech, before he turned the knob off.

The noise stopped.

'You're kidding!'

He wasn't ready to accept what his mind already knew, so he turned the switch again, in hope there was silence in the cab.

It wasn't to be. Another loud shriek from behind the dash and Dave sighed.

Bloody air-con wasn't working. The ten-day forecast was telling him the temperature was going to be above forty degrees every day. He wound down the window so at least the wind would dry his sweat and backed out of the car park. Instead of the snack bar on the edge of town, he headed for the garage.

Chris was the mechanic, as Bob had reminded him, and Dave hoped like hell he'd be able to fix the air-con. Very quickly.

The trees that lined the back streets seemed to droop in the heat and there were small black clouds hovering underneath them. Flies, trying to find the moisture in the leaves and ground to keep themselves cool.

On the school oval, a lone trigger sprinkler watered the only green spot, and it looked like the entire population of budgies, galahs, willie wagtails and magpies were making the most of the coolness.

Another street back and Dave found the petrol station and garage, on the corner next to the windmill maintenance business. Further on from that was a yard for the shearing contractor. Dave could see a mobile crutching trailer parked neatly next to three minibuses used to ferry the shearing team from shed to shed.

The fuel station cum garage had a faded Ampol sign out the front and two very old bowsers; the sort that, at the top, had a wire guard around the glass cylinder to indicate the gallons that had been pumped. They'd been decommissioned and not replaced with modern ones. The large windows of the station were filthy, thick dust covered them, and the sign above the store that read *Barry's Mechanics* was peeling.

Annoyed once again with the lack of trees, Dave parked next to the bowsers and got out, heading towards the side of what had been a small shop. The iron doors were flung open wide, obviously in the hope it would create a breeze. The light at the other end of the dark shed would have certainly created a tunnel, if there had been a breath of wind to flow into it, but no. Just a mass of hot, still air wherever Dave walked.

Mopping his forehead, he called into the dimness. 'Chris? You here, mate? I'm Dave Burrows from the police.'

A clanging from inside told Dave someone had dropped a spanner onto the cement floor. He waited.

'Be right with you.' The voice echoed out from deep under a ute.

Dave heard a certain amount of puffing and panting as a large man heaved himself up a ladder from the pit the ute was parked over. His head appeared first, then naked shoulders, chest and arms, and finally the waist and legs. Dave was relieved to see that Chris's lower body was clad in navy blue shorts, grey socks and boots. His face was shiny with sweat, which also ran in between his large breasts and down his stomach.

'G'day, I heard you fellas were around. Come into the office where it's cooler.' Chris didn't break stride, just walked towards a corner that was enclosed roughly by HardieFlex. 'Get you a drink?'

Dave followed. 'No thanks, mate. Looks like you're busy here?'

'Always busy.'

'Need to ask you a few questions, but also the air-con in the troopy is making a hell of a racket. Wondered if you'd have time to have a look at it for me? No one wants to be without air-con in the middle of summer.'

Chris didn't answer, and when Dave entered the make-shift office, the mechanic was standing in front of a fan, eyes closed, letting the strong breeze cool down his body. In his hand was a can of cool drink. It was touching his forehead.

Dave didn't think the scorching air being moved around by a fan meant that the atmosphere was cooler. In fact, he was sure the temperature had gone up a couple of degrees inside the office. He dug into his pocket and pulled out his hankie to wipe his forehead again.

'Fuck, it's hot today,' Chris muttered, before cracking the can and slugging down the contents. He smacked his lips and crushed the can. With casual practice, he tossed it at the woolpack in a frame that seemed to be half full of empty soft drink containers. It bounced off the wall and into the back of the woolpack. Then he turned and held out his hand. 'Chris Barry. Sorry, need to keep hydrated.'

Dave shook his sweaty hand, and then Chris took a towel hanging from the back of the chair, which was pushed into a wonky laminated kitchen table, and rubbed it across his hair, face and stomach.

'Yeah, that heat has sting in it, for sure,' Dave said. 'Been here long?' He looked around and noted a calendar with a naked woman's upper body staring from the wall. It was dated two years previously, so it was safe to assume that it was still hanging for the photo, rather than anything else. There was a microwave on the bench and a fridge up against the wall. From the ceiling, a radio hung from a coat hanger, silent, but moving just slightly when the fan turned its face towards it.

'My dad was the mechanic before me,' Chris said, now pulling out a chair and sitting, a second can of soft drink in front of him. 'I took over from him a few years ago, when he retired. There's enough here to do for one person.' Chris seemed to be taking Dave in properly for the first time. 'So, air-con, you said? What about Leo?'

Dave grinned at the country spade is a spade sentence. 'My air-con is screeching and I was hoping you could look at it while I ask a few questions about Leo. Two birds with one stone.'

'Course I can. Give us a few minutes to cool down. That bloody pit down there, it's like being in an underground mine.'

'Ever worked underground?' Dave pulled out a chair and sat.

'What? Oh. No,' Chris gave a boyish grin. 'Just saying that there's no airflow down there.'

'Don't know how you work in this place, to be honest. The tin must heat it up twofold to what it could be.'

'Guess I'm used to it. What else am I gonna do? Put in one of those flash air-conditioning systems for sheds? Ha! I'd go broke tomorrow if I tried to do that. Interesting though, Leo suggested it once. A while back now, but he was telling me one of the machinery dealers had one put in and how much of a difference it made to their work-shop.' He gazed at the ceiling. 'By god, I wouldn't mind, you know.'

'You and Leo are mates?'

'Yeah, we are. Me, Andrew 'n' Bruce, we all knock around together. Well, we did when we were single blokes. Changes a bit when the girls come along, you know, then it varies again when the kids arrive. But yeah, we're still good mates.' He took a long sip of his drink and wiped his face again.

'You grew up here?'

'Sure did. Been here since I was five days old. Mum had to go to a bigger hospital to have me, of course, but brought me back here after that, and here I am. Love the place.' Chris gave a grin and threw the towel over his shoulder.

'Had you seen Leo much lately?'

'Now, here's the thing. Leo's taken to being a bit of a recluse. Not afraid to use the phone for a yarn, mind, but just didn't get off the farm that often. Not sure why, before you ask. And yeah, me and the boys, we'd noticed, wondering what was going on. We tried to get him more involved and away from the farm, you see. Come to bowls or tennis, coz he wouldn't play footy anymore. Said his knees hurt. And he always hated basketball, so there was no point in trying to get him to join a team. But no, he wouldn't come to bowls or anything else. Leo was just hell-bent on trying to make that farm work for his olds and family. Wanted to have it right by the time he took it over.'

'So, he was going to take it over in time?'

Chris paused, taking another drink. 'Well, that was my understanding, but I guess we never really had a conversation about it. Assumed maybe that's why he was working so hard. And Leo did have a lot of problems with water that he was trying to fix, and he'd been in conversation with the power company. They'd promised to install some generators, but nothing had happened and so Leo was still stuck having to start the petrol gennies every time the power went out. We kept trying to get him to buy a solar pump but his father wouldn't have it. Too expensive and not proven enough in their pumping ability, in his opinion, which isn't true.

'He'd never leave the joint when the power went out. Petrol and summer don't play well together, and he was always frightened there'd be a fire and he wouldn't be around.' Chris gave a small, quiet harrumph. 'What's that Alanis Morissette song? "Ironic"?' He focused on Dave. 'You got any idea what's going on?'

'Yeah, well, the fire was caused by the petrol pump being overfilled. The fire started on the outside of the pump, on the exhaust, so the petrol had been spilled there. Other than that, we haven't been able to find Leo or his dog, Coffee, and that's causing us some concern.'

'Never went anywhere without that dog.'

'What can you tell me about his relationship with his parents?'

'Not a lot lately. Back when they first retired, I think things were a bit tense. His old man wasn't ready to hand over the reins, but his health dictated otherwise. Stephen insisted on being involved with every decision that was made.' Chris made another A-plus effort in can throwing and pushed back the chair, indicating for Dave to follow him. 'Even down to what sheep were being shifted into what paddock. I always thought Stephen's extra involvement was unhealthy, and it certainly gave Leo the shits.'

'Did he talk much about it?'

'Early on he did, because it took up all his waking energy. But as time went on there seemed to be some type of acceptance on Leo's behalf, and obviously, he got into a routine that he was happy with, so it didn't consume him the way it had before.'

'Was there any other tension between Leo and his parents? Or was it all business-related?'

Chris seemed to consider his words before speaking. 'Well, I think there was more than just business. Neither of Leo's parents liked Jill, and Leo was convinced they'd poisoned Elliot and Sally against her as well.' He paused and looked over at Dave. 'The fact his family didn't like his wife really hurt Leo.

'And to be honest, none of us ever understood why. Jill's a top chick. Always working at something in the community, a great mum. I know my wife thinks the world of her. They're really close.'

'Funny how friends and in-laws see different things,' Dave said, his words laden with irony. 'How do you get on with Leo's folks?'

'They're okay. When we were kids, they were the strict parents; the place you didn't want to go when you were trying to sneak a few beers on a Saturday night.'

Dave laughed. 'Better places to go?'

'Shit yeah! Mine.' He grew serious. 'When Mrs P had the stroke, that was the turning point for everything. Jill had just turned up with Leo and they were wanting to move in together, and Mrs P didn't want them living in sin in her house. I know it sounds pretty old-fashioned, but that's what they are—old-fashioned.'

'What about Elliot and Sally? They got along with Leo?' Dave braced himself for the smack of heat as they left the shed and walked towards the troopy.

Chris gave him a look. 'Neither of them fit in around here very well. Too good for us hayseeds.'

'You don't like them?'

'We all tolerate them, coz they're Leo's family, but they don't spend a lot of time here and neither do they want to.' Chris grinned as he looked at Dave and indicated for him to pull the lever to pop the bonnet. 'You know, when I was a young bloke, I thought I might be able to convince Sally to stay here and marry me.' He spread his arms out. 'Sometimes what you wish for isn't what should happen, and as you can see, this is one of those times. I'm glad Sal didn't stay. It wouldn't have worked out. Yorkenup is too small for her. And Tina, my wife, likes living here.'

Dave leaned against the troopy and watched Chris as he worked. 'Have you got any idea where Leo is at with the relationship with his family? It strikes me there might have been a bit more than angst there.'

'Yeah, there was. Between the farm and shit with Jill, us boys had a few drunken nights at the pub where we talked shoulder to shoulder. But, look, all of that was a while ago, and I think more recently some of it had settled down.'

'Why do you say that?'

'Only that it hadn't come up in conversation for a long time. For a spell there, that's all Leo could focus on. The one thing you need to know about Leo is that he wore his heart on his sleeve. If there was something bothering him, you'd know about it quick smart.'

CHAPTER 12

The cold air blowing in Dave's face made him grateful that Chris Barry kept a large stock of parts for air-conditioners.

When Chris had finally lowered the bonnet and wiped his hands on a rag, he'd nodded towards Dave and told him to start the engine and have a try.

The silence and cold air had been bliss. Dave smiled as he drove towards Bruce Cameron's snack bar on the edge of town.

Chris had been adamant Bruce would still be there, preparing for the next day. 'Just go round the back and bang on the door,' he'd said. 'Brucey'll be restocking the fridges or something like that.'

The snack bar was on the main road, just on the outskirts of town. A bright blue store with lots of lighting at the front and two large windows that showed the inside plainly. A tall backlit sign told everyone who cared to read it that food was available from four am and the kitchen closed at three thirty pm before the doors at four pm. Long hours for an owner–operator.

Dave followed the road around to the back of the shop and parked next to a dusty Subaru Brumby ute.

From inside, a radio blared, so Dave followed the noise, knowing there would be no point in calling out over the sound. He pulled open the flyscreen door, letting himself inside.

The storeroom was filled with oil drums, freezers and large squeezy bottles with tomato and barbecue sauce inside. The smell of old cooking oil made Dave crinkle his nose.

'Hello?' This time he called out loudly, then banged his fist on the wall for good measure. 'Hello? Bruce Cameron?'

The radio was shocked into silence and a tall man appeared in the doorway that led through to the shop. Dave found it hard to believe that a tall man like Bruce Cameron would be able to get his body inside the tiny Subaru cab outside.

'You right, cobber?' Bruce asked. 'We're closed, so I can't help you with any food.'

'Dave Burrows, I'm a police officer,' Dave held out his hand.

Bruce's face relaxed into a smile, before it was replaced with concern. 'You've got some news on Leo?'

'Unfortunately, no,' Dave said. 'But I'd like to ask some questions. You got the time?'

'Sure, anything to help out. Come this way.' Bruce disappeared and Dave followed him in and around the deep-fryers, stainless-steel benches and cooktops lined with leftover bread to behind the counter and out into the customers' side of the store. Crates of drinks were stacked up here and Bruce was placing them carefully in the four fridges lining the walls.

'I'd do anything for Leo, so whatever I can help with, fire away.' He swung a crate of Coke down and took out two bottles in each hand, before looking expectantly at Dave. 'You talked to Chriso and Andy?'

'We spoke to Andrew last night. Tells me that Leo was a good bloke, but found it hard to get off the farm. Chris echoed the same sentiments when I spoke to him just now.'

'Yeah, Leo was always busy. Always something to do, but—' Bruce gave a laugh '—that just seems to be farming.' He stopped and frowned. 'Maybe not farming as such, but working for yourself. I have trouble getting away from this place in time to see my kids before they go to bed and I never see them eat their breakfast. There's always something. If it's not physical, then it's the bloody paperwork. Bloody hell, the GST has made a huge extra load for us self-employed people. I know it's been in for two years now and we should be getting used to it, but it's taken me some time to wrap my head around all the rules and regulations that go with it.'

Dave nodded his understanding. 'Are your kids the same age as Leo's?'

'Me and Carmel got an early start. The oldest is ten. Youngest seven. And the tearaway in the middle, she's nine.'

Dave let out a whistle. 'Those first two are pretty close.'

Looking slightly embarrassed, Bruce said, 'Yeah, you would've thought we'd worked out what caused the first one and slowed it down. There were a few troubles having two in nappies, I can tell you. Carmel told the doc when she went back after the six-week check-up with Tia that he'd better figure out how to stop her getting pregnant or there'd be trouble.' Bruce gave a belly laugh. 'Doc told her to keep her legs shut and there shouldn't be any more problems!' He laughed again. 'Good thing we're mates with that Doc Grant.'

'I'll say,' Dave agreed. He couldn't imagine Melinda putting up with that type of talk from her doctor.

The Coke part of the fridge was now stacked neatly and to the edge of the shelves, so Bruce started on the lemonade.

A timid knock sounded on the front door and Bruce looked over. 'Ah, little buggers,' he said, affection in his voice. Walking over, the tall man made shooing actions with his hands. 'On your bike, Tyson. You know I'm shut.'

Bruce didn't seem to mean the words he'd spoken.

'Just a drink, please, Mr Bruce? It's so hot.'

Dave thought the little boy standing at the door with his bike did look very hot. His face was a bright red and his fringe wet with sweat.

'Got any money?'

Tyson put his hand in his pocket and brought out four painted stones. One bright red, two blue and a yellow. 'Is this enough, Mr Bruce?'

Reaching into the closest fridge, Bruce took out a chocolate milk then clicked the lock open. 'Are you going to share it with your sister?' he asked, but before Tyson could say anything, Bruce took an orange juice box and handed them both to the boy. 'Give Frankie the juice, okay? Oh and wait there.' Bruce turned and went back into the kitchen, returning quickly with a loaf of bread. 'Take that with you.'

Tyson's face lit up. 'Thank you, Mr Bruce, thank you.'

Bruce held out his hands for the stones and the exchange was over in a matter of seconds.

Locking the door, Bruce stood watching Tyson ride off, his hands on his hips. 'Rough and tumble lad, that one,' he said softly. 'Dad's not around and Mum lives off the government. She tries so hard to make ends meet, but . . .' He shrugged and turned back to the job at hand. 'I think life is pretty tough for them.'

'You make him pay?'

Bruce smiled. 'That boy goes to the creek every day and collects as many rocks as he can. Then he begs a bit of paint from school. Teaches him he's still got to earn his way.'

A warm feeling swept through Dave. Country people looking out for their own. The conversation turned back to Leo. 'Ever have any heart-to-hearts with Leo about his relationship with Jill?'

Without pausing, Bruce answered, 'Yeah, a few. There was trouble between his family and her. His folks didn't like her.' Shrugging now, he continued. 'God knows why, she's the salt of the earth type and she made Leo happy! Surely that should be enough for any family.'

Again, as with Chris, Dave found his 'Oh yeah' filled with longing and irony.

'Jill is a bit expensive to run, you know, likes the nice clothes and always has to have her hair and nails done when she goes over to Northton to do the shopping. But that's not a crime, and Leo didn't mind. In fact, whatever made Jill content, made Leo happy. I'm sure you know the saying—happy wife, happy life.

'Still, Jan and Stephen see that sort of thing as wasteful and they weren't going to give her one penny for her "upkeep". That's what Jan called it.' He moved quickly, stacking the lemonade as he spoke. 'I guess our parents grew up in a different time where putting food on the table and earning a crust mattered more than nails and hair. They made do with what they had, didn't they?'

'She obviously didn't come from a farming background and Jill tells us she didn't work on the farm. Was that ever a point of contention between them?' Dave pushed the crate of water bottles over to Bruce and leaned against the counter.

'Nah, Jill grew up back in Perth and worked for some kind of specialist. That's how they met. Leo went to see . . .' Bruce frowned. 'Might've even been a skin specialist, maybe. Anyway, he snapped her up from there. Leo is a man of few words when it comes to women, but he told all of us blokes that he knew right from when he saw her that she was perfect for him.'

Dave smiled and nodded. 'So, no problem then? Leo wouldn't have expected her to work. Some farmers need their wife to work alongside them.'

'Leo was happier working on his own. Didn't have to put up with other people's stuff-ups was what he used to say. Course, he had to have people in during harvest and seeding. Can't drive the header and chaser bin at the same time.' He gave a laugh at his own joke and Dave smiled.

His words weren't funny, but what Bruce lacked in humour he made up for in kindness, Dave had decided.

'That dog of his. Coffee. When they went to work sheep together, they were poetry in motion. The two of them love each other. Leo is never anywhere without Coffee and Coffee is never anywhere without Leo. If you find one, you'll find the other.' He paused and swallowed hard, before giving his nose a hard rub. 'Leo didn't need Jill's help; he had Coffee.'

'You don't know where Leo is, do you?' Dave asked, watching the man's face carefully.

Bruce turned around and eyeballed him. 'I wish I did, because I'd go and get him and ask what the bloody hell does he think he's playing at, upsetting everyone the way he is.'

Dave frowned. 'What do you mean by that?'

'Well, is he dead, or isn't he? If he was alive and I knew where he was, I'd go and get him. Put everyone that's worrying about him out of their misery. If he's dead, I'd do the same thing, coz I'd get the same result. We'd know what happened and we'd be able to bury him. This not knowing is stuffed.

'Leo isn't selfish. If he's alive, he's not getting in contact because he doesn't want to. I reckon he can't. He would never leave any of the people he loved hanging like this.' Bruce made sure he held Dave's eye again. 'One way or the other, he can't.'

'Do you mean because he's dead, or can't as in he's made some enemies recently and they've caused Leo a problem?' Dave asked.

Bruce sighed. 'I don't know the answer to that question either. What I do know is Leo didn't have any troubles. If he did, we always knew about them. You could never accuse Leo of not sharing details. Even if he was busy on the farm, he'd ring up when he was going for a drive and have a chat. And yeah, over the last few years he hadn't been coming into town as much, but he still knew how to use the phone. My mate is pretty much an open book. Transparent really.

'A few times after the kids were born, he told me about how he had a bit of trouble you know, um . . .' Bruce indicated towards his groin. 'Wasn't interested in sex after seeing the kids breastfeed. Turned him off completely. So you see . . . Open book.'

'Chris said something similar.'

Bruce nodded before turning back to refilling the fridge. 'Yep, he is, our Leo, he is.' His voice was soft and sad.

'Is there anything you could tell me that might help? How did he get along with everyone in town?'

But Bruce was shaking his head. 'Leo is the nicest bloke you'd ever meet. He's got this charm that made most people gravitate towards him. And a loud—nah, *booming* laugh. It seems to come from deep down here.' He patted the lower part of his stomach. 'I'm sure that was what made people come over and talk to him. Look, he's a good bloke and I can't think of a damn thing that would have made him disappear like this. If that's what he's done.'

CHAPTER 13

'He's a contradiction, from what I'm hearing,' Dave said to Bob as he took a sip of his beer.

They were back at the same table as the previous evening, except this time, they were the only ones in the restaurant. There were about five blokes in the front bar and that was it.

'Yeah, I hear you, son,' Bob said, scratching his head. 'Interesting they all mention the dog.'

'Perhaps we should see what Jill has to say about her. She hasn't mentioned Coffee at all.' Dave gave a snort of laughter. 'I think I like Leo's sense of humour when he named his dog. Good coffee, bad coffee, could go either way.'

Bob gave a chuckle, then his face became solemn again. 'Maybe we should check the animal pounds and vets within a hundred kilometre radius. See if they've had any injured dogs taken into them.'

'Good idea,' Dave said. 'We should have done that at the start.'

Bob held up his beer to Dave and they clinked glasses.

'What are you doing?' The female voice came from the front bar and Bob and Dave turned around in time to see a flash of colour, then a woman come striding into the restaurant.

'What are you doing?' Jill asked as she drew herself up as tall as she could. 'Why aren't you out there looking for my husband?' She was dressed in a linen skirt and freshly ironed shirt, and even though her makeup was done perfectly, it didn't hide the angry flush that was spreading across her cheeks. 'How can you sit here drinking beer when he's probably lying on the side of a road or worse?'

Dave started to stand. 'Jill—' He put out his hand, but she batted it away.

'Leo is out there, somewhere . . . missing!' Her voice had become a screech. 'I can't believe . . . I'm going to make a complaint. Who do . . .'

'Mrs Perry.' Bob was standing now, his voice soft but commanding attention. 'Mrs Perry, how about we go outside and have a chat.'

'What?' Jill screwed up her face as she looked at Bob. 'So no one hears that you're not doing your job? You were brought down here to find my husband and—'

'Mrs Perry.' This time Bob didn't allow for an argument. He took her elbow, preparing to escort her outside.

A few faces stared through the gap in the bar, watching the commotion. Dave went to Jill's other side and started speaking quietly. 'Jill, we are doing our best. Sometimes these things take time—'

'But you're not even looking!' Her eyes stared wildly at him, and Dave had trouble matching the woman he'd met previously to the one who was screaming at them now.

'We don't have time!' Jill shouted at him.

Bob leaned back and brushed her spittle from his face. 'Why is that?' he asked.

'I've read that if you don't find a missing person within twenty-four hours, you never find them. It's been much longer than that now.' Her voice dropped. 'Much, much longer. Does that mean I'm never going to see . . . The kids won't know their . . . uh . . .' her voice wavered before tears spilled down her cheeks and she grasped at her waist, bending over as if she was in physical pain. 'They'll never . . .' The wail that came from her was high pitched, thin and full of grief.

Bob leaned forward and spoke gently. 'Mrs Perry, what you've just told me is not correct. We continue investigating until every possible avenue is exhausted.'

'Then why?' She reached out and grasped Dave's hands so tightly that they were white where she gripped him.

'Jill?' Andrew came into the restaurant, holding Charlotte's hand. Instantly he turned and left the room, re-entering seconds later, this time without Charlotte.

Bob ambled casually towards the front bar. 'Charlotte's out here?' he asked Andrew.

'I've left her with Bernie. The barman,' he added at Bob's questioning glance.

Bob nodded and kept going.

'Andrew . . .' Jill drew the word out and reached out her hand.

154

Such a broken woman, Dave thought, keeping his hands outstretched around the perimeter of her body in case she fell.

'Hey, hey,' Andrew said. He stood firmly in front of her and gripped her hands in his. 'What's wrong?' He glanced at Dave, hopelessness crossing his face. 'Have you found him?' he asked, his voice low and desperate. 'Is this what this is about?'

Dave shook his head. 'No. Jill is a bit—'

'They're sitting here drinking beer and not looking for him, Andy. For Leo.' Her wide, reddened eyes stared at Dave with anger.

'Oh, Jill,' Andrew said, drawing her into a hug. 'They've got to eat, love. Just like we all do.' He looked over at Dave. 'Nicola is back at the motel with Noah,' he told him. 'We've just popped down to pick up takeaway pizza for all the kids and some meals for us. It's too hot to cook and we thought that the little ones might like a bit of a run in the playground since everyone has been cooped up in a small room all day.' Andrew looked down at Jill, whose tiny frame was still shaking against his tall body. He kept his arms tightly around her as if trying to protect her from all the bad in the world.

Andrew spoke into her hair, as if she were a small child. 'Come on, love. Let Bob and Dave have their dinner and we'll all go and have ours down at the playground like we organised. Noah and Charlotte will be hungry by now. All good?'

Jill frowned and took a couple of hiccuping breaths. 'No, it's not all good,' she said desperately. 'Nothing is good.' She turned away from him.

Andrew nodded and put his hand on her shoulder, gently guiding her towards the door. 'Sorry,' he said to Dave. 'Nicola and I thought it would be a good idea to get her out of the room for a little while. We didn't know this . . .' He raised his hand helplessly and kept going after her.

Dave waited until they were out of the room and sat down with a heavy sigh. He drained his glass, then went to the restaurant side of the bar, making sure he was out of Jill's sight, and ordered two more drinks, thinking about the exchange.

A few moments later, Bob joined him and emptied his glass, too. 'Holy hell,' he said.

'Yeah,' Dave agreed, and they both went back to their table as the waitress appeared with their two steaks.

'These might be a bit cold,' she said. 'Sorry, we didn't want to come out while that was going on.' The curious stare said she really had wanted to, but someone had stopped her.

'Thanks for being considerate,' Dave said.

'Looks like anything could have happened.' The words were out of the young girl's mouth before she could stop them.

'Always best to leave situations alone that don't concern you,' Bob said. 'Now, that steak needs eating and look at that mushroom sauce.' He smacked his lips together in delight.

The waitress's face flushed and she put the plates down with a little extra force than needed. 'Let me know if you need anything else,' she said, not sounding like she meant it, before she flounced back towards the kitchen.

'We were probably a bit harsh,' Dave said, looking after her.

'Nope. If we can discourage that sort of behaviour then hopefully they'll tell their friends they can't get anything out of the two detectives eating their dinner, and we'll all be sweet.'

Dave picked up a chip and dipped it in the gravy. 'I wonder why Andrew brought Jill to the pub. It's usually the girls doing that and leaving the blokes at home?'

'Is anything normal in this kind of situation?' Bob asked.

Dave ate another chip. 'Did you see that shirt she was wearing?'

Bob was quiet for a moment then asked, 'The waitress?'

'Jill.'

Bob raised his eyebrows. 'Oh, yeah, yeah, I did. Cashmere mixed with wool and silk and something else I missed, was it?'

'Fuckwit,' Dave said mildly, picking up his knife and fork.

'Well, seriously, son, as if I'd know anything about that shit.' Bob gave a half smile and reached for his glass. 'Tell me what you'd like me to know about the shirt Jill Perry was wearing.' He leaned back casually and looked at Dave over the top of his glasses.

'Bruce said today that Jill was a bit—' he made quotation marks '"expensive to run". I've seen Melinda wear a shirt like that. It's some fancy brand that's sold only in department stores or exclusive shops. I don't know what they're called.'

'Thank god for that, son. I was beginning to think you'd turned into some type of fashion expert and I didn't know you at all.'

157

Grinning, Dave continued. 'How much do you think a shirt like that might cost?'

'Surprise me.'

'Three fifty.'

Bob's glass halted halfway to his mouth. 'I'm assuming you don't mean three dollars fifty. It must be thirty-five dollars?'

'Three hundred and fifty dollars.'

'For a shirt? Surely not.' Bob was incredulous. 'How many of them could she afford on what she and Leo were pulling out of the farm? That's more than half of their weekly wage.'

'If it's the same as the brand that Mel wears.'

'Bit expensive to run all right.' Bob took a sip. 'But how . . . ?' His brow was furrowed. 'How could Leo be comfortable with Jill spending that much when there's food to buy and kids to look after?'

'Not sure whether it's about Leo being comfortable. Jill could have spent the money anyway, but you're right about their weekly pay cheque. I can't see how it could have stretched that far. I guess she might've scrimped and saved especially.'

'Jill might come from money?' Bob suggested. 'Could the shirt have been a present? Has she got any savings from her previous job?'

Dave shook his head. 'No, that can't be it. Everyone else is indicating she's a spender. That thick silver necklace looked like it was worth a bomb, too. Neatly dressed and makeup done. Even with Leo missing. Classic Blue Blood thinking.' He raised his finger. 'Now, here's the thing. Most mums would spend any extra money they had on their kids, right?'

'Mmm.'

'Charlotte and Noah look like their clothes come from Target or a discount department store . . .' Dave left his words hanging.

Bob nodded thoughtfully and cut himself a large mouthful of steak. 'Maybe that was the real reason Leo was skimming money from the farm.'

'No word from Fraud.'

'If you haven't heard from them tomorrow, give 'em a call.'

'You went to see Charlotte?'

'Yeah. Didn't get much. Poor little mite was crying, wanting her mum. I asked what she was having for tea and she said pizza, so I bought a couple of ice-creams for them to take away. That dried the tears. I wanted to ask her about her dad. Unofficially of course.'

Dave wondered if his kids ever cried for him at night. Probably not. He doubted he even rated a mention during their bedtime routine. Or at any time of the day.

He unfolded a piece of paper from his pocket and pushed it towards Bob. Cutting into his steak, he said, 'I've drawn this timeline up and made a note of the most obvious points we have. There's the fire and then no sign of either Leo or Coffee. We've been told by his mates that neither dog nor man would be apart from each other. We've got the fake invoice that Leo must've made up himself, and money going from the farm bank account into this other account we're waiting for information on, and we've found a spot under the header where something was stored that isn't there now.' Dave ticked each item off on his fingers, after putting down his knife and fork.

Bob was reading what Dave had given him, his glasses perched on the end of his nose. He was chewing slowly, nodding.

'As far as we're aware all utes are accounted for and there haven't been any confirmed sightings.'

'Dead end,' Bob said.

'We've got to find out where the money was going.'

'Follow the money, and you'll usually find the answer to most crimes.'

Bob's mobile phone rang, and he dropped his knife. 'Bloody phone,' he grumbled, reaching into his pocket. 'Who would want one? Holden.' Pause. 'G'day, Robbie, what's going on?' Pause. 'Aha. Yeah right.' Pause. 'Okay, see you at the station.' He closed the phone and looked at Dave. 'Eat up, we might have a break.'

CHAPTER 14

'Tell me again how you found this ute.' Bob had one bum cheek leaning on the desk and his arms crossed, as Robbie pointed to a spot on the map.

'A farmer from over near Hunter Rock called it in. Apparently, this ute's been sitting there for about three days and hasn't moved an inch. He thought it was weird because it's hidden behind a patch of bush. Decided to take a look, so he stopped off there tonight on his way home. With Leo in the wind, he thought it would be good to ring us.'

'Right. The ute is still out there?' Bob glanced out into the darkness. 'And have you checked the rego? Got an owner?'

'It's not registered now, but it has been. The last company to have it registered was Perry Pty Ltd, and that goes back to Leo and his family.'

Dave glanced over at Bob. 'All those utes in the shed,' he said.

Bob pointed his finger at Dave like a smoking gun and said, 'Right, well, let's go for a look. This farmer, did he touch anything?' he asked, looking over at Robbie.

The constable looked down at his notes. 'He opened the driver's side door and then the glove box to see if there were any rego papers in there.'

'Better get him fingerprinted then so we can discount his prints. And were there any?'

'No rego papers.' Robbie went to leave, then turned back. 'The ute is clean of everything,' he said. 'Could Leo have faked his own death?'

'That's one of the options we're pursuing at the moment,' Dave said. 'I'm waiting for some information to come through from Fraud, which will help with that theory. Of course, there's still the one where he has memory loss, or maybe he has died and we haven't found his body. We're just following through every lead that comes to us to see where that takes us.

'Now we're going to need a tow truck. Can you get one organised for us?' Dave asked.

'Yeah, Chris has got one down at his garage. I'll give him a call.'

'Thanks.'

Robbie nodded.

'Good lad. Thanks for letting us know about the ute, mate,' Bob said and clapped the young man on the shoulder.

'Too easy.'

'Right-oh, Dave, let's get on the road. At least the sun's gone down and it's cooler.' Bob walked out the door, and Dave followed.

In the troopy, Bob used a pen-sized torch to read from the paperwork that Robbie had given them. 'Okay it's a 1983 HiLux with a canopy on the back. Bull bar and three spotlights mounted on the roof.' He turned to Dave. 'Three spotlights on the roof would make the ute stand out. Windscreen is cracked. That's all this bloke noticed. What's his name . . . Brendon Coward.'

On the open road, Dave flicked his headlights to high beam and drove carefully, keeping an eye out for kangaroos. He reset the speedometer at the town edge so he knew exactly how many kilometres the spot was away from Yorkenup and how much time it took to drive there.

Bob was unusually silent, and more than once Dave glanced across at him. His face was impassive, and he stared out of the windscreen. Bob might look as if he wasn't doing anything much, but Dave knew his brain would be turning over all the facts they had and trying to piece them into order or possibilities.

Bugs smacked into the windscreen, their tiny bodies splattering over his view. He wanted to turn on the windscreen wipers but that would make more of a mess than leaving the insects caked across his line of sight.

'Got the directions there?' Dave asked when they were ninety kilometres out of town. The road had been quiet, not a single car had passed them in either direction, and he thought how easy it would be to disappear in the dead of night.

Bob turned to Dave. 'All those utes,' he said. 'Did we do a reconciliation as to which ones were registered and which ones weren't? Have we got a list of the vehicles that aren't registered?'

Dave shook his head. 'I don't think we took any notice of the ones that weren't registered. We've got no way of checking them off against anything. Jill made it clear she didn't seem to know.' Dave lifted his foot and watched for a sign that was going to send him towards the tiny township of Hunter Rock.

'Then how the hell are we going to tell if we're missing one or ten? Or there's, I don't know, some random number more than there should be.'

'Ask the old man? Do you think he would know?'

'We can try, but I wouldn't reckon. I know he keeps an iron grip on things, but as to every old ute that was bought at a clearing sale . . . He'd have to have a memory like an elephant. Or at least be able to put his hands on the invoices for the clearing sales.'

'With the way he keeps records he should be able to do that. Might be worth having another chat to Chris Barry, the mechanic. See if he knows why Leo needed so many.'

'Yeah, that's a good idea. Leo could have been looking for some sort of advice from a mechanic. And he had one on tap. You need to turn here.' Bob indicated to a side road that was advancing quickly and Dave lifted his foot. 'Another three kilometres down here and there's a turn to the right, then a clearing, which is where the ute is.'

'Have you noticed how quiet the road is?' Dave asked. 'Yeah.'

'I know it's not a Saturday night, the same day as the fire, but even if it was, I'm thinking the road would be similar.'

'Especially after we turned off the main road,' Bob agreed. 'There wouldn't be anyone to see him leg it across a paddock to a different vehicle, or to see if someone was waiting for him.'

They were silent for the last part of the drive, then the reflection of a tail-light caught their eye and Dave slowed to a stop.

Outside, the night was warm and still. Mozzies the size of jet planes started to dive-bomb them as soon as they smelled the warm skin of humans. Dave slapped at his face a couple of times then found the mozzie repellent in the glove box. 'What the hell do they feed these things out here?' he muttered as one collided with his forehead.

'Fertiliser in the blood, I'd reckon,' Bob said, holding his hand out for the tin.

Dave handed it to him, and then they walked towards the ute, torches in hand, stopping just shy of the vehicle. They both observed the scene, continuing to slap their ears where the mozzies were buzzing around.

'Why wouldn't he have hidden this ute better, if he used it as a getaway vehicle?' Dave asked.

'I was just thinking the same thing, son. Wouldn't have taken much to drive it deep into some bush, or park it in an unused gravel pit. Bury it in a dam, even. Set the thing in first gear and put a block of wood on the accelerator. I guess it would have been found soon enough but not within the first few days. Given him a longer lead time, if he has shot through.'

Camera in hand, Dave snapped a few photos of the ute where it was parked under a tree. The windows were wound up, and it looked as if it were waiting for its owner to come back to collect it. No flat tyres, and the bonnet hadn't been propped up to indicate there was a mechanical problem.

Pulling on a pair of gloves, Bob opened the driver's side door and peered inside, Dave taking photos of every step. Nothing underneath the visor. The ashtray contained absolutely zero—not even a speck of dust—while the glove box held an owner's manual. Bob pulled it out and flipped to the front where the details of the owner were usually noted.

'Someone doesn't want us to know who owned it,' Bob said, pointing to torn stubs near the spine. Reaching down he felt under the seat, finding a spanner, and when he pushed the seat forward, he saw the jack and winder. 'Clean as a whistle, son,' he said, popping the bonnet. 'Here, look, the VIN and engine number haven't been ground away. Got your pen?' He called out the numbers as Dave wrote them down. 'We'll cross-reference that with what's noted on the expired rego and see what we come up with.' He glanced up at Dave. 'What are you thinking?'

'That this is getting stranger by the second. I've been leaning towards the idea that he's left, but if he's driven here, someone else is involved because he would've been picked up. I'm sure Leo wouldn't walk from here to another town and risk being seen if he's trying to make his great escape. And yet, I'm still not convinced that I've found enough problems in his life to make him want out.'

'What if he'd hidden another getaway car?'

'Sure, but he would have had to have left the farm and parked it earlier, then got back again. Still showing there's another person involved.'

'Might need to go and have another chat with his mates.' Bob slammed the bonnet and bent down, his knees cracking. On his back, he shuffled underneath the engine and shone his torch upwards. Nothing seemed to be out of place and there wasn't anything hidden in any of the nooks and crannies.

'I don't think we're going to find anything here, do you? I've never seen the inside of a farm ute so clean,' Dave said, looking under the tray. He adjusted his torch and carefully looked over the top of the aluminium, trying to see if there were any signs a dog had been on the back. 'But the outside isn't.'

'I agree.' Bob winched himself out and groaned as he tried to stand, using the bull bar to help him up. 'I'm getting too old for this shit,' he said as he shook off the dirt hanging on his knees. 'Right-oh, let's get this old girl dusted for prints, then head for home.'

Dave flashed his torch over the ground then back up at Bob. 'You're bleeding again,' he said. 'Where's the first-aid kit? I'll get a bandaid. Get your shirt off.' He went back to get the fingerprinting kit he always had on hand and carefully brushed the dust over the door handle and any other shiny surface he could find. Half an hour later he'd lifted five prints.

'Right, that's done, now let me have a look at you.'

'Don't fuss, son. It's fine. Like I said, it's just a pimple that's itchy and I keep scratching the head off it.'

'Just give us a look.'

Bob shrugged out of the sleeve of his shirt and turned around.

'It's infected,' Dave said the moment he saw the red welt the size of a fifty-cent piece. Hang on, I'll whack some Dettol on it.' He went back to the first-aid kit and found the tube of cream, put a blob on Bob's arm and stuck the bandaid over the top. 'Better keep an eye on that.'

'She'll be right. Thanks, son.' Bob put his arm back into his shirt and helped Dave pack up.

'Okay, in the morning, I'll tackle the father,' Bob said then cocked his head. 'Ah, that sounds like the tow truck. Excellent.'

Headlights flashed across their view and the truck came to a halt a long way from where they were standing. Chris jumped down, his face drawn tightly.

'He's not . . .' he yelled as he stood jiggling next to the truck. 'He's not in there, is he?' Panic radiated from him as he moved from foot to foot, and stared at the vehicle.

'Nah, mate. Clean as a whistle. You're good to go,' Bob called back.

Chris climbed back into the cab of the truck and ground the gears, trying to find reverse. Slowly he winched the ute up onto the tray and chained it on, all the while his eyes avoiding the inside.

'We'll come and catch up with you in the morning,' Bob told him. 'And Dave here is going to have a few more questions for you.'

Chris nodded. The jovial man from the afternoon had disappeared. Now his shoulders were slumped, and grief lined his face. 'Did he die in there?'

Dave put his hand on the man's shoulder. 'No. There is nothing to indicate that at all, Chris. Nothing, okay? If you look in the window, it'll be like looking at a very clean ute. Okay? There's nothing to be frightened of. We can't even be sure Leo has been in here.'

He let out a deep breath. 'You sure?'

'Promise, mate.'

Chris relaxed, but he still didn't smile. 'Where is he?' he asked, more to himself than the other men. 'Right-oh, fellas, see you tomorrow.' He got back behind the steering wheel and crunched the gears, causing Dave to wince as the truck lurched forward and onto the road.

'Geez, wouldn't want to be that gearbox,' Bob said as Dave started the troopy.

'Come on, let's get a bit of shut-eye and get ready for tomorrow,' Dave said. 'It's near enough to midnight.'

They followed Chris down the road, watching the tail-lights glow red as did the brakes when occasionally he applied his foot to the pedal.

'You happy enough to talk to Andrew, Bruce and Chris again?' Bob asked.

Dave nodded. 'What about having a word with the wives, too?' he asked thoughtfully. 'Probably should have done that before now.'

'Great idea. And I think we should follow up on the angle that neither Jill nor the family got along. I'll talk to Stephen as well.'

From the side of the road, there was a flash of grey-brown. Dave reacted by slamming his foot on the brakes and the back of the troopy slid out sideways. There was the sickening thump and bump of a roo tumbling under the wheel.

They came to a sudden stop and silence filled the air.

Bob looked over at Dave, his hand holding on to the Jesus bar. 'Now, son, if you don't like what I'm saying, just tell me, okay? No need for all the dramatics.'

Not able to help himself, Dave gave a short snort, then got out and went to make sure the roo was dead before dragging it off the road.

Bob opened his door and inspected the bull bar, lights and radiator. 'Nothing. Geez, you managed that well. Not a mark on the vehicle!'

'Let's make sure there's no damage underneath,' Dave said grimly, crouching down and hoping they didn't have to call Chris back out again.

He shone the torch on the dirt and then from side to side. 'Nothing leaking, anyway.' Gingerly, Dave started the car and watched the temperature gauge. Five minutes later, there was no sign anything was amiss.

'Right, well, as I was saying,' Bob said, as he snapped his seatbelt into the latch, 'if I talk to the father, how about you make a visit to Andrew, Chris and Bruce? See what they can tell you about the excess of utes on Leo's farm. Then we'll follow up with Jill and the rest of the family.'

'Yeah, that sounds like a plan. I also want to come over to Hunter Rock and have a look. This ute was, what, ten kilometres from the town? I might just go and flash his photo around to see if anyone has seen him. Robbie said there's only about ten houses in the town and a pub, so it shouldn't take too long.'

'Great idea.' Bob looked over at Dave with a grin. 'God, I don't know who you were trained by, but by hell they've done a good job.'

Dave raised his eyebrows. 'Anyone told you that you're a nob lately?'

'Ah now, son. You keep all that loving to yourself. Don't want anyone getting the wrong idea about us.'

CHAPTER 15

'Sorry to bother you again, Chris,' Dave said, as he gave the ute another once-over in the daylight. 'I've got another couple of questions that you might be able to help with.'

'Go for it,' Chris said as he shrugged into his overalls.

The day hadn't warmed up to the severe temperature of yesterday, so Chris was still wearing a T-shirt and shorts underneath the overalls. He was quieter than the previous day and the sparkle had gone from his eyes.

'When Bob and I were out at the farm, we found eight Toyota utes. All old and clapped out. Doesn't look like they're used much, just stored in the shed. We were wondering if you had any ideas why Leo would have had so many?'

Chris gave the ghost of a smile. He was pale and his hair hadn't been brushed that morning. Picking up the ute last night had obviously upset him deeply and had made the ordeal very real.

'Yeah, Leo never goes to a clearing sale without buying a ute. Uses 'em as wreckers. Sometimes I'd go out there and grab some spare parts, when I couldn't get what I needed. He's restoring a couple of old HiLuxes. God knows why, they're a dime a dozen. He buys up, then uses them as parts.' Shooting a nervous look towards the HiLux, his eyes swung quickly back to Dave.

Gently, Dave said, 'Chris, I want you to know there is nothing linking this ute back to Leo, other than it had been registered to him three years ago. The rego has lapsed so, as I told you last night, we can't be sure if Leo was even in it. I've dusted it for fingerprints, and my forensic crew are running them at the moment. This vehicle could also have been stolen. Or Leo sold it after it was deregistered. We're still working through some options. You seem as if finding the ute has rocked you.'

'No need to run the fingerprints,' Chris said quietly. 'That's his ute. I checked when I got home last night. Don't worry, I didn't touch anything. Used a rag to open the door. Recently, a fella brought a HiLux in that needed a seatbelt replacing and he wanted it done yesterday. Like they all do. Anyway, it was going to take a couple of days to get the part down from Perth, so I rang Leo and asked if I could grab one out of one of his. He said to come on out. Took the passenger's side one. You'll see the casing is still there, but there isn't a seatbelt inside. It's his ute for sure.'

Dave nodded slowly. 'Right. And when was this?' He fished in his pocket for his notebook.

'About three weeks ago. This one was parked outside the shed, so it was the one I attacked when I got there.'

'I see.' Dave swivelled on his heels and looked again at the ute. 'Leo left it out for you? You didn't see him?'

'I don't know if there was anything special about this one. He just said he'd get one and leave it at the front of the shed because he was up the back of the farm shifting sheep from one paddock to another. But I'd reckon this would've been at the front of them all. You've seen how tightly they're stacked in.'

In broad daylight the ute seemed unremarkable. A banged-up, rusty HiLux that had dents in every panel, dust covering it, and a filthy windscreen with a crack that made the sunlight warp as it shone through. The canvas canopy was dry and worn, a few small holes where it had rubbed through on the frame. A contrast to how clean it was inside the cab.

Dave bent down and ran his fingers over the tyres. 'Still plenty of tread.'

'I used to think he paid too much for these wreckers. Coz they were more than that. Mostly they were good solid utes that would be fine out on a farm, even with just farm plates on. Some used to have a few vibrations if you pushed them over eighty kay an hour, but—' he shrugged '—still can drive 'em, just got to hang on a bit tighter, and sometimes he'd grab a tyre or part off it, too.'

'Did Leo ever lend any of the extra vehicles to anyone? Friends? People whose cars had broken down that you were fixing?'

'Like, as in, did I send people to him? Nah, and I don't think he lent them out.'

'And did he drive the ones that were roadworthy?'

Chris thought for a moment. 'I don't remember ever seeing him doing that off the farm, unless he was bringing them home from the clearing sale. He really liked his new Nissan ute. Has that been found?'

'Yeah, that was at the farm when the fire went through. Down at the pumphouse. Burned. That's how the Arson squad worked out it was a spillage rather than deliberately lit. There's nothing but a shell left.'

'He wasn't in there?'

'No. Even with how hot the fire was, there would have been some remains if he'd been caught inside the vehicle when the flames went through. There was nothing.'

'Uh-huh.' Chris looked around and went towards his tools, grabbing a spanner from the shadow board. He turned back to Dave, slapping it into his palm.

Realising this was his cue to leave, Dave said, 'Great. Thanks, Chris. And don't let anyone near that ute, okay? I'm going to have to work out where we can put it to keep it impounded. Doesn't look like the police yard here is big enough. Can you get it out of sight? Behind the shed or something?'

'Yeah, can do.' Chris nodded and turned away.

Dave waited. There was more coming from Chris.

'He's gone off somewhere, hasn't he? Shot through?'

'Why do you ask that?'

'That's what the word on the street is.'

'I know I've asked before, but I'm going to ask again: do you know why Leo would want to do that?'

Chris ran his hands through his hair and looked over his shoulder. 'No. No, I don't. This type of behaviour is very out of character for Leo.'

'You and Bruce said yesterday that Leo wore his heart on his sleeve . . .' Dave left the sentence hanging.

Anger and hurt lashed out from Chris. 'And this is exactly why we don't understand what is going on. He always talked to us. Told us what was going on. We all did. Us four blokes: me, Andy, Bruce and Leo. One of our group—our *mate*—died by suicide when we were kids. We were all so young and most of us hadn't even heard the word suicide. His death ripped us to pieces and we made a pact that we would always talk to each other, no matter how hard. Whatever problems we were going through, we agreed that none of us would be judged, only supported.' He wiped the back of his hand over his nose then rubbed his eyes. His throat worked up and down as he tried to control his emotions, then he looked at Dave with imploring eyes. 'Yet there was nothing from Leo. He was normal. Phone calls, yarns. We didn't get to see him much, but that wasn't unusual anymore. There was absolutely nothing indicating anything was wrong. Nothing to give him a reason to do this.'

Dave put his hand on Chris's shoulder. 'It's tough when there aren't any answers,' he said. 'But we're doing all we can.'

His phone rang and Dave moved back to check the number. 'Better grab this,' he said, and Chris nodded.

'Burrows,' he answered as he walked towards the troopy, holding his hand up in a goodbye.

'It's Shannon. How are you?'

Dave paused for a moment and squinted across a brown paddock where the wind had kicked up a small whirly-whirly and it danced across the ground picking up dry bushes in its path. 'I'm okay, how are you?' he asked.

'Busy. I'm just letting you know I've sent the results back on the fingerprinting. Good thing I was here early this morning so I could run them for you. Results are on your email. It's your man. Where did you pull the prints from?'

'Door handle, gearstick, steering wheel.'

'Was the handbrake on and did you dust it?'

'Ah, no,' Dave said slowly as he thought back. 'Not engaged, and no, I didn't dust it.'

'Mirror?'

'I didn't pull any prints from there.'

'Well, all those other places are consistent with him driving the vehicle.'

'A detective in the making. Thanks, Shannon.' Dave didn't feel the elation he should, because Chris had already confirmed what Dave and Bob had suspected.

'Need anything else?'

'Not for the time being.' He took a breath. 'You going okay?' He could hear the rustle of her cheek against the phone and remembered how she had felt against him during their nights together.

'Yeah, fine. Any word on when you're going to be back?'

'Not yet, we're not getting very far. Without a body or a sighting . . .' His voice trailed off. 'The fella in the hospital didn't amount to anything and we can't find Coffee, the dog. The ute was a breakthrough, but I'm not sure what that will end up telling us since Leo decided not to leave us a map as to his whereabouts.' Tiny black flies kept bombing his eyes and nose, looking for moisture, so he pulled some grass from the soil and used it as a fan.

'They never do. Don't worry, something will turn up. It usually does.'

'GPS coordinates?' he joked.

Shannon laughed, and he felt the warmth he always did when he was speaking to her begin to flow through him. The slow hot lava of desire, conversation and intelligence. Three aphrodisiacs.

'What have you got on your plate?' he asked, wanting to keep her on the phone.

'Ah, Dave, just the usual. About to scrub up and go into the mortuary. If I get home at a decent hour, I'm going to try to go to the gym.'

'Sounds like a plan.'

'I'd like to ask if you might be home by the weekend so we could organise to do something, but it's too hard to guess, isn't it?'

A smile played around Dave's mouth. This was the sort of conversation he'd always wished he could have had with Mel, but she had never understood the job and why, at any moment, plans could be cancelled.

'Hit the nail on the head. I'll let you know if we get any breakthroughs, or if we've done all we can here and are heading back.' He paused. 'You do know I'll ring you, don't you? And we'll have dinner.'

'Good,' Shannon's voice whispered through the line.

Dave imagined her long dark hair falling over her shoulders and caressing his chest. He didn't want to break the spell, but he had to move on. 'I've got to go,' he said. It wasn't just the warmth from the sun heating him up.

'Hmm, me too. I'll hear from you later.'

'You will.' He paused, but Shannon hadn't hung up. 'Talk to you soon,' he said.

This time the phone line was disconnected.

~

Dave drove along the main street and flicked the indicator on as he came to the entrance of the motel. In the car park, he glanced across to Jill's room and then to where Bob was sitting on the verandah with Stephen and Jan.

Stephen was leaning forward as if pleading with Bob, while Jan sat back, her fingers clasped to her mouth. Perhaps she might have been crying.

He parked further down the row of rooms and walked back to Jill's room. From inside he could hear the blare of the TV—the *Bananas in Pyjamas* theme song, he thought. A little girl's voice called out 'Muummmy!' and Dave put his hand to his chest without even realising his heart was sore. Not just sore, his whole body *ached* for his kids. He could still feel Bec's hand in his and Alice's soft skin as he kissed her cheek.

He raised his hand to knock.

Noah gave a cry and then said, 'Daddy, Daddy.'

Jill opened the door, anticipation on her face. Her smile fell away when she saw Dave and she had the grace to look embarrassed. 'I'm sorry about last night,' she told him, adjusting her designer label skirt. 'Andrew made me see how badly I behaved. I didn't realise.' Her eyes lowered to the floor, but not before Dave noted her makeup was done and she looked as if she was ready to run out the door to an appointment.

Noah was clinging to her leg, while Charlotte sat at the table colouring in. She'd looked up curiously when she saw Dave in the doorway.

'No problem,' Dave told her. 'No one can know how they're going to react until they're in a situation.'

'Would you like to come in?'

'Thanks.' Dave stepped into a clean room, toys all in a basket and the dishes washed, draining in the sink. A vast improvement from the chaos that had greeted him and Bob a couple of days ago. 'How are you all getting on today?'

Jill glanced around. 'Well, I feel as if it's the first time I've been half organised since all this happened. I decided last night after we got back from the pub that I can't feel sorry for myself. I'm just going to have to keep chipping away at what normally goes on. Going to head back out to the farm today to see if I can work out what needs doing.

Andrew said he'd go with me, and we'll have a look around. He can probably guide me, being a farmer and all.'

Dave raised his eyebrows. 'That's something you want to do?' He took in her clothes again. Jill wasn't dressed as if she was going out to the farm.

Her hand strayed to Noah's head and she stroked him gently. 'If this little one is going to be a farmer then I don't have any choice, do I? I don't want him to miss out.' She stopped and glanced down, swallowing hard.

'Would Stephen have an idea of what program Leo was going to follow for this year?'

'I asked yesterday, but it hadn't been decided. So maybe I can make those decisions.' Then she leaned towards Dave and whispered, 'That's if they'll let me.'

Dave didn't want to tell her that if she'd never farmed before and didn't know wheat from barley it was very unlikely her in-laws would let her have anything to do with setting the program for 2002. Jill had no claim over the farm because it was still owned by Leo's parents. *Did she realise that?* he wondered.

Instead he asked, 'Stephen and Jan?'

Jill nodded.

Indicating he wanted to speak to her privately, Dave tipped his head towards the tiny patio, and waited while she asked Noah to stay and watch the TV and got Charlotte a drink.

Outside, they kept their voices low in case Stephen and Jan heard them, even though Dave knew they were out the front with Bob.

'How have you been getting on with Leo's parents since they arrived?'

Jill sank down into a chair as if she was exhausted. It was still early in the morning. A hand went to her mouth and she rubbed her lips as if deciding whether to say something or not. 'Difficult,' she finally said.

Pulling up the spare chair, Dave put his elbows on his knees and leaned towards her. 'Want to tell me about it?'

Jill was quiet, smoothing out the hem of her skirt, even though it didn't need it, then she sat up and crossed her legs. 'Sometimes it's okay and other times it's not. I understand they're feeling lost, too, not knowing where Leo is. Jan loves the kids, but Stephen is pretty "you will be seen and not heard" with them. Then, when the kids get upset, he gets angry. And Jan keeps shooting me these looks as if I know something about Leo, when—' she spread her hands out, tears brimming '—clearly I don't, because I'm in the dark with the rest of you.'

'It's a horrible time for all concerned.'

Sweeping her hair from her eyes, she got a tissue from her bra and dabbed underneath her eyes, the way Dave had only ever seen movie stars do. 'Unfortunately, Leo's family haven't liked me from the first moment we started going out together. We met when I was a medical receptionist ten years ago, when I was twenty and he was twenty-one. I know it's a bit weird, a country bloke falling for a city girl and vice versa, but that's what happened. Leo had to come up a few times to have some suspect moles cut out, and we got talking. One day he asked if I wanted to go for a coffee.'

Dave got out his notebook and wrote down 'extra scars'. They might be helpful in time, as would the one on his chin.

'And you said yes?'

'I did. About a year later, I resigned from my job and moved up here. It was around that time Jan had the stroke and the family were trying to work out what was going to happen. Stephen didn't want the farm to be sold, and Leo certainly didn't. I don't know what he would have done if his dad insisted that it was listed on the open market. Leo was freaking out for a while, sure that's what was going to happen.'

There was a cry from inside the room and Jill got up, curving her hands around her face at the glass door. She motioned for Charlotte to sit down, then smiled and gave her the thumbs up when she did as she was asked.

'Farming was Leo's life,' she continued as she sat back down. 'Having a new girl on the scene at the same time wasn't easy. It seemed to them I'd just left the city to come up and swan around as a rich farmer's wife. That I'd seen the money, not the man.'

'Acre Chaser,' Dave said.

Jill gave a little laugh. 'Yes, if you like. I thought it was more the Hectare Hunter these days. Those words have been tossed at me a couple of times.'

'You might be right.' Dave smiled back. 'I'm old school.'

'The trouble was, I got pregnant about two months after I moved here and that's when the knives really came out.' She swallowed again, the hurt on her face obvious. 'I couldn't believe it, you know?' Her voice rose a little. 'I was so sick. Vomiting all day. Morning sickness is never just in the morning when I'm pregnant. Could barely lift my head from the pillow.' At the mention of the nausea, Jill seemed to go a little green. 'And one day, Leo came in and said his parents were asking for a medical certificate to prove I was pregnant.'

The words lifted into the silent air and bounced off the brick walls.

'Sorry?' Dave asked, his notebook still in his hand.

'Yeah, crazy, right? Actually, down right *insulting*.' Insulting was said a little louder and Dave thought it might have been intended to fly over the fence and land on the right person's ears.

'You had to supply them with a medical certificate to prove you were pregnant?'

'Yeah. And that's when they decided to put Leo on wages and Stephen had to check everything—every invoice, purchase, sale. Whatever.' She flapped her hand as if casting all the horrible things that had been said to her aside. 'Anyway, I said fine. No problems. I'll get a certificate. Leo didn't want me to. Said we should just tell them to get stuffed, but I did. Wanted to prove that I was here for the long haul.

'So, I made the appointment and the day before I was due to go, I miscarried. Unfortunately, I wasn't far along so it looked like a very heavy period.' The tears were back. 'I couldn't prove anything to them. That was the icing on the cake. They were still convinced I was gold digging, so nothing changed. If anything, they made Leo report back to them in more detail than before.'

'You and Leo weren't receiving any other money than your wages?'

Jill shook her head. 'We get free fuel, meat and power as any farm employee does, but nothing else. It was barely enough to live on once we had the kids. Leo had to go back and ask for a pay rise, and it took a bit, but he got one.' She tossed a furious glance over her shoulder towards Stephen and Jan's room.

'Jill, I need to clarify. Other than the wages you were receiving from the farm, the, ah—' Dave referred back to his notebook '—five hundred and fifty dollars a week, you weren't getting any other money from the farm?'

'No. Nothing.' She frowned. 'Well, not cash, just some extras as I said. Like fuel. I guess that would add up to a fair bit, especially since I go into town most days. The power bill isn't excessive, and meat, again, I don't have to buy it because Leo kills the lambs on the farm. I don't know how much any of that would be worth, but we have to pay for all of our own car registrations and vehicle services. Why do you ask?'

'We've been through all the invoices and reoccurring payments, crosschecking everything, and we've found that there has been money going to a bank account which isn't a hire purchase account. I'm waiting for Fraud to get back to me, but it looks as if Leo was transferring money out of the farm through a fake invoice and depositing it in another account.'

Jill stared, unable to say anything, although Dave noticed her fingers clenched tighter around the hem of her skirt.

'Do you know anything about that?'

With tears running down her perfectly made-up cheek, she shook her head and whispered, 'No. Nothing.'

CHAPTER 16

Dave wanted to offer some kind of comfort, because Jill was bending over, her arms wrapped around her waist, rocking herself.

'How could he?' she whispered. 'How could he?'

Instead, he had to ask another question. 'Jill, I need you to be very clear with me on this. You don't know anything about money being transferred into a different account from the farm?'

'I told you, no,' she muttered. 'I was never involved with payments or any type of office work. Nothing. Why would he have done that? So he could leave? To be—' She broke off.

'Mummy?' Charlotte was standing at the door.

Dave got up and went to her, squatting down and giving her a smile. 'Mum and I are having a talk, could you go back inside for a little while? What's on TV?'

'*Bananas in Pyjamas* has finished.'

'Should we find something else to watch?'

Jill appeared at Dave's side, her face pale. 'Come on, darling, I'll get you another colouring-in picture. Noah, are you hungry, love? Want an apple?' She looked at Dave. 'Just give me ten minutes to get them sorted.'

'No hurry,' Dave said, heading back outside. He heard her moving about in the kitchen, talking quietly to the children. *What a transformation*, he thought, from shocked to sad to tears, that were suddenly gone and she was off doing normal things. He wondered if that's how Mel had dealt with the situations that had been sent her way.

His phone rang and he checked the screen. Fraud. *Perfect timing*, he thought.

'Burrows.'

'Jamie Patterson, Fraud Squad. Got what you were looking for.'

'Fast work, thanks for that.'

'Okay, the money is being paid into a smaller bank, not one of the big four. It's the Country Rural Bank. Only has branches in Western Australia. Very small and not well known, except for rural customers.'

'Whose name is the account in?'

'A Mr Leo Stephen Perry.'

'That's my missing man.'

'Well, he's been paying into this account for three and a half years and there's an eye-watering balance. Nearly four hundred thousand dollars. Some of that is interest, but there are payments of thirty thousand going in quarterly.'

'Geez, he's certainly made up for the money he's been missing out on from the rest of the family. And yeah, that adds up to the amounts that are being taken from this bank account. Nice work.'

'So, there's—' Jamie drew out the word as he found the information Dave would be looking for '—two transactions that went out every month and that was two thousand dollars, so it never really put a dent in the balance. One thousand each withdrawal. That's the maximum amount of cash that can be withdrawn in one hit from an ATM.'

'One thousand per transaction, twice a month?'

'Yeah, and it comes out on the same date each month. The second and the fourteenth.'

'Is it withdrawn from the same place every time?'

'Yep. The same branch where the account is held. It's an ATM transaction, not an in-bank one.'

'There'll be CCTV footage?'

'Banks usually have that, for sure. Guess it will depend on how long a smaller bank holds the vision for.'

'Right, I'll see what I can get out of them. There are no other transactions?'

'Correct.'

'And where's the branch situated?'

'Ah, in Mowup.'

'Mowup? Where's that? Not too far from here, I think?'

'Mate, you're the stock squad guys, we're the ones who sit and look at computer screens all the time and don't know what the sun looks like. I'm sure you can read a map.'

'Thanks, Jamie. All that information is great. Talk soon.'

Dave closed the phone, thinking. What would be at Mowup?

Jill came back out again, looking ashen. Before Dave could say anything, she said, 'You have to believe me. I know nothing about that money. I didn't have access to any of the farming bank accounts, except our joint one and my personal one. I don't know passwords or—'

'I hear what you're telling me, Jill,' Dave interrupted her. 'I had to ask, though, okay? All these questions are normal procedure. We need to gather as much information as we can to put a full picture together.'

'Yeah.' Her voice was low, but not defeated. 'And I'm just telling you, there is no way that Stephen would have let me have access to the Perry bank accounts.'

Nearly halfway through the morning sky, the sun had started to heat up the land, and Dave could feel a sweat coming over his brow. He needed to change tack with her. 'What do you do during each week, Jill?' he asked. 'Do you have any reoccurring appointments? Things you don't change?'

'Wait a moment,' she said and disappeared back inside again.

Dave fought the urge to peer over the high brick wall and make sure that Jan and Stephen weren't there listening, but he hadn't heard any doors closing to indicate that Bob had finished with them yet. He glanced at his watch. Jill and he had been talking for nearly fifteen minutes.

A moment later, Jill returned with a leather-bound diary and held it out to him. 'Here you go. Look through that.

That's my bible. All my appointments are in there. I've got nothing to hide.'

Dave took it and tucked the book under his arm. 'Thanks, I'll get it back to you as quickly as I can.' He paused. 'Jill, last night we found a ute that had been registered to Leo, or at least to the farming company. It had been abandoned over at Hunter Rock. Do you or Leo have ties to that town?'

Slowly, Jill shook her head. 'No. Not that I know of.'

'No friends?'

'No. But I guess I can't speak for Leo, can I? I would never have thought he would take money from the farm, and here we are, so I don't know if he knew anyone there.'

Dave ignored the sarcasm that was overriding her hurt. 'What about a place called Mowup?'

'Mowup? It's about thirty minutes' drive from here. On the road to Northton. That's a two-horse town if ever there was one! No, I don't know anyone there. What I just said about Leo applies there, too.'

'Okay. Now, look, you might not like this, but I'm going to have to ask about your personal bank accounts. Can you show them to me, so I can see that there isn't any money from the farm being deposited into them?' He paused as he heard her take a deep breath. 'If you don't want to do that willingly, I can apply for a warrant.' He said the words softly to take the sting out of them.

'Which bit of I've got nothing to hide don't you get?' Jill asked, her tone edged with disdain. 'You can look at them. You can look at my diary, you can go through my underwear drawer if you like.'

Dave felt a snap of annoyance as she spoke.

'There's no money from the farm going into any of my accounts.'

'Great, then you won't mind giving the statements to me.'

'They've all burned, but I can give you my bank's log-in details.'

'How about you log in and get everything printed off for the last twelve months and bring me the statements that way? How many accounts do you have?' As he asked the question, he made a note in his book to get Fraud to check the details.

'One. Oh, two if you count the one for the kids. That's in my own name but we put fifty dollars a week aside for the kids' later education. It's a savings account and no withdrawals can be made unless there are two signatories: Leo and me. The other one I've had since I was in school. My wages used to go in it when I worked.'

Dave made another note while he thought about the next question. 'Do you have your own income?' he asked.

'As in?'

Dave raised his hands. 'Do you get paid for any of the community work you do, or receive any share dividends? Those types of things?'

Jill raised her head defiantly. 'When I came here, I gave up everything. I sacrificed my career, the ability to be independent. I had to rely on Leo for everything, apart from a small amount of savings. I haven't worked for a wage since. I look after the kids and the farm is supposed to look after me. I don't see anything wrong with the farm doing that, with what I've had to give up, do you?'

Dave felt a pressure around his heart as he heard echoes of Melinda. He remembered one awful argument before they found out she was pregnant with Bec.

I've given up everything for you, she had told him. What Dave remembered about those words was how anger had dripped from every syllable. *I might never get a job like my old one. All the training I've done will be for nothing.*

'My wife, ex-wife,' he corrected himself, 'felt the same way. It's huge, leaving behind everything you know. Family, career. It's the ultimate sacrifice, isn't it? Love does funny things to a person. I wouldn't have thought any less of you if you had asked for more than what the family had been providing for you.'

Jill's mouth twisted into a grimace that could have been a smile. 'Ex?'

'Yes. Ex. For some of the abovementioned reasons.'

'Do you understand now?'

'I understood before. She made a choice. Just as you did, coming here.'

Dave recognised her anger and was trying to get her back onside.

'Yeah, well, it's nice of you to notice. I guess if your ex is your ex then you didn't fix it in time.'

Biting his lip, he heard Spencer in his mind: *Still tongue in a wise head.* Dave desperately wanted to defend himself. Tell Jill that fixing a marriage required two people to want to work at a relationship. Instead, he said, 'I notice your clothes are very good quality.' And then wanted to bite his tongue off.

Jill scoffed. 'Ah, so this is where that's coming from? Do you think I'm stealing from the farm so I can buy clothes and lead the good life? You sound just like my in-laws, going back to the gold-digging references.' She turned away, her shoulders heaving with anger.

'I'm sorry, Jill. This is my job and these are all routine questions.'

'Well, let me tell you, that when you buy decent quality clothes, they're timeless and last for years. If you look after clothes, they will last.

'Anything extra I have goes on the kids. And,' she turned around and pointed her finger at him, 'my parents always give me gift vouchers for Christmas and birthdays. That's when I buy new clothes.' She looked at him as if he was dog shit that she'd stepped in.

Dave, knowing he had stuffed up with the last question, wanted to shrink. Still so much to learn.

'Where did you find the ute?' Jill asked after a stony silence.

'It was parked in a little clearing off the main road going into Hunter Rock. Behind bushes so it couldn't be easily seen.' They were back on safe ground, and Dave was relieved.

'Who found it?'

'Another farmer had noticed it. He waited a few days before he called it in. Just making sure that someone hadn't left it there for an overnighter.'

'Was there . . . um, any sign?'

Dave shook his head. 'No, the ute was clean. But Leo's fingerprints were on the steering wheel, and I've also got an eyewitness report that the ute was owned by Leo.'

'He's alive then?' Hurt covered her face. 'He's *alive*?'

'Until I see him, I can't say for certain, but yes, one of the possibilities we're looking at is that he's alive but doesn't want to let anyone know.'

'This isn't Leo,' she said despairingly. All the fight and anger left her now. 'Why would he do this? I just don't understand. Obviously I didn't know him the way I thought I did.' Her shoulders slumped a little.

'I'm going to have to ask you this, Jill. You don't know of any reason why Leo would want to leave here, abandon you and the kids? We know the farm side of things was pretty restricting for you both, but it's sounding like the position was workable.'

Jill had fire in her eyes now. 'I'll say this once and once only. My husband is a good man. We love each other and I know of no reason why he would want to leave me, the children or this godforsaken farm.'

~

Dave and Bob met out in the car park and stood facing each other, their faces grim.

'I really don't think Jill knows anything,' Dave said. 'She's given me access to her bank accounts, her diary,' he held up the book, 'and I can't see any red flags.'

'I'm the same with the family, but there is one thing. All of them—Stephen, Jan, Sally and Elliot—they are all convinced that Jill is out for herself in this. That she didn't marry Leo for love.'

'Yeah, she told me that she had to supply them with a certificate from the doctor saying she was pregnant. I mean, who does that?'

Bob nodded. 'That matches with what they told me. If that were me, I wouldn't be admitting I'd stooped so low. Anyway, their reasoning was that they were in the process of working out how the succession plan was going to go and they felt that Jill wasn't marrying for the right reasons. Once she had made the appointment with a doctor . . .' He opened his notebook. 'And I quote: *She conveniently miscarried. By then, Leo had already asked her to marry him and they were engaged. There was nothing to be done.* Jan said that. She also went on to say there was more to the story, but she wouldn't be repeating that now. I asked why. Jan said she didn't see the point in dragging up dirt, and I said that everything was important to the investigation. Still, she remained tight-lipped. Couldn't get it out of her. I reminded her that I could interview her at the station, and she said she knew.'

'So, what made them ask for the medical certificate? They were concerned she wasn't pregnant? That's not something you can fake.'

'They didn't really expand on it.' Bob continued, 'Interesting though, that both Stephen and Jan now say Leo and Jill seemed happy in their relationship. I think it cost them a lot to admit that to me, but if that's what they're seeing, after all the angst they've had with Jill, the comment holds a lot of weight. They tell me she's a good mum, but they still wouldn't trust her to have anything to do with the farm finances.'

'Money. The root of all evils.'

'Ain't that the truth? And look, their comments around money aren't unusual, until a succession plan is complete. I mean, so many farmers make sure the in-laws—be it women or men—can't sign for anything, or that they don't have any claim over the land, so families can't lose what they've worked so hard for, until it's their time.'

'Yeah. Wealth and land are just one great big evil in some families, especially if someone doesn't agree with the decisions that are being made.'

Dave kicked at the dirt with the toe of his boot. 'I don't know, something isn't sitting right here. Jill says there're gift vouchers from her parents and that's how she buys her clothes, but say she bought three shirts, a skirt and a pair of jeans each time, there wouldn't be much change from a couple of thousand a year. That's a lot of gift cards. Where else could she be getting the money from?' Dave frowned, then his face cleared. 'Fraud rang while I was talking to Jill.' He quickly summarised the outcome.

Bob tapped his pen on his mouth. 'Hmm, well, something has possibly pushed Leo to the edge and we need to change our thinking. We are looking for Leo alive. We've established that there's money going missing from the farm, the ute has his fingerprints; to all intents and purposes, he's done a runner.'

'But why? We haven't found a motive.'

'Well, son, that's what we're going to have to work out. Let's have a quick brainstorm: why do people disappear?' He looked at Dave over his glasses. 'The most common reason is someone wants to start afresh. Two, he or she has a debt that is about to be collected due to drugs, criminal activities. Three, mental illness. Four, escaping an unhappy situation. Five, victim of crime and has to testify. Six, scared. Seven . . .' He frowned, thinking. 'Fall in love with another woman or man. Do I need to go on?'

'So, which is it?'

'From what I've gleaned about Leo, it could be any of those, but my gut feel is either four or seven. Two could feature.'

'Debt?'

'Yeah, drug dealers don't usually issue invoices for the amount owed. Just because we haven't found a debt yet doesn't mean he hasn't got one. Doesn't have to be drugs. Could be gambling, or the fact he wanted to go on holidays—his honeymoon even—and he borrowed from the wrong person.'

'I haven't asked anyone whether he'd do drugs or not.'

'Make a note. Always worth a question.'

'I'm going to head over to Hunter Rock and have a bit of a dig around there. See what I can find out,' Dave said, as he wrote *drugs* in his notebook.

'Good. I'll go through the statements when Jill brings them over and see what I can find there. And I'll follow up with the bank and see what CCTV footage there is of the withdrawals.'

Dave's phone rang. 'Fraud, again,' he said glancing at the screen. 'G'day, Jamie.'

'I made a call to the bank to see what CCTV they had there. I was lucky because usually they video over it within a week. I've had it sent to your email. Hopefully you'll find something there that's useful.'

'Thanks, mate. My partner was about to make those calls. We'll check it out.' He hung up and looked at Bob. 'Right, let's get back to the office.'

They got into the troopy and headed back to the station.

Once he was at his desk, Dave brought up his emails and waited for them to download. Red and Robbie were hovering in the background, keen to be brought up to speed.

Bob told them the ute was Leo's and now they had changed the search parameters.

'Anything that you could help with about Leo?' Bob asked.

'You know, we hardly ever saw him,' Red said, leaning back in a chair. 'Once in a blue moon, maybe. But we'd see Jill all the time; well, her car was always parked at the tennis club or the school. She'd be with their group of friends, Bruce and Carmel Cameron, the Barrys and Pearces. I often see her car going between Andrew Pearce's farm and her own. I think they take it in turns to carpool with the kids.

'Sometimes I'd see Leo in at the stock agent's getting chemical and the like, but not too often. Always had his dog chained up on the back of the ute. He's a bit like a ghost. We knew he was there but didn't see him. And I can't remember the last time I saw Jill and him together.'

Dave motioned them all over. 'Okay, is this him?' He pressed play and they watched as a tall man came into the shot, his hands deep in his pockets. Then he withdrew a hand from his pocket. They saw him insert a card into the ATM and punch a few buttons. Dave let out a frustrated sigh when he realised they were only going to see the back of the man's head. The money arrived in the slot and he reached out and took it, glancing over his shoulder, before folding the notes into his pocket.

The man turned and Dave hit the pause button and stared at the screen, hoping to see the scar, or his blue eyes. Some identifying feature. All he could see was half a cheek and a whole ear.

'Do you know who it is?' he asked.

'That's Leo,' Red said softly. 'That's him. When was this filmed?'

Dave pressed his finger to the date stamp. 'Two days ago.'

CHAPTER 17

Bob gave a cackle and rubbed his hands together. 'Well, well, well, we were on the money, son,' he said to Dave. Then, with a burst of energy, he stood up. 'Right, as of two days ago, Leo was alive. Robbie and Red, can you take this footage over and get a statement from Jill that the man in this video is in fact Leo Perry?'

'Course.' Red stood up and reached for the computer.

The room buzzed with adrenalin as the news filtered through that Leo was alive and the case had changed.

Dave held up his hand. 'I'll email it to you. Print some copies off and see if you can get a clear picture to show Jill. If not, get her to come into the station.' He turned to Bob, the anticipation in his voice making him speak faster than normal. 'I'm going to head to Hunter Rock now and see what I can find out.'

'Sure, I'll talk to the wives. See what they can tell me about Jill and Leo's relationship.'

Dave almost ran out of the office. Leo only had two days on them, and the withdrawal was taken from a town that was only a short drive away. So, the ute being left on the road going into Hunter Rock meant that he had to have someone helping him from near there, or that was where they'd decided to meet.

Who was helping him? Dave wanted to jump to the conclusion it was a woman, but as Bob had always said, and Spencer before him, a slow and methodical investigation was the only way to go. Perhaps Leo had had enough, and he just wanted out. By himself. Perhaps a mate had helped him and was keeping quiet.

What other options were there? That he was sick of his family controlling his life? Yep, Dave could certainly see how getting away from that could be enticing. But, as a father, Dave still could not reconcile that Leo would walk away from his young children. No one would do that.

Was he in a situation that he couldn't get out of? Blackmail?

Dave hopped in the car and wrote down a couple of questions before he set off for Hunter Rock:

Any further CCTV around the ATM or the main street of Mowup?

Date is different from the other transactions, but the place is the same: Mowup.

How did he get there? Pressure on mates.

Coffee? Where is she?

And the big one that had only just come to him. There had been something niggling at the back of Dave's mind for a day or two and he hadn't been able to tease it out, but as he sat in the troopy, scribbling notes, the thought finally revealed itself.

If Leo didn't spend much time away from the farm, how did he get over to Mowup to withdraw cash twice a month?

Dave sat back, staring out of the window but not seeing anything. He imagined Leo reversing one of the HiLux utes from the shed. Leo leaving the farm when Jill was . . . Where? At the school or tennis club? Shopping in a different town? How did she not know that Leo wasn't where he said he was; and how did Leo ensure Jill left the farm on the same day at the beginning of every month so he could make the withdrawals? Maybe she was on the farm but didn't know Leo had left? Then how did he get away for the second time? He scratched another note that Leo would've kept to the dirt roads, keeping away from the main highway. Perhaps he used a different HiLux ute every time.

Dave shook his head, running everything over in his mind. They were close, he could feel it. He just needed to eyeball Leo. Let him know that if he was unhappy he didn't need to come back. If that was what Leo wanted, he and Bob would go to Jill, Stephen and Jan and say that Leo was alive and well, but wasn't in a position to be put in contact with them.

Dave already knew that wouldn't be enough for Leo's family, for any family, but it was the way the system worked.

They couldn't make Leo go back to a situation he'd willingly taken himself out of.

The same way that Dave could have never made Mel come back to him. People had choice and free will.

Although, as he rolled the thoughts around and around, testing for holes and problems, one came to him. Leo had been stealing as a servant. If Stephen and Jan wanted to press charges against their son, Bob and Dave would have to arrest and charge him. They already had the evidence of that.

Reaching over to the back seat, he grabbed Jill's diary and started to leaf through it, checking the pages. Her handwriting was strong and bold, so heavy that the writing had pushed through to other pages. He felt tired just looking at the amount of community work she did:

15 Feb: Tennis club AGM

16 Feb: Charlotte Dr

17 Feb: Library duty 2–4 pm

He flicked to 2 February and read the entry.

Perth.

Nothing more, nothing less. He flicked back to 2 January.

Perth.

Turning forward to 2 June showed the same entry.

Perth.

Why was Jill going to Perth on the second of every month? Dave supposed that could be immaterial if, indeed, she didn't know the money was being withdrawn that day.

If she did know, perhaps Leo and she had concocted an alibi for Jill so she couldn't be implicated if they were ever found out.

The CCTV footage he'd just seen didn't match these dates either.

He started the car, his mind still processing the diary entries. Would there be any CCTV for the second withdrawal? Was it only Leo who had access to the account?

There was a niggling feeling in his stomach as he started the troopy. A hypothetical. Jill spends so much time off the farm. Could she be a great actress and have a bank card linked to that account? Could it be her who makes the second withdrawal?

The drive to Hunter Rock took less time than he expected and he was glad of the freedom of the road. The previous night, they hadn't been sure where they were headed to, and the road had seemed to be nothing more than a long black ribbon without an end.

At the eighty-kilometre sign, Dave lifted his foot and the troopy slowed, doing sixty by the time he'd crossed over the town boundary.

He didn't have any trouble finding a park on the main street. His was the only car in sight. Five houses on one side, five on the other. Further down was a small town hall, which looked well maintained but unused, and a corner store. On the edge of a tiny RSL park was a monument to the fallen soldiers from the two world wars.

There were empty buildings; one was a blacksmith's and the other a railway station, with a tall water tank against the train line. Dead weeds and grass waved at him from the middle of the tracks, confirming Dave's theory that the rail hadn't been used here for a long time.

Some of these smaller towns died when businesses like mines or railways were taken away from them, and it seemed that Hunter Rock was nearly one of those. Nearly, because there were still a few people living here.

He imagined that a school bus would turn up twice a day, picking up any kids who lived here, ferrying them to another town to go to school and then dropping them off in the afternoon. Families would collect their groceries from a bigger town, getting only the essentials at the corner store. As in so many smaller places, the cost of living was twice as high as the larger towns. These shops didn't have the buying power.

The photo of Leo and Coffee was burning a hole in his pocket. Clenching his fists in anticipation, he hoped someone here would have seen them. Give him the head start he needed. Dave decided the corner store would be the first place he went to, wondering if there was a pub on a back street. A no-pub town would be unusual, even if the pub was closed.

Taking in the houses, Dave noticed most of them were clean and tidy, if not worn from the relentless heat of the sun during summer. The small patches of lawn were either bright green or a dull brown, depending on the amount of water they were getting.

An old man sat on his verandah in a swing chair. He raised his hand in greeting. 'You lost, mate?'

Dave stopped and leaned against the wire-netting fence held up with white wooden posts. A narrow cement path led straight from the street to the front door, and the mailbox showed a toothless, empty gap as he opened the gate and walked in past it.

'G'day, I'm Dave Burrows. Can I come on up?'

'Sure thing, young fella. If you've got the time to talk to an old man.'

Dave grinned. 'My favourite thing to do.'

'You must be short of a quid then or have too much time on your hands.'

'Nah, you blokes are interesting. Nice, quiet town. Lived here long?' Dave indicated to a chair that was empty.

'Take a load off, young fella,' the older man invited. 'Sam Dooney.' He held out his hand.

'Great to meet you, Sam.'

Sam assessed Dave through rheumy eyes. 'You must be here for a reason,' he said. 'No one comes to Hunter Rock for the hell of it these days.'

Dave smiled. 'I was close by last night and got curious about the town. Thought I'd come back during the day and see what I could see.'

'Looking for someone, are you?' Sam leaned over and picked up a stained mug full of black tea. Steam rose into the air, and he took a sip. 'Want one?'

Dave couldn't think of anything worse, drinking something hot when the temperature was close to forty. 'No, but thanks,' he said. 'Why do you think I'm looking for someone?'

'Unusual to get strangers walking down the street without a caravan attached to their vehicle.' He nodded to Dave's troopy. 'Looks like you're set up for something, but it isn't camping. Aerials and the like.'

Dave looked at the troopy and had to agree with him. 'Do you get many tourists through?'

'Not at this time of the year. Too warm for them and no wildflowers.'

'Many strangers stop in?'

Sam looked over at him, his cup of tea still in hand, curiosity in his expression. 'Old mate from Yorkenup has gone missing, what's his name? Parry? Perry? Anyhow, we're not that far from there.' He seemed to ignore Dave's last question.

'That's true. Know Leo Perry, do you?'

'Nope.'

'Ever seen him around here?'

'Nope.'

'Wouldn't mind finding him just for a yarn,' Dave said casually. 'He's not in any trouble.'

'Guess you'll have to work out where he is to be able to talk to him.' He gave an old-man cackle. 'Not sure I can help you there.'

Dave grinned at Sam's infectious laugh. 'True enough,' he said, then he leaned back in the chair. 'Tell me about your town.'

Sam looked across the road, a sadness filling his face. 'Used to be a hectic place when the trains still ran through here. Ah, they'd come in, all full of noise and puff, dirty buggers, they were, but we loved them. They were exciting! Us young fellas, we'd race about loading them, filling the carriages with grain from—' he moved his arm around in a sweeping gesture '—everywhere around here. Beaut area to grow grain. Safe as houses if we don't get a frost.

'Then we'd send them on their way and go back to do it all over again. And again and again . . .' His voice trailed off. 'But our siding was too small to be kept up and the powers that be shifted the silos and loading to the bigger towns.' He shrugged. 'The work wasn't here, so slowly Hunter Rock died off to a dribble. Course the stalwarts stayed! Like me and the families across the road. We just couldn't up and leave.' An arthritic finger pointed across the road. 'Mr and Mrs Thompson lived there until he died about two years ago. Her family packed Mrs Thompson up and shifted her to a Perth nursing home. Scandalous if you ask me. She'd never lived anywhere else and suddenly her life was upended. No friends, nothing familiar. Died within six months, too, poor love. From a broken heart, I'm sure.' He stretched out his legs and looked with love across the wide, dusty street. 'By golly, I was dirty on her family for being so mean to the old dear in the end. That won't be happening to me. They'll be carrying me out in a box,' he said firmly. 'But I do understand that she needed more care than was possible here.'

Dave didn't answer. Families made different decisions for different people and, if there was one thing he knew, no one had a right to voice a judgement unless they were the people living the life.

'Jack Flannigan, he lives in the next one. Runs the corner store. Got bowsers out the front, but not too many people stop to buy fuel here. No real reason to stop unless you're in real need of a toilet break or a coffee. Probably a bit on the expensive side here, too. Not on the road to anywhere and we don't have any tourist attractions.'

Dave's gaze swept along the street to a small house that had the blinds pulled down and a swing set in the front yard.

'Still got young families though?'

'Ah, young Sophie lives there. Lovely girl. Single mum to a little boy about four. I think she lives here because it's cheap rent. She told me a couple of nights ago that she was off to visit her mother in Perth for a few days.' He smiled. 'That girl is a breath of fresh air. Brings a bit of life back to us all. We all keep an eye out for young Charlie. The other day I caught him trying to climb the fence. By golly, he's a quick 'un. Soph had only ducked inside for a mo' or two and he was off.' The old man smiled at the memory. 'I'm not as fast as I used to be either, so by the time I got down there he was just about over and gone! Cheeky monkey.'

'Sounds like he'd be a handful. Where does Sophie work?'

Sam steepled his fingers and regarded Dave over the peaks. 'Well now, young fella, I'm not sure what business that is of yours.'

Giving a one shoulder shrug, Dave didn't answer. The old man was protecting his town. 'You didn't tell me how long you've lived here for.' Dave repeated an earlier question.

'Since my teens. Once the railway closed, I got work out on the farms, helping at harvest and seeding. Sometimes with the livestock. When I retired, I had nowhere else to go. Don't know anywhere else. Don't want to *be* anywhere else.'

Behind the houses, the farming land stretched out to the horizon and the stillness of the air was freeing. Dave could see himself living somewhere like this when the time for him to leave the police came. *The peace would be addictive*, he thought. *And I'd be able to see the criminals coming.*

Still, the excitement of being close to Leo was still fizzing in his stomach. He needed to get on. 'You're right,' he said. 'I'm a copper looking for Leo.'

'I know that.' Sam dabbed at a spot of blood that had sprung up on his hand as he'd brushed it past the chair. Paper-thin skin that would bleed when it brushed against anything. The blood made him think of Bob. He must remind Bob to get Betty to look at that infected mark on his arm.

Dave took the photo out of his pocket. 'You sure you've never seen this man? Or his dog?'

Sam took the picture and stared at it for a long time, before giving it back. 'No. Not here. I've seen him on the TV, when the fire went through and you couldn't find him then, but I've never seen him here on the main street.'

'We found his ute nearby and wondered if he had any contacts in the town.' He handed another photo to Sam. The ute in situ from the night before.

'Yeah, that's down at Coward's turnaround. The school bus used to stop in there when we had enough kids for them to pick up. Bit more overgrown than it used to be, but I guess that's what the bloke was looking for. Not to be seen.' He glanced at Dave, looking for confirmation, then continued on. 'If he knows anyone here, it's not me and I haven't seen him in the area.' He stared at the second photo longer than the previous one. 'Dime a dozen those HiLuxes.' Sam gave the photo back.

'Would you tell me if you had seen him?'

Sam grinned, then let out a chortle. 'Yep, young fella, I would. I was brought up not to lie to the police.'

'Just thought I'd check,' Dave said. 'You seem to want to protect the town.' He liked the old man and his loyalty. 'How about this then, if you see him, will you ring me?' He held out his card and repeated his earlier words. 'Leo isn't in any trouble and if he doesn't want to return, we won't make him.' Dave didn't make any comment about another possible charge for fraud. That was up in the air, depending on what they found, and Dave couldn't help but feel that Leo was only taking what was owed to him.

'Sure, I can do that. Though,' he paused and shook the card gently at Dave, 'ever thought he might have a good reason for disappearing?'

'He might well do, Sam, and if he has that's okay. But it's our job to make sure he's not a danger to himself or others. Then he can be left alone.'

Sam gave a small nod. 'Part of the reason I never left,' he said softly. 'The missus wanted me to move back to Northton once the trains stopped, but I liked it here. Didn't want to move, so she left and I stayed.'

'I can understand that.'

'Can you? I wonder.'

'What I don't understand is how a father can leave his children.' Dave was surprised the words came out of his mouth. 'Because that's what he's done.'

'Ah well, young fella, not all fathers are cut from the same cloth and some are better than others.' He had a faraway look in his eyes now.

Dave's mobile phone rang, and he saw it was Bob. 'I'd better go, but thanks, Sam. I appreciate all the information that you've given me.' He shook the old man's hand and walked down from the verandah onto the path, catching the call just before it went through to his message bank.

'How're you getting on?' he asked.

'Well, well, well,' Bob sounded like he was the cat that had got the cream. 'Interesting the things you find out. The baby who was coming along before Jill and Leo got married? It wasn't Leo's.'

Dave squinted.

'She got all pissed on champagne at their engagement party. Jill was telling Sally what an amazing man Leo was because she had been having someone else's baby and he still wanted to marry her. Sally told Mum and Dad and that's when they really got more cagey about letting her have anything to do with the farm money. Then of course she miscarried.'

'Leo knew about this?'

'Apparently so.'

'What the fuck? She told Leo's sister? No wonder there was an outcry. And their mates know about this?'

'Yeah, they do. They were there that night. The skeletons weren't hidden very well. And maybe that was the point. She made a mistake and was up-front about it. Leo took her at her word, his family didn't.'

'And we don't know who the bloke was?'

'Someone she never saw again.'

'Convenient.'

'Right.'

'So, hang on, was she pregnant to someone else before she and Leo got together or after?'

'After. Jill's side of the story is that she went up to Perth for a weekend and she got herself into a little bit of trouble. Guy came on to her and before she knew it things were getting hot and heavy, and she couldn't get away.'

'Oh yeah?' Dave knew he sounded cynical.

'Like I said, never saw the bloke again but—whoops!— wrong timing.'

'Interesting. No wonder the family did what they did. Although you'd think they'd ask for a DNA test, not a medical certificate.'

'I agree. How are you going in Hunter Rock? What have you found?'

Dave looked back to Sam who was still sitting on the porch. 'Nothing of value, except that I can't place Leo here. I've got a couple more people to ask, but I think it's a dead end.'

CHAPTER 18

Red threw down his notes on the desk and looked at Bob. 'Jill has confirmed that the man in the footage is Leo.'

'Has she? That's good news. How did she react?'

'Pretty teary when she saw him. It took a little while for it to register that Leo was alive and wasn't with her. Shocked is the best word.'

Bob shook his head, then asked, 'How'd you get on with the vets and animal shelters. Anyone seen Coffee?'

'No, not that I've found,' Red said. 'I've spoken to all the animal pounds and vets within a couple of hundred kilometres radius and no one has seen a dog that looks like Coffee. If she's fallen off the back of a ute, then she's dead. Either that, or she's still with Leo and no one has noticed her.'

'Right.' Bob jotted a note down. 'Well, still circulate the photo to the TV stations and see if they'll run another story.'

'Already done. All stations are running with the photo on the six pm news, and then again at the ten pm update.'

'Good work. Where's Robbie?'

'He's gone to follow up how much money was made at the auction and how the transfer was being made.'

'Right,' Bob said. He turned as he heard boots on the steps and saw Dave. 'This fella's been over at Hunter Rock checking out if anyone had noticed the ute from the other night.'

'Get anywhere?' Red asked.

'Doesn't sound like it.' He grinned as Dave walked in. 'How'd you get on, son?'

Dave threw his notebook on the desk and ran his fingers through his hair. 'Not too much. Met a bloke by the name of Sam Dooney. You know him?' He looked at Red.

'Old Sam sitting on his verandah? Yeah, nice old bloke. Never moves far from there. I think the town would fall down around him and he wouldn't leave.'

'Yeah, I got the same impression. But he seemed a little cagey. I asked a few questions about the other people living in the town, and he closed up. There's a young single mother living just across the road from him and I reckon he'd protect her until the cows came home.' Dave looked over at Red. 'Do you think he would have told the truth about not seeing Leo?'

Red was nodding before Dave had finished the question. 'He's as trustworthy as the day is long. Whatever he tells you will be the facts. I've known Sam since I moved here. Sometimes he rings up because there's a strange car hanging around a little too long, or he calls in an accident. I had to go and help him a few weeks ago. Needed a ride across to Northton to get to the doc. Had a chat and made sure the world was a better place by the time I brought him back again.'

'Guess I'll have to take your word on that.' Dave pulled the computer towards him and opened the screen.

Red got up and stretched, not seeming to be affected. 'Well, I'm going to get a coffee. Anyone want anything?'

'I'm fine, thanks,' Dave said.

His partner shook his head. 'So, you discovered nothing?' Bob aimed his question at Dave.

'Not a damn thing. I'm going to pull the records on who lives in the town and see what I can find out about them. It appears that most of them are older and been there for a long time. Town died when the railways fell over.' He paused and looked over at Bob. 'Anything more to the story about the baby and the miscarriage?'

Bob leaned forward. 'I spoke to Carmel Cameron, Tina Barry and Nicola Pearce and all of them say that Jill and Leo were tight. Not a problem anywhere except Jill would have liked for Leo to spend a little more time with her and the kids off the farm.

'Nicola made mention that Jill seemed to go to Perth about once a month, to see her parents. When her bank statements came through, I checked the transactions against the times she'd been away and there wasn't any outside of the route I think she would have taken to get to her parents' house.

'There are a few restaurants she's visited, but the dollar amount is enough for four or five people. I rang one of the places and they remember her with her parents. They eat there regularly.' Bob sighed. 'The bank accounts are clear. She's not receiving any money that she shouldn't be.' He paused. 'At least, not on the accounts we're seeing.'

Dave raised his eyebrows at those words, then spoke. 'Interesting those trips to Perth have come out, because Jill gave me her diary this morning. I've been wondering how Leo could get off the farm, considering he didn't go away that often, and withdraw the money in Mowup.'

'You're assuming it's him making the withdrawal?' Bob replied.

Dave paused. 'Yeah, I was. Although I did have the thought, and you must have, too, from what you've just said, that it's Jill who goes off the farm all the time. Perhaps she has been given a bank card by Leo and makes the second transaction. We need to check with the bank again. But, for all intents and purposes, let's keep that idea in the back of our minds and go with what we have evidence on at the moment.

'Jill has just the word *Perth* written in her diary on the second day of every month, which coincides with the withdrawals. Again, I'm making assumptions, but perhaps we can play with the idea that Jill was taking the kids to Perth with her, Leo is left on his own and can do what he wants, so he drives across to Mowup and withdraws his cash.

'Now, if he's kept the cash from every withdrawal, he's got a shitload of money he needs to stash somewhere—maybe under the header guard—and if he's home before Jill, there's no questions asked.'

Bob rolled this idea around for a while. 'He won't need to access that bank account for a while if he's been keeping the money.'

'No. Going to make him harder to track without a sighting.'

'What is she going to Perth for?' Bob wondered. 'Is it just to see her parents or something else? Because wouldn't she want Leo to go with her for a family lunch or dinner? Especially if the kids are with her. It can't be an appointment; every second day of every month? That would fall on a Saturday or Sunday at some point across the year.'

'There's no other information in the diary. We'll have to ask her.'

'Right—' His words were interrupted by the angry voice of a man.

'Where are they?' Stephen was at the front desk.

Bob sighed and got up.

Robbie's quiet, calming tone started to speak, but Stephen's overrode his.

'I want to speak to both of them. Where are they?'

'Mr Perry,' Bob said, from the doorway leading into the back offices. Dave stood behind him and took in the scene.

Stephen and Jan were standing at the desk, their faces angry, but Jan's crumpled as soon as she saw Bob and Dave. 'Is it true?' she asked, her voice breaking as she stepped towards them. 'Is he alive? Why isn't he here then? Has he lost his memory? Please. What is going on?'

Bob held up his hands in a calming gesture. 'It's okay, Mrs Perry, it's all right. Come and sit down.'

Robbie held the door open until they'd both entered behind the desk, and Bob indicated for them to come further inside. In their office, he helped Jan into a chair, and Dave passed her a glass of water, while Stephen stood ramrod straight next to the table.

'Could you please update us, detectives,' he said. 'How come I've had to hear from friends that you have images of Leo alive from two days ago?'

'I'm sorry you've found out that way, Mr Perry,' Bob said. 'We were on our way to talk to you.' He indicated for Dave to get out his laptop and show them the footage.

Dave tapped on the grainy image and let it run.

Jan put her hand up to her mouth, then held it out to the screen as if begging the man to turn around and look at her. 'Leo,' she whispered. 'Leo.' She turned to Stephen, whose face hadn't altered. 'Did we do this?'

Stephen scoffed. 'What are you talking about, woman? It's got nothing to do with us. Leo has made his own choices.' He shot a furious glance towards the motel, a long way away. 'More likely to do with her.'

Bob leaned forward. 'But you've stated that Leo and Jill had a good marriage and relationship.'

'Yes, and she is a good mum,' Jan said softly. 'But why else . . . Maybe we were too hard on him, Stephen. We forced him to answer to us, when perhaps we shouldn't have. I always had doubts . . .'

'You know why we needed to.' Another angry glance towards where the motel was.

'But that was their business, not ours. I've tried to tell you . . .' The stress was causing Jan's speech to be more slurred than usual.

Bob invited Stephen to sit down.

'Look, we have yet to find a reason as to why Leo wanted to leave,' Bob said. 'But what we do know is he's been planning this for a while. Let me tell you how we know.' He started off as gently as he could, telling them about the money going into the extra account. He told them how all of Leo's friends didn't think there was anything wrong and, as of yet, they hadn't been able to find something that would make Leo want to leave. 'Is there anything you can tell us? Had he fallen out with someone? Were all of your relationships still intact?' Bob asked. 'Has he made any enemies? Did he gamble? Drugs perhaps?'

Leo's parents looked at each other for a long moment, then Stephen sighed and leaned his elbow on the table.

Dave leaned forward, expectantly.

'I want to have something to tell you,' Stephen said. 'But I've been back over and over our phone calls, our emails, our correspondence from the past six months and there is nothing out of the ordinary. Nothing.' He swallowed hard. 'Look, we have been tough on him and Jill.

'Jill, in particular. Maybe too tough. Trouble is, I've seen families lose everything they've worked for when a marriage breaks up. I'm not sure you could have any idea what it's like to build up a business then have the fear of losing everything you've worked towards because some floozy comes along, ready to fling her leg over for a bit of money.'

Jan gasped. 'Stephen!'

He held up his hands in defence. 'I'm not saying that was Jill, only stating a scenario. One that's happened many times over.'

'But that's how you saw Jill when she and Leo first got together?' Bob asked. 'As a threat?'

Stephen hesitated. 'Yes. That's not how I see her now, though,' he conceded. 'You need to be clear on that. But that's exactly how I saw it when she first arrived on the scene. And yes, we asked for some evidence that perhaps wasn't right of us to do. We're not the Mafia.' Now he looked Bob in the face. 'Although Leo did call us that once. I don't know why our son has done this. As far as I'm aware everything was okay within his life. He didn't gamble and he certainly didn't do drugs. I haven't heard anything else that would indicate he had made enemies; Leo got along with most people so . . .'

It was Dave's turn now. 'Had there been any machinery bought recently?'

'No.'

'Any business transactions that didn't go according to plan? Hard negotiations?'

'No.'

'Had you looked at buying more land?'

222

Stephen raised his eyebrows. 'Yeah, we did have a conversation about the next-door neighbour's farm about three weeks ago. We knew it was going up for sale in March. I was keen and so was Leo, although he was a bit worried about staffing over harvest and seeding. Still, if we'd wanted to buy it, that wouldn't have been enough to stop us. We would have made it work.'

'And did you decide that you wanted to?'

'We'd done some prelim work on it. A few back-of-the-envelope budgets, but we hadn't made a final decision.'

'What entity would the farm have been bought in?'

'The same as everything else. Jan and I would own it, until it was time to work out whether the land would be sold and the profits split between the three kids or if Leo would take the whole lot on and pay out the other two.'

Bob nodded and made a note. 'Was Leo happy with that entity?'

'Of course. He understood. Look, detective, you might think we've been too tough on them, but everything Leo asked for, he got. When he wanted a pay increase, we gave him one; when he wanted a new ute or a new car for Jill, they got one. The farm paid for that, I might add. So, you might sit back here and judge us, thinking Leo and Jill were getting the raw end of the deal, but they were not. We took care of them.' He looked down at his hands. 'And now you're telling me our son has been stealing from us. From his own family.' Stephen cleared his throat loudly, but both men heard the devastation in his words just before he did.

'Thanks for your honesty, Mr Perry. We do appreciate it, and, yeah, families are hard to deal with sometimes. That's why we're just looking for any little chink that might have pushed Leo over the edge, enough to want to leave.'

'Well, I have nothing further that I can help—'

Jan broke in. 'Are you going to tell him about Elliot's conversation with Jill?'

Stephen's face fell but Jan looked determined.

'Elliot asked her straight out. Had Leo and her planned to leave together?'

'What was her answer?' Bob asked.

'She spent a bit of time screaming and yelling at him but her words were, "Clearly not, because I didn't know he was alive, did I? And I didn't know he was stealing money. So how the hell could I know he was planning to disappear?"' In despair, Jan looked at Bob, her head shaking slightly. 'She said, "Please, please understand, I didn't know. I just want him to come home and explain why he's hurting us all so badly. The kids aren't sleeping. They're continually asking where Daddy is and when is Daddy coming home. What am I supposed to tell them?"'

The office clock ticked loudly as Bob took in everything Jan told him. There wasn't an answer to the question the kids kept asking.

Dave shifted uncomfortably as he thought about Charlotte and Noah, who morphed into Bec and Alice. What were they saying to Melinda?

Finally, Bob said, 'We're sorry for everything that you're going through, Jan, and please do understand that all Dave and I are trying to do is find Leo.' He paused. 'There is something else you need to know . . .' Bob took a breath and glanced across at Dave.

Jan recoiled. 'There can't be anything worse than what you've just shown us.'

Stephen reached for her hand and drew his wife close.

The kind smile that Bob used made his eyes crinkle at the corner, then he looked at her seriously. 'If your son has made a conscious decision to leave, then there's nothing that we can do to enforce him to return home.' He sighed. 'He's within his rights to inform us that he is well, but not wanting to be contacted or have contact with you, family members, friends and the like. I'm sorry.'

'What?' Jan gasped and her eyes flew to Stephen's. 'They're wrong, aren't they?'

Dave cleared his throat. 'Unless, Mr and Mrs Perry, you want to press charges. As we've told you today, we've got evidence that he has been stealing as a servant. You're well within your rights to ask for your son to be charged.'

CHAPTER 19

Dave walked into the pub and ordered two beers. Bob wouldn't be far behind, but Dave needed some time by himself for a few minutes. He couldn't get Jan's words out of his mind.

When is Daddy coming home? Where is Daddy?

Had Bec ever asked Melinda that? He was sure she had. What had Mel told Bec? And Alice? That he didn't want to come home? Or that he couldn't? Dave hadn't any idea, but it was probably more down the lines of: *He can't be here.*

Frustration hit him hard, as did the sorrow that went with the guilt of what he'd put his family through. There were days he couldn't blame Melinda for not wanting to be married to a cop. After all, it was his work that had brought Bulldust into their lives and ended Melinda's mother's. But there were other days that he raged against the injustice. The hatred that was hurled from his father-in-law, the indifference from Melinda. All thrown at him, as if he solely caused their family's demise. Mel and Mark couldn't really think Dave had wanted this to all happen? Surely, they couldn't believe that.

He thanked the barmaid who put the glasses down in front of him, but then she just stood there. Annoyance flashed through him as he waited for her to leave. When she didn't, Dave asked if she wanted something.

She smiled and leaned against the counter. 'I'm Jacinta. How's it all coming along?'

'All what?'

'The investigation.'

'Sorry, I can't talk about an active inquiry.'

Jacinta changed her position, her arms either side of her breasts now, pushing them up so Dave had nowhere else to look. 'Such a shame, what's going on.' She eyed him again. 'Who would have thought someone like Leo would do such a thing.'

'What do you mean by that?' Dave asked, moving back. He managed to keep his eyes on hers, when all he really wanted to do was take his beer and go and sit in the corner and brood.

'Well, someone who's got it all, you know. Nice bloke, lovely wife. Great kids. Farm. Why would you want to shoot through? He must've been hiding a big secret for a long time.'

'Got any hints for me?' As soon as the words were out of his mouth, Dave wanted to groan. Wrong ones, idiot.

'Oh, honey, I've got some hints for you, but you'll need to be up for them,' she said, a smile playing at the corner of her mouth. 'You got anyone waiting for you at home?'

Dave blinked and took in her blonde hair streaked with strands of silver and her smile, which, if he hadn't been so shocked, may have been pretty.

'Sorry,' he said. 'I'm not interested.'

'Ah, come on, now. You never know what information I could have.' Jacinta lifted her eyes towards him. 'You could arrest me,' she said suggestively.

'Yeah, I could and if I did that, you'd be in a world more hurt than where you are now.' He picked up his drinks and moved away. 'If you've got information that we need to hear then I'll get Bob to come and have a chat. If not, then this conversation is finished.'

He sat down, annoyed that his peace had been disturbed. Then his thoughts flew to Shannon, Melinda and the kids, in that order. Suddenly there was a hand on his shoulder and he flinched, turning away. 'Don't—' Then he realised the owner of the hand was Bob.

'You haven't lost it with the ladies, son,' Bob said with quiet humour. 'Don't get cranky.'

'Fuck off,' Dave said, gulping at his beer. 'Not what I'm looking for.'

'I know. Thanks for the beer.' Bob picked it up and went over to the bar to talk to Jacinta, leaving his partner, whose chest was heaving with a ridiculous fury. Why was he getting angry over a few stupid comments?

Needing to move, Dave got up and wandered through the pub to the back where there was a room reserved for the RSL meetings. The room was dark, the heavy curtains drawn to keep out the heat, while the thick carpet was a deep blue, adding to the heaviness of the room. A couple of glass cabinets filled with mementoes lined the walls: photos of men dressed in uniform, some medals, red hardcover books about World War Two, a compass in a wooden box, perfectly preserved from what Dave could see—no scars or cuts to the screen. A collection of hand-knitted beanies and socks made Dave stop and think about the women and children who had been left behind. Every stitch would have contained love and care.

He turned his attention to the photos. A group—five men, young, wearing stiffly starched uniforms, guns hooked on to their belts. They hadn't experienced war at the time the photo was taken. The eagerness and anticipation were still too bright in their eyes. The horror was to come.

Reading the names, he saw they were all local: Copple, Hunter, Mason, Mayfield and Pearce. He studied the faces trying to see if there were any similarities to the young men he'd met during his time in Yorkenup. Perhaps there were still sons and grandsons here.

His phone rang and he answered.

'Yeah, I'm looking for Detective Dave Burrows,' the woman's voice on the end of the phone said.

'You got him,' Dave replied. He continued to stare at the photos.

'Ah, yeah, Senior Constable Karly Hepworth from Meekatharra Police Station here.'

Her words made Dave pay attention. 'How can I help?' he asked.

'You heading up the search for Leo Perry?'

'Yeah, me and Bob Holden. You got something?' Dave's antennae went up at the sound of Leo's name.

There was a silence and Dave could hear sirens wailing in the background. An emotion that he couldn't name trickled through his stomach.

'Are you there, Senior Constable?' Dave raised his voice.

'Ah yeah, look, I think we've got your man here.'

'In custody?' His heart leaped at the good luck he'd just been handed. Meekatharra wasn't that far away. A cool eight- or ten-hour drive. Dave glanced at his watch. If they left now, they'd be up there by early morning and be able to interview Leo first thing. He started to walk back to the bar, looking for Bob, a quickness in his step.

'No. Unfortunately he is deceased.'

The plummet in Dave's stomach was quick, like a stone sinking to the bottom of an algae-covered pond. 'Deceased? Care to explain that?' He grimaced at his words. *Care to explain that?* The man was dead, what more explanation was needed!

'I'll send you some photos, but we've found him leaning against a tree, gunshot to the forehead. The weapon wasn't found at the scene, but there were so many people about that anyone could have picked it up, so we're not sure if it's murder or suicide.'

So many people at the scene? What the hell?

'Senior Constable, you are going to have to explain this a little more. Where was Leo Perry found and how have you identified him?'

'He was at the agricultural showgrounds. The show was on yesterday and today, so all the outlying station people have come to town, plus some blow-ins. Cue lots of people. When everyone was clearing out after the fireworks one of the security guards went to ask your man to leave; that's when the guard realised he was dead. The deceased was sitting, leaning up against a tree, right next to the bar. The security guard thought he'd fallen asleep and was trying to wake him. Got the shock of his life when he realised that wasn't the case.

'Anyhow, at this stage, everything is pointing to him being shot during the fireworks, to hide the noise of the gun, because no one we've interviewed so far heard a shot.' Her tone took on a new decisiveness. 'Now, like I said, whether this was suicide or murder, we're not sure. To me, the wound looks typical for a suicide case, but the gun hasn't been found. Still, anyone could have picked it up if it had fallen out of his hand after the bullet had been fired. The ID in his pocket was for a Mr . . . Ah, wait a moment. Mr Stephen Perry, but a DL for Leo Perry was still in his wallet. I matched the photo you sent out on your release to this man. He's on his way to Perth for a post-mortem.' Her voice was rushed as if she needed to get as much information out as quickly as she could.

Dave was having trouble keeping up. 'I see. What other details do you have? Was he with anyone? Where was he staying?'

'We're just starting to investigate all of that, detective. I'll get back to you when I have more information. At this stage I don't have anyone sighted with him and we are yet to find his vehicle.'

'Okay, well, I'll wait to hear from you.' He paused. 'You've already got the body on the way to Perth?'

'Yeah, so happens the plane was here so we got him on board as quickly as we could.'

'Can you send me through what you've got ASAP?'

'Will do.'

'Are you still at the scene?'

'Yeah.'

Dave could hear her talking to someone and he waited before asking another question.

'Sorry,' she said coming back onto the line. 'I'll get the photos emailed so you can see what we're looking at.'

'The scene is going to be very hard to contain with a lot of people there, Senior Constable. You should be calling in Major Crime.'

'Understood, and I have, however they've asked us to investigate at this stage. They're unable to send a team. Geraldton detectives will be coming over as soon as they can, but they're under the pump, too. There's been a dispute between some families over there and they've got a couple of bodies. My team is doing the best we can in difficult circumstances. We've got the area cordoned off, and most of the people are on the oval now, giving statements, but we've got a lot of people and very few coppers.' She paused for breath. 'This is my worst nightmare,' she added.

'Have you got police coming from other towns?' He couldn't help but ask the obvious questions. Meekatharra was a small town and he was sure the police there wouldn't have dealt with a case like this before.

'Yeah, but they'll take a while to get here. Like I said, we're doing the best we can.'

Dave felt a flicker of annoyance now. He shouldn't be such a long drive away from the scene, he'd be better on the ground, carefully going over Leo's final resting place, looking for evidence, rather than leaving it up to the locals. He knew it wasn't his jurisdiction and he shouldn't . . . But . . . 'I'm leaving now. Don't touch anything further around the scene. I want it exactly as you found it when I get there. I'm eight to ten hours away.' He started striding towards the front bar, purpose in his step.

'Would you really come all this way?'

Dave heard the disbelief in her voice.

'Yes. I just need to organise a few things here and I'll be on my way. Could you organise somewhere for me to stay? And text me your details so I have a contact when I get there.'

'Sure. Drive safe.'

'Before you go, Leo always had a tan kelpie with him. Coffee. Have you seen a stray dog running around?'

'No, and I haven't had one reported to me. I'll check with the vet and shire to see if one has been impounded.'

'Keep an eye out. The dog might lead you to where Leo was staying. I'll flick you a photo of her.'

Dave said goodbye, while making a mental list of things to do. He needed someone to organise to make the ID on the body and . . . Really, what the fuck had just happened?

Dave found Bob putting out some money for the two beers that were in front of him on the bar.

'What's up, son? You look like you've seen a ghost.'

'Not a ghost, let's talk in here.' He pointed back to the RSL room.

Bob picked up the drinks without another word and followed Dave.

'I hadn't finished telling you my story,' Jacinta called to Bob.

'It'll have to wait, love,' he called back. 'Shouldn't be too long.'

Dave turned just inside the door and Bob almost ran into the back of him.

'What's happened?' he asked.

'Meekatharra. Leo's been found with a bullet wound to his head. He's dead.'

Bob's face drained of blood. 'What did you just say?'

'I know. I've had a phone call from Senior Constable Karly Hepworth telling me she had his body there. He's on PolAir headed for Perth for an autopsy now.' He quickly told his partner all he knew, and they both stood staring at each other. Each of them knew how difficult it was going to be to tell Jill, Stephen and Jan that their husband and son had gone from being alive to dead in the space of a few hours.

'Right,' Bob said finally, scratching the back of his neck. 'Well, how about we check your emails, and then see what else comes in. We can't notify the family until we have a positive ID, so our hands are tied for the time being. We have nothing to investigate.' He paused. 'Wouldn't mind heading up to Meekatharra, though. What about you?'

'I've asked for her to preserve the scene. I want to go up there. Maybe you can grab a car from the station here and go to Perth. That way you'll be there when the body lands and in the morgue with Shannon when she does the autopsy. I can be in Meeka by morning and get some feet on the ground. She said they hadn't worked out where he was staying, so once I've been to the scene and looked at that, I can walk the streets, talk to the locals. See if I can find a HiLux ute parked somewhere, or a dog looking lost.'

'Yeah, that's a good plan.' But Bob's hands moved in a way that told Dave he wasn't comfortable with the decision. 'Bloody hell! I hate not being in control. Still, if we split up we can cover both areas.' He paused for thought. 'What about the local dees? Major Crime really should be looking at this. Not us. We'll get our arses kicked.'

'Yeah, I had a discussion with Karly about that. They're snowed under. No chance of getting the boys from Perth up there, and by the sounds of it, even less with the ones from Geraldton.'

'You'd better clear it with the boss. You know what the hierarchy are like if we step on another squad's toes.'

Dave shook his head. 'And have him say no? I'll tell him when I'm back.'

CHAPTER 20

It was only a few hours later when Dave's phone rang again. By then he was three hundred kilometres north of Yorkenup, and the white lines were slipping away under his gaze. He didn't feel tired. In fact, the adrenalin was pumping long and strong and Dave felt like he could drive forever.

He looked at the screen warily, then realised it was Shannon. 'Hey, how are you?'

'Guess you've heard?'

'Well, I've heard some things. Nothing that makes too much sense to me,' he said.

'I have your missing man on my morgue table. Look, it's not protocol to talk to you, but I knew you'd want to know. Plus, the locals are directing this more towards you and Bob than the dees, who they think might arrive from Geraldton at some point.'

'I'm on my way up there now.'

There was a slight pause. 'To Meekatharra?'

'Yeah. I want to check the area myself.'

'Good thing, then, I can tell you it's Leo, isn't it? Otherwise, you would have just wasted a lot of your time.'

'You're sure it's him?' Dave asked, pressing his finger into his ear. The roar of the tyres on bitumen was loud.

Shannon spoke in the same confident tone she always used when she was on her turf. 'Well, of course we need a visual ID, but yeah, for all intents and purposes, it's him. I've only done a very quick once-over and I want dental records and so on to be completely sure, but comparing to the photo you've supplied . . .' Her voice trailed off. 'Yeah, I think it's him. Right age range, colouring, et cetera. There is a scar on his chin. And I've found a couple of scars where some moles have been removed. I noticed you'd written them up in the description. Haven't matched fingerprints yet, but there's enough to go to the family and ask them to come in for an ID.'

'Bob's going to see the family and organise for someone to go to Perth with him or at least get the family to Perth for the ID. And he'll be there for the autopsy.'

'Okay, I'll wait for Bob to get here before I start. Is he coming tonight or in the morning?'

'Morning. He needs to talk to the family first.' Dave watched the road as the troopy ate up the kilometres between him and Meekatharra. His company on the road now were the long triple road trains that carted freight to the north part of the state, and although it was dark, he knew the countryside had started to change from the long open paddocks where crops were grown to the bushy, prickly shrubs and the deeper red dirt.

Dave felt as if he was going home.

'Shannon, I've got him on CCTV two days ago, eight to ten hours from where he's been found. How's he ended up with you?'

'The fact he has a bullet in his brain is mostly the reason.'

Despite the black humour, Dave laughed. 'I was meaning, how did he get to Meekatharra? Why was he at the show? Who was he with? Who would have wanted him dead?'

'Dave, that's your job, not mine. I'll give you what I can forensically, but everything you've asked is not for me to track down.' She paused. 'You okay? You're sounding really rattled.'

'I'm okay.' Dave dropped his head briefly, then stared back at the road. 'Leo's death has completely thrown me. Nothing about this case makes sense or is straightforward.'

'Hey, that's not the Dave Burrows I know. What's the difference with this case?'

Dave paused, not wanting to tell her the real reason, but not seeing a choice. 'He left his kids.'

'For good now, from what I can see,' Shannon said briskly. 'So, what I've done is emailed you some more photos and the rest is up to you and Bob.'

She was right, of course, but Dave wanted her to tell him she had something concrete. That the person who had shot Leo was in custody. That the reason Leo had disappeared was because . . .

'Do you know what type of gun yet?' Dave asked.

'Everything I'm telling you is completely off the record, and like I said, I've only given him the once-over. A *very quick* once-over,' she emphasised again. 'But I'm suggesting it's a handgun of some kind. I'll have more for you once I open him up to see if there's a bullet still inside. I haven't found an exit wound. Right now, though,' she yawned, 'he's not going anywhere so I'll put him back in the box until tomorrow when Bob gets here. I'll get as much info as quickly as I can once we start.'

'Time of death?' Dave pushed.

'Not one hundred per cent sure. I don't have all the details from the doctor who was on the scene. It's hard when I'm not on the ground because I've got to rely on information getting through to me.'

'I hate that, too,' he said. 'If I'm not in charge of the scene I get frustrated and annoyed. And if there's one thing I don't like much, it's the feeling I don't have any power.'

'The mighty Dave Burrows does have a chink in his armour. That's good to know.'

Dave chuckled softly. 'So you're headed home?'

'Yeah, I'll clean up here and make for the door. What time is it?' He heard a rustle as she pulled up her sleeve to look at her watch. 'Ten o'clock. Be home by eleven and back here by seven. Mmm, that's enough sleep. What time will you arrive in Meekatharra?'

'Probably between four and five tomorrow morning. The locals have got me booked into the pub and they've left the key in the door for me. I'll grab a couple of hours' sleep while it's still dark then go to the scene. They've put someone there to guard it tonight.'

'You don't have any idea why he was up there?'

Dave shook his head then cleared his throat. 'No. I wonder if Leo was trying to put a fair bit of distance between him and the family, but if that was the plan, I'm not sure he'd be happy to be seen out in the open at a show. Too many people might recognise him. His face has been splashed across the media in the past few days.'

'I agree. In the cases I've had, if someone up and leaves with no intention of returning, they lay low for a bloody long time. Change their appearance—have plastic surgery if they've got the money, dye their hair, stick a stone in their shoe to make their gait different. They don't go and play happy families at a show.'

'Happy families?'

'Well, he wouldn't have been there by himself, would he?'

'Why not?' Dave saw a parking sign and started to slow, putting on his indicator. The high-vis reflectors of a truck flashed across the beams of his lights, and he pulled the wheel to the side so he didn't wake the truckie who was camped there for the night.

Bringing the troopy to a standstill, he got out and pulled out the twelve-volt kettle and plugged it into the socket. Shannon was still talking.

'Shows are for kids, mostly. Or families. My gut is telling me he had a reason to go. Someone with him he couldn't say no to. A kid, a woman. I don't know, something like that. And, look, he hasn't changed his appearance at all;

no different coloured hair, his original driver's licence was still in his wallet. I don't think he was planning to visit the show, it just happened.'

The kettle boiled and Dave poured the water into his travel mug, stirring hard as he made a coffee. From the fridge in the back of the troopy he added a dash of milk, put the lid on and stowed the kettle away again.

'If he wasn't prepared to stop at the show, how could someone have known he was there to kill him? Or, if he had a kid with him, why would he shoot himself?' The jigsaw puzzle pieces looked all the same size, colour and shape to Dave. In other words, there weren't any answers yet and that was why he needed to get on the ground.

'All excellent questions. And ones a detective of your calibre is more than capable of finding the answers to.'

'God, you're starting to sound like Bob.'

Shannon laughed. 'Well, if I'm going to get home, I'd better go. Drive safely, won't you? Can you text me when you arrive?'

'Yeah, I'll do that,' Dave said softly. It had been a long time since anyone had cared enough to ask him to text when he reached his destination.

There was a longing in his chest to see Shannon, to wind her long hair around his fingers and draw her into him, to kiss her and to have her rest her head on his chest. Just so he could feel like he was home.

Home? Shannon?

That was an interesting thought.

Dave sent a text to Bob, giving him a time to get going in the morning and a brief update on Shannon's information, then opened his laptop to check his emails. He wanted to see if the senior constable at Meekatharra had sent him the photos of the body, as well as what Shannon had emailed through. That would give him thinking time before he saw it all in person.

He tried to connect the internet through the police-issued modem, but the signal was looking too faint. Adjusting the position to the roof of the troopy and the computer to the back seat, he tried again.

Success! For a moment, Dave wondered how they'd ever coped without the internet. Information that was imperative to an investigation was right at their fingertips now.

The first photos had come in from Senior Constable Hepworth only five minutes before. Tentatively, Dave clicked on the first image and Leo's head came into view. Dried blood had dribbled down what was left of his forehead and cheek. The hat he was wearing was crooked and almost tipped off his head.

Click.

This time the whole scene came into view. Leo was leaning against a tree, a bottle of water next to him and his hands flopped down on the ground. If it hadn't been for the blood, he could have been asleep, just as the security guard had thought.

Leo's head had fallen forward and there was dried blood on his shirt and jeans.

The pocket of his shirt bulged, a spot of brown peeking out the top. Dave assumed that was the wallet that they'd found his ID in. He hoped that it had been taken in and catalogued as evidence and not left in the pocket.

Click.

Close-ups of Leo's fingers, clothes, the water bottle. A showbag—one full of chocolates and another one with fairies. That caught his attention, after his conversation with Shannon. He zoomed in and saw they were quite a way from the body; hard to tell exactly how far, but perhaps five or six metres. Maybe someone had left them there and they weren't related to Leo. Could be kids torn away by their parents when they realised the man wasn't moving and there was blood.

Pondering how he could find an answer, he kept clicking through. Then there were photos of the crowds. People with faces, shocked, pointing, horror oozing from innocent bystanders who had gone to the show to have fun but had ended up in the middle of a nightmare.

Dave enlarged the gathering shots and carefully looked at the faces, trying to see if he could recognise anyone. No one stood out, but the photos had been taken from a distance.

He'd ring IT tomorrow and see if the photos could be enlarged with a decent clarity to them. Get them printed off.

His phone dinged with a message.

Do you think you'll have time for dinner when you're back? You'll head home tomorrow or the next day? Shannon asked.

Dave's fingers hovered over the keys, unsure of what to write. Who knew what tomorrow might throw up. No one had expected what had happened today.

I hope so, he wrote back. Dave wanted to spend some time with Shannon. He should just make it happen.

There was a silence and finally he put the phone down.

The next photo showed the body bag being loaded into the ambulance and then more crowd shots. Whoever was wielding the camera hadn't had a lot of experience. Normally crowd shots weren't in the brief. The images were supposed to be close-ups of the body and any evidence that was nearby. Still, in this situation, Dave thought it was a smart move to take photos of the crowd because someone could have slipped away without being interviewed. These photos were a good record, even if they weren't perfect. Hopefully some locals would be able to name the people in them. Dave also hoped that the witnesses had been asked if they had any photos of the scene on their phones, too. Someone somewhere could have inadvertently taken a picture of their child with Leo in the frame.

He waited for Shannon's photos to come through, taking another sip of coffee as he walked around the troopy to get the blood moving.

In the still darkness, Dave felt a sense of sadness in his chest. What had happened to Leo? How could he have been on camera withdrawing money only two days ago, and now be dead, cold and stiff in the fridge? Had he been on the same road that Dave was on now? Had Coffee been in the front seat, her head hanging out the window, the wind in her face. Had the radio been playing country music?

Or had it been as Shannon had described? A woman and child with him. Had they been playing children's songs instead of country music? Had the gun been under the seat or in the glove box?

Or hadn't Leo known about the gun at all?

Picking up the phone he sent a text to Senior Constable Hepworth.

Got a statement from this Dean Setter who found him?
Yes.
Please email through. What content was in the wallet?
Will send through report.
Any suicide note?
Not that has been found.

His email dinged, and he checked the sender. Shannon.

This time Dave found himself staring at a cold and clinical steel table, a man laid out, his head held in a steel arch. The red hair pushed back from his damaged forehead and his clothes still bunched around his shoulders. Shannon's words echoed in his mind: *They lay low for a bloody long time. Change their appearance—have plastic surgery if they've got the money, dye their hair, stick a stone in their shoe to make their gait different.*

Leo had done none of those things. He still looked exactly like Leo Perry before the fire—farmer, father and husband.

Tomorrow, Shannon would undress him, record his weight, height, eye and hair colour. Note whether he had any tattoos. Then she'd move on to look for gunshot residue, run X-rays, see if there were bone fragments somewhere, before turning to the internal investigation.

Dave had seen Shannon in action before and she was gentle, professional and respectful, but there was nothing respectful about cutting a large Y-shape into a chest cavity.

Anger whirled inside Dave, and he promised the photo of Leo Perry that he would find out what happened, because it seemed to him there was so much more going on here than a man wanting a new life.

CHAPTER 21

'So there was five hundred dollars in cash, two different driver's licences, one for Stephen Perry and the other for Leo Perry. I can see what he's doing there,' Dave said, trying to stay focused on the road. He was only about half an hour away from Meekatharra now. 'Keeping as close to the truth as he can, so he won't slip up.' He propped the phone up on the dash and had it on open speaker so he could talk to Bob. 'Why wouldn't he get rid of his original licence?'

'Hmm,' Bob said. 'I'm looking at the photos of these now. I don't know. I would've thought that was the first thing he'd do.'

'Shannon mentioned that she didn't think he intended to go to the show. Leo hadn't changed his appearance in any way. He certainly wasn't acting as if he were trying to hide from anyone.'

'Right.'

Hearing Bob's pen scratching across the page, Dave continued. 'Okay, so back to the contents, also in the wallet was the debit card to the bank account he withdrew money from, but no other credit or EFTPOS cards. Nothing else that could be used to ID him.'

'No photos?'

'Nothing. A very thin wallet with hardly anything in it. No suicide note that they've found, but they haven't discovered his vehicle yet either,' Dave said. 'Or Coffee. I told them to keep an eye out for a hungry-looking, friendly stray kelpie.'

'He used to keep a diary?'

'Leo? Yeah, Jill told me he wrote in one religiously every night after dinner.'

'See, if this was a suicide, I would imagine that he would have left a note. He didn't mind writing.'

'But who to?' Dave asked. 'He'd just left his family.'

'I understand that. I'm not sure. Haven't put everything together yet, but that's my first impression. What about a phone?'

'Yeah, he had one and they've kept it at the station for me along with everything else they took from the body. I've asked them to touch nothing else until I'm there. Karly has contacted Telstra, looking for the numbers that are on his phone, inbound and outbound, and to see if we can get information on which phone tower Leo's phone has pinged off. We might get an idea of his movements before he was found in Meeka, that way.'

'Good idea. What are they like? The locals?'

'Karly seems to be fairly thorough, from what I can ascertain through our phone calls tonight. I was concerned to begin with because I didn't think whoever was stationed there would have enough experience, but I might have to eat humble pie,' Dave said briskly. 'Anyway, it's not like the dees from Geraldton are going to be able to get there anytime soon after what I've heard about the family feuds.' He changed the subject. 'You'd better get Betty to have a look at that thing on your arm when you see her today.'

'Who said anything about seeing her today? You got plans that I need to fit in with, son?'

If Dave hadn't been so worked up about Leo, he would've laughed and put Bob back in his place. Instead, all he did was look ahead and keep driving.

'The locals are going to hit up the hotels and caravan parks, see if they can find someone matching his description. Which will be fine if he was here, but he could have been swagging it out in the bush or staying with a friend for all we know.'

'Okay. It'll be interesting to see what Shannon finds,' Bob said.

'I think that the old man doesn't know jack shit about his son,' Dave said.

'I believe you're right. Now, I'm also sure the answers we need will be in Yorkenup and Meekatharra. That's where he left from so that's the cause of the problem. Going to Meekatharra screams to me that he's heading as far away, and as quickly, as he can.'

'I think Shannon is right, the local show isn't the place to turn up. Anyone could have noticed him. His face has been flashed over every TV station for the last few days. I've said this so many times since we found out that Leo was dead . . .' Dave heaved a sigh and went on to tell Bob about Shannon's theory.

He wanted to thump the steering wheel in frustration.

Bob seemed to sense his anger. 'Son, often there isn't anything that makes sense when someone is battling with mental health.'

'You reckon that's what's going on?'

'It's possible. Not everyone decides to move on and make a new life when there's a fire at their farm.'

'Well, there could be something in that, I guess,' Dave replied.

'I mean, Arson is right in that this was an accident, but the fire created an opportunity for him to run. Leo was as prepared as he could be. He's probably been hoping for this opportunity. All that preparation and time waiting for the perfect chance, and he still ends up dead. What has caused that?'

'Could it be something as simple as being in the wrong place at the wrong time?' Dave could hear Bob tapping on something.

'Anything is possible, but my gut says no. As you've said before, there's a missing link here and we have to find it.'

'Nothing about this case is making any sense to me.'

'Sometimes logic doesn't fit in, son.'

Silence filled the car as Dave continued to drive. He couldn't stop his mind from forming all sorts of scenarios about what could have happened to Leo, but he knew they wouldn't help. He needed cold hard facts, so instead, he let his mind drift towards Shannon and the hope of seeing her tomorrow.

Having danced around each other for a few months, they had sort of settled into a friends with benefits relationship. Dave protected his broken heart that way, but Shannon, well, he knew she wanted more. He wasn't capable of that yet. So, they kept going this way, but as Bob had informed him earlier in the week, Shannon would get sick of that soon enough.

'Have you heard anything from the girls?' Bob asked, cutting through his thoughts.

'No, nothing.'

'Grace been in contact about another visit?'

'Nope.'

'Maybe you should give her a call and ask about seeing Bec and Alice when you get back to Perth. How long will you be up there? Two days tops, I'd imagine.'

'Shouldn't be any more.'

'Right, well, I'm going to get on the road. I'll ring once the autopsy has been completed.'

They said their goodbyes and Dave punched the disconnect button and blinked tiredly. He'd had to stop a few times, refill his coffee mug and take a short walk, interspersed with some star jumps to keep the blood flowing. Tiredness was beginning to seep through his body as gently as the pinks, reds and golds were spreading across the horizon heralding the dawn of the new day.

A sign telling him Meekatharra was only twenty kilometres away flashed by, and Dave gripped the steering wheel. He would have to be careful. It was usually within the last fifty kilometres of a long drive that an accident could occur, and he didn't intend on becoming a statistic for Leo Perry.

Dave's phone rang and his hand shot forward to pick up the handpiece.

'Detective Burrows, it's Senior Constable Karly Hepworth.'

'What have you got for me?' he asked, putting the phone on the dash and making sure it was on speaker.

'We haven't found any evidence of a Leo Perry or a Stephen Perry staying anywhere in town. That seems to be a dead end.' She sounded tired, as if she'd worked through the night.

'No vehicle?'

'None that we can find that's registered to either of the licences.'

'And there aren't any abandoned cars on the showgrounds?'

'No, nothing like that.' She gave a giggle that was formed from overtiredness. 'That would be too easy.'

Dave tapped his finger to his mouth as he thought. 'Are there any places where people with nothing but a swag would camp on the outskirts of town? I reckon Leo was travelling pretty light if he was by himself.' As he said the words, Shannon's comments about the family and show came to him.

'Couple of spots about ten kay out of town. I could send a patrol to check.'

'Do that. I'm about fifteen minutes away. But I'm going to have a sleep for a couple of hours and then come to the station. You sound as if you haven't been home either.'

'I haven't. Too much to do.'

'Send your patrol to check the camping places, while you and your team go home and get some shut-eye. Let's catch up, say—' he looked at his watch: five am '—let's go with nine. You can take me to the showgrounds after that. Okay?'

'Sounds like a plan. Before I head off, I've got the statements from the interviews and more photos to send to you.' She paused. 'There's a bit of media interest already. Have I got an official line?'

'No. Other than you've got a body. No ID or anything more to add at this stage.'

⁓

Bob's footsteps were heavy as he climbed the three small cement steps to Stephen and Jan's motel unit. The sun had yet to slip above the horizon as he knocked on their door. It seemed unfair to have to pull them from their beds with this type of news. But the investigation had to keep moving forward; it couldn't stop still.

There wasn't any answer, so he repeated the heavy tapping.

'Coming.' Stephen's voice was hoarse from sleep, and when he yanked the door open, he was knotting a dressing-gown around his waist.

His eyes widened, then he stared, and his knees began to buckle. 'What is it?' he whispered, backing away from the door.

Bob felt his stomach drop. God, he hated informs.

'Stephen?' Jan was suddenly next to him, her cotton nightie above her knees, her expression dazed. 'What's going on?'

'I'm sorry to bother you so early in the morning. Could I come in?' Bob smoothed down his shirt as he spoke.

Neither of Leo's parents seemed able to move, frozen in the moment before they knew their world was about to change forever.

'It's important that I come inside,' Bob said gently.

'Ah, yes, of course.' Stephen stepped away and put his hand on Jan's arm to help her across to the kitchen table. 'Can I get you a coffee?' His good manners were instilled in him, even after being woken before dawn.

Bob didn't answer, but walked to put the kettle on himself, then went back to the table. 'I'm sorry to come knocking on your door so early,' he said again, 'but I have some bad news.'

Jan's intake of breath was audible and her hand flew to her chest. A little whimper escaped, and Stephen reached for her hand.

'We had a phone call last night informing us that there was a man's body matching Leo's description discovered in Meekatharra.'

Jan and Stephen sat stock still. Upright, silent. Not able to grasp what they were hearing.

'I would like it if one of you, or both, could come to Perth and confirm that it is or isn't Leo. I thought that doing this might be too difficult for Jill with the kids.'

'No,' Stephen said. 'No, it can't be him. You told us yesterday he was alive. I've seen the footage. How can—' A hiccup escaped and his hands flew over his mouth as the tears started.

Stephen looked at his wife and she reached out to him, united in their grief.

'We're unsure of what has happened as yet,' Bob told them quietly. 'The phone call came late last night, and the pathologist has been in contact—' He broke off as Jan let out a moan that seemed to come from deep within her.

'He's dead?' she mumbled.

'We have a body that matches his description,' Bob told them again gently. 'Although, until this man is identified then we won't know for sure, but we have enough information to ask you to come to Perth. Dave has gone to Meekatharra to talk to the local people and see what he can find out.'

Stephen shot up and looked wildly around. 'Right, I'll have a shower and get dressed. Jan, no need for you to come. Stay here with Jill. Bob's right, she'll need help with the kids. Actually, better idea, ring Andrew and his wife and ask them to come over and help her. I'll get Elliot to drive me.' His need to be in control was clear and a reaction that Bob had seen many times. 'We can be there in—' He glanced at the watch on his wrist.

'Mr Perry,' Bob said, 'we won't need you until later this afternoon, so please, just take in what I'm telling you. I can organise for a constable from here to drive you there and back again. You have my number. When you get to Perth, call me and I'll take you in.' He looked at them both, the shock spreading across their whole bodies, which were crumpling as if they were a newspaper being scrunched into a ball.

'Did she have anything to do with it?' Stephen bit out.

'Who?' Bob leaned forward.

'Jill, of course. How can he be alive one moment and then not the next?'

'Let me make you a cup of tea,' Bob said, pushing Stephen gently back down into the chair and going to the kettle that had already boiled. 'The man matching Leo's description was found in Meekatharra.' He got out three cups and found the tea bags.

Stephen unexpectedly let out a laugh and his shoulders relaxed. 'Meekatharra? It won't be Leo. He doesn't know anyone in the north of the state and he hates the heat. It'll be as hot as hell there now.' His back straightened and he nodded, as if his expert opinion was going to change the outcome. 'God, it's hot enough down here. No, whoever that poor person is, it won't be Leo.'

'Okay. Why do you think he didn't know anyone in Meekatharra?' Bob put a cup in front of Stephen, then Jan, going back for the milk, sugar and his own cup.

'Because he was from down south.' Stephen looked at Bob as if he were demented. 'He's always lived here, never travelled or holidayed up north. Never shown the slightest interest in heading that way. No, I think you've got the wrong man, detective.'

'I see. Well, unfortunately, we don't believe that to be the case. The man in question had two driver's licences in his wallet: one stating he was Leo Perry and the other a Stephen Perry. We believe this is the identity that he was operating under. He also has a scar on his chin.'

Stephen's bravado fell away.

'Would you like me to organise for a constable to drive you to Perth? Or would you prefer to get there yourself?'

Stephen didn't look as if he were capable of making a decision, so Bob did it for him.

'I'll organise the constable to take you there,' Bob told them.

Stephen gave a short nod and glanced across at Jan, who seemed to be frozen in time. Stuck between the time when her son was alive and laughing and loving his parents, and when they were never going to see his smile again.

Stephen seemed to hesitate. 'What are you going to do now?' he asked.

'I'll be heading to Perth so I'm there when you need me,' Bob told them. He didn't want to mention that he would be in the autopsy suite, waiting for any information that Shannon could hand out, which he could then use to help find who did this to Leo. 'Is there anyone I can call for you?'

Both parents shook their heads.

'I'm going to head along and tell Jill now. Would you like to be there?'

'I'll ring Andrew and Nicola and get them to come over,' Jan said softly. 'They seem to be the two who are here most.'

'Maybe someone who lives in town. They'll get here quickly. I'll see you soon.'

Bob left them to their grief. Outside he blew out his cheeks and ran his hand over his face. Should he wait for Jill's friends to arrive? He really didn't relish dragging the poor woman from sleep or having the kids there when he told her.

Still, sometimes there weren't options.

He glanced to Jill's door, then gave himself a little shake and walked towards it, just as a car pulled into the parking lot.

Chris's wife, Tina, parked in front of Jill's unit and got out, her face still bleary from sleep, and her hair unbrushed.

'I came as soon as Jan rang,' she said to Bob as he moved towards the door. 'This is terrible.'

'I'm about to tell her. You got here quickly.'

'Not far from my house. I live two streets away.'

Bob knew this from when he'd visited her previously.

The door opened and there was no turning back from the news Bob had to deliver.

'What's going on out here? Tina? What are—' Jill's eyes went from Tina to Bob and back to her friend. She took a few steps backwards, holding up her hands as if to ward off any news.

'Jill, let's go inside,' Bob said firmly as Tina reached out to take Jill's arm.

'No,' Jill whispered, staring at Bob again. 'Please, no.'

'I'm sorry, I have some bad news.'

CHAPTER 22

Shannon washed her hands and dried them on a towel as she looked over at Bob. 'I believe the gun should have been alongside of him, if it was suicide, but because the firearm wasn't recovered from the scene, I can't be sure. There were so many people all over the area; god, there're about fifty witness statements, from what I've been told. Have you seen them all?'

'Not yet, but Dave told me there were sheafs of them. The senior constable had them all printed and delivered to Dave's room when he first got there. I reckon he only got about an hour's sleep before he started going through them.' Bob paused. 'I worry about that boy, sometimes. He works too hard. Anyhow,' he focused back at the body on the table, 'what are you saying, Shannon? Have we got a murder or a suicide? Surely, it's murder if the gun isn't there.'

'I can't discount suicide, Bob,' Shannon said softly. 'Because the shot is in the side of his head, a typical suicide shot, and there's gunpowder and burns on his hands consistent with that finding. But I can't discount murder yet either. Tricky one.' She paused and looked down at the body covered by the sheet.

'There are no other wounds or any trauma to say he was fighting off someone, although I can see where his hair has been singed from the fire. The fact he's been found just leaning against a tree makes it feel like suicide, but the setting is wrong. In among a heap of people. Kids having fun. I can't see a father, or anyone, doing something like that, can you? Usually, suicide is a very personal decision and they take themselves away from the public eye, or family, or anywhere they can be found before attempting it. I'm uncomfortable with the fact that his death was so public.'

'I've thought that from the minute I heard where he was found,' Bob said. 'I think the fireworks were used to mask the sound of the gun. And Dave also mentioned you wondered if Leo might've had people with him.'

'I don't see any reason a single man would attend a show when he was trying to hide from his family. For all the reasons I told Dave.'

Bob wanted to argue. To find another reasoning behind Leo's trip to a show, but he couldn't.

'Now, back to the fireworks, which would be a perfect cover for the noise,' Shannon said as she went to stand behind Bob. 'What could have happened—' she shaped her hand into a gun '—is that he was standing watching the fireworks, looking at the sky and someone popped him that way.' She used her hand to touch the side of Bob's head

261

where the shot would have been made. 'He would have crumpled and the man—it would have had to have been a man, or at least a woman who was strong enough to hold him upright—held him there before lowering Leo to the ground and leaning him against the tree.'

'How would he have got the gunpowder on his hands then?'

Shannon placed her hands in Bob's as if she was still holding the gun and shaped his trigger finger around. 'Just like that. Not hard.'

Bob nodded. He already knew the information Shannon was giving him, but he wanted to hear her say it. Make sure there could be no mistake. 'Or he could have gone to meet someone and was just leaning against the tree and they surprised him from behind.'

'Yep. But there is an element of danger with that. Someone would have seen them or noticed Leo slump when he was shot.' Shannon frowned. 'The whole scene has a feeling of not being quite ready or organised. Like it was a bit of a spur of the moment thing, but also not quite. Does that make sense?'

'That's the whole feeling about this case. I asked Leo's wife this morning if there was any reason for anyone to want her husband dead, and of course the answer was no. Didn't get anything different out of the parents this morning either. And where is Coffee? I don't think the dog would have left him from all accounts.'

'Tell me what you've got here,' Shannon said. 'A bloke who was planning to pack up and shift on, then we've found him dead, is that the crux of it?'

'Basically. He's certainly been planning to leave,' Bob said. 'The fire seems to have been the opportunity he's been waiting for. But not one of his mates can think of a reason he'd like to leave, neither can the wife or parents. Leo's got a secret that we're yet to find.'

'The secret would work well with my family theory.'

'He never left the farm. Where would he have found another family?'

Shannon shrugged. 'He left often enough to make the withdrawal at Mowup.'

Surprise showed on Bob's face.

'Dave told me last night when we were throwing some ideas around.'

'And that's a true statement,' Bob said, scratching his arm. 'Once a month isn't enough time to find another family.'

'Have you checked out online dating websites?'

'Have I what?' Bob took a step back.

'Websites that hook people up together. There's a few beginning to pop up since the internet is easier to get these days. People sign up and then somehow they're matched up with people who have similar interests and so on. Maybe he's got a secret online life.'

'I wouldn't even know how to start investigating that,' Bob said, clearly out of his depth. 'As far as I know, the fella finds a lady at the pub or church or somewhere and asks if she'd like to go to dinner. Then the fella rocks up in a car, takes her out and then home again. Then they work out if they want to do it again. Or not.'

Shannon smiled and went to her computer. 'Here, look at this.' She tapped a few keys and pointed at the screen. 'Online dating started to get a bit of a following at the end of the nineties. It's the way time-poor people meet others.'

Bob looked over her shoulder at a computer screen that showed a couple looking at one another with smiles that wouldn't be out of place on a toothpaste commercial.

Looking for love? We can help you was the caption that covered the top of the screen.

'You put your details in here.' Shannon tapped a couple of times on the mouse and brought up the sign-in page that asked for name, age and interests.

'Are you on this site?' Bob asked.

Shannon didn't turn or react, she just kept explaining how the website worked.

'So, perhaps, if Leo had a laptop or a computer that Jill didn't have access to, he had joined the world of internet dating,' Shannon finished.

'Can you put his name into that thing?'

'No, the way you get notified with a match is by email. And then you only get their first name and photo until you make contact.'

'How do we find out if he's on there then?'

'Guess you'll need a warrant or you'll have to get Computer Crimes to enact being a single girl looking for love using Leo's interests. Actually, Computer Crimes may have a way of getting in and seeing if he's on there that I wouldn't know about.'

'Well, thanks for that, Shannon. Certainly a different route to investigate.'

'What's with your arm?' she asked, nodding towards the dried blood on Bob's shirt.

He felt up under the sleeve and realised the blood was warm. He was bleeding again. 'I've scratched something that's got infected,' he said. 'You got a bandaid?'

'Let me look.' Shannon lifted his shirt sleeve and used a sterilised wipe to clean the area.

As she worked on him, Bob's phone rang. One-handed, he pulled it from his pocket and looked at the screen. 'It's Stephen. Are you ready for him to ID the body?'

'I will be in fifteen minutes,' she told him.

'Hi, Stephen, how are you?' Bob asked. 'Was your trip okay?'

'Fine, thank you.' Stephen Perry's voice was croaky as if he'd been crying the whole way to Perth. 'Your constable was very kind.'

'Is it just you, or have you brought Jan?'

'Jan is with me and would like to be there when we see him.'

'Sure, no problems. And where are you now?'

'At the address you gave us. In the foyer.'

'Right. I'll be right down.'

He disconnected the call and closed his eyes, suddenly feeling bone weary. 'Here we go,' he said.

Shannon put a piece of sticky plaster across his arm. 'That will stop it from bleeding,' she said. 'But I want you to go to the doctor as soon as possible and get it looked at.'

There was something in Shannon's tone that made Bob turn and look at her. 'Why?'

'I don't like the look of that mole, Bob,' she told him bluntly.

'It's not a mole, it's a pimple.'

'No, it's a mole with a jiggered edge and two different colours inside. You can't see it because it's around the back of your arm, so you'll have to trust me when I say, you need it looked at as soon as possible. Especially since you've scratched it enough to make it bleed.'

Nervousness ran through Bob's stomach, but he kept his face passive. 'Right, I'll do just that, then.'

'Good.' Shannon washed her hands. 'Right, better do this.'

Bob nodded and went into the hallway towards the lifts. He stood there for what seemed like an eternity, waiting for the lift to arrive. When it did, the doors slid open silently, then he stepped in and pushed the ground-floor button.

Mole? Didn't those things cause that skin cancer, mela-noma? He'd ask Betty, she'd know, but he was sure that's what it was. And if that was right, he knew four or five fellas who had died from that.

Maybe Parksey wasn't the only one who needed to look after his health a little more. He fingered the sticky plaster that Shannon had wrapped around his upper arm, fear making his stomach churn a little.

The lift slid to a stop and Bob swallowed, before stepping out, focusing on Stephen and Jan who were sitting on a fake leather lounge in the waiting room. 'Thank you so much for coming,' he said quietly. 'Can I get you anything? Tea, coffee, water?'

'No, thank you,' Jan said. 'Let's just do this so we can go home.'

Jan looked like she had aged ten years in the space of hours. Her eyes were red from crying and her hands shook as she held the tissue, swiping at her nose every so often.

'Yes, of course,' Bob said, 'but before we do, I'll let you know what's going to happen. When we get upstairs, I'll take you into a smaller room, which has a window. There will be a curtain covering it and when you're ready to see, let me know. Behind the window, in another room, will be a man covered by a sheet. Again, let me know when you're ready for the pathologist to lower it. Then, have a careful look and when you're sure about the identity of the man, tell me.'

Stephen nodded, while Jan's expression made it seem as if he was speaking a different language.

'Do you have any questions?'

Both shook their heads, but Bob knew that wasn't true. The anguished confusion on their faces asked every question.

Why them?

How had this happened to their family?

Why had Leo decided to leave?

Had they caused this?

Could they have done something better as parents?

'Okay,' Bob's voice was gentle. He hated this side of policing. He wasn't sure how many of these IDs he'd been present at, but each one was so similar, he knew what was going to happen. 'This way.'

He ushered them into the hallway and then over to the lift. Stephen and Jan walked as if they were heading towards their own execution. Nothing was going to stop what they were about to do. There was nowhere to get off this tread-mill now.

In the lift, Jan slipped her hand into the crook of Stephen's elbow and held tight, while her husband covered her hand with his.

Bob stood, his hands clasped in front of his waist, head down, waiting for the doors to open.

Melanoma?

Bob chided himself on jumping to conclusions and being so dramatic, everything he counselled Dave against doing.

The lift stopped with a bump and the doors slid open.

'This way.' He indicated the entrance, which led into a small room. Stephen walked slowly with Jan, who stopped seemingly unable to make her feet walk any further inside the room.

'Come on, love,' Stephen said.

But Jan didn't move. Bob understood. If the curtain was drawn back and the person behind it really was her son, there was no going back. Until those final seconds when the sheet was turned down, Leo was still out there some-where. Living a life that didn't include them, but at least he was alive and happy.

Not in here. In this sterile environment, with a Y wound down his chest and a bullet hole in his head.

Bob moved forward and indicated the couch that was in the passage. 'Jan, you're more than welcome to stay here, if you don't want to go inside.'

Her mouth was moving but there weren't any sounds coming out. Gently, Stephen took her hand and placed it on the couch. 'Stay here,' he said, his voice gruff.

Quickly, he took three steps and was inside the room. Bob stayed for only a moment longer to make sure Jan sat safely down and then he followed Stephen inside.

The man, this father, was standing, chewing his cheeks from the inside, but he nodded to Bob before he could ask the question.

Bob discreetly pushed a button and the curtain slid open, revealing a covered body and Shannon standing next to the head.

Stephen took in an audible breath and once again nodded.

Shannon gently turned back the sheet.

CHAPTER 23

Dave looked down at the tree that Leo's body had been leaned against. He crouched down, keeping his hands tucked behind his back, and carefully looked at the dirt, trying to see if there was any blood or fluids that had been missed by forensics.

The scene had been managed as well as possible considering thousands of people had tramped around a murder or suicide scene. He glanced around and noted the empty beer stubby that had been tossed nearby.

'The bar isn't far away,' Karly told him. She seemed refreshed from her short sleep and was dressed in a crisp uniform, including her hat. Her handshake had been firm when Dave had introduced himself to her. 'And this area here—' she indicated to where Leo had been found '—is on the way out of the grounds, so . . .' She stopped talking and let Dave connect the dots.

A high traffic area.

'This way?' Dave pointed.

'Yeah, alcohol isn't supposed to get outside of the fenced-off area, but even with guards on they seem to manage to get some outside. I'm not surprised that there are a few stubbies and cans around here.'

Sideshow alley hadn't been packed up yet and Dave could see some uniformed coppers walking to each caravan, talking to the occupants and taking more statements.

'Better bag it as evidence. Where's the cattle shed?'

'One hundred and ninety metres this way.' Karly pointed in the opposite direction.

'Have you interviewed the exhibitors?'

'We have. They're in the statements I had delivered to your room. Only one bloke recognises him from the photo you gave to me. Said that he checked out a few of the stud bulls that were being judged, but didn't speak to anyone. He didn't stay long, perhaps ten minutes and then he left. Leo wasn't noticed by anyone we've taken a statement from since then.'

'I see.' Casting an eye around, Dave played some ideas out in his mind. He tried to imagine the man leaning against the tree, drinking his last beer and watching the fireworks before putting a gun to his head and pulling the trigger.

Someone confronts Leo from behind, there's a tussle that no one takes any notice of, or ignores, not wanting to be involved, and bang, Leo goes down. But could this have nothing to do with Leo at all? Maybe he was in the wrong place at the wrong time. 'Were there any incidents at the show?' he asked. 'Anything get out of control? Fights? What about the showies over at sideshow alley?'

Karly shook her head. 'It's one of the quietest shows I've ever been involved with, I have to say. Normally there's a brawl at the bar, or some little shithead trying to nick motorbikes or something from the outdoor displays, lost kids, even, but this year there was none of that. Everyone has behaved in an exemplary fashion.'

Dave's phone rang. He answered without looking at the screen. 'Burrows.'

'Positive ID. It's Leo,' Bob said.

Dave was silent a moment. He'd felt a kinship with Leo— similar age and similar backgrounds. 'Right, well, I'll keep looking here then.'

'Good-oh.' Bob paused and Dave sensed there was more, so he stayed quiet. 'Listen, son, you might have to take over this one for the moment. I've had a bit of bad news.'

Again, Dave stayed silent, but he squeezed his eyes shut and breathed deeply. Something had told him Bob hadn't been firing on all cylinders, not just during this case but for a month or so.

'Shannon wanted me to go to the doc when she had a look at that thing on my arm and so she rushed me through to see one of the copper GPs. Testing didn't take as long as I thought it would. Only got preliminary results but its sounding more and more like I've gotta have an op. It's melanoma in that arm there.'

'Melanoma?'

'Yeah, not quite what I expected, but I don't think I anticipated anything at all. Anyway, op has tentatively been booked for tomorrow, so are you right to carry on by yourself? Lorri will be able to help you if needs be, but we're going to be pretty short-staffed here for a while. Parksey won't be back for ages. If he even comes back. His missus might have something to say about that.' Bob breathed heavily, muffling the phone line. 'Good thing the coppers have access to doctors who can do this stuff pronto, hey, son?'

'Jesus, Bob.' Dave couldn't find any words to make anything feel better. He stood up and walked away from Leo Perry's final resting place, sadness flooding through him.

'Ah, she'll be right, son. Take more than something like that to keep me down. Might have a bit of a recovery period though. Especially if they've gotta take the lymph nodes out.'

'Lymph nodes?'

'Oh, you're asking the wrong bloke, son. They were some words the doc threw at me today. Didn't take it all in.'

'I'll finish up here as quickly as I can,' Dave said. 'The case is really closed, isn't it? I mean we have a body now.'

'Ah, no. No, it's not closed. You're looking for a murderer. Even though Shannon can't say for certain that it is murder, suicide doesn't wash with either of us.'

Dave was quiet again. 'Shit,' he said.

'Indeedy.'

'Okay, well, I'll be home tomorrow to see you when you come out of surgery. Then I'll go to Yorkenup.'

'Don't hurry anything, son. You've still got a case to solve, and I'll be fine. Okay?'

Dave wanted to yell at him. No one had any idea if Bob was going to be fine! What if the melanoma had spread to other parts . . . Other *organs*!

'No shadow-boxing now, son. Wait until the doc has got all the info.' Bob's voice was stern and Dave automatically gave a smile. His partner already knew what he was thinking before he voiced it.

'I'll ring you in the morning,' Dave said.

'Good job, talk to you then.' Bob's voice was all business now. 'Catch you 'ron.'

Dave looked at the phone as Bob disconnected. Emptiness spread through the pit of his stomach. That was his mate. His go-to man. The one who had been looking out for him and educating him over the last three years. The bloke who had been his only friend when Ellen had been shot, his only support at Ellen's funeral and afterwards when Mark had slapped divorce proceedings and child custody papers on him only moments after the coffin had been lowered into the grave.

This was his partner.

'Everything okay?' Karly was standing behind him, curiosity on her face.

Dave took a breath and summonsed up his professionalism. 'Yeah,' he said, turning to her briskly. 'Yeah, we've got a positive ID. It's Leo.'

Karly let out a breath it seemed she'd been holding for hours. 'Well, that fixes that, doesn't it? You know where he is now.'

'Sure do, except the pathologist thinks it was murder. So, we're still on the hunt.'

Her eyes lit up. 'I've never worked on a murder investigation before.' She eyed Dave. 'I researched you, because your name was familiar.' Drawing herself up tall, she looked him straight in the eye. 'I'd like to learn from you.'

Dave shook his head. He didn't want to deal with her now. Winding this case up as quickly as possible and getting home to Bob was more important. 'You can shadow me while I'm here, Karly, but your job is in Meekatharra. You'd need to apply to do the dee's training if you want to become a detective.'

'I know all of that. I've got my name down on the list, but you can still talk to me about the case, can't you?'

'Like I said, I'm happy for you to shadow me while I'm here, if your sarge can spare you. I don't want to be stepping on anyone's toes.'

'I'll clear it. Anyway, you need to come back to the station and meet him soon.' She shoved her hands in her pockets and rocked on her heels. Even feeling as sad as he did, Dave wanted to laugh. So much self-confidence came from working in a small town and knowing everyone. Karly would find being a detective very different in Perth, or places where she wasn't a local.

'Show me where the CCTV is on the grounds?'

'On the grounds? There isn't any,' she told him. 'The footy oval here has some pointed on the change rooms. Few years back a mob decided they were going to lynch the umpire that called a point a goal in the final quarter and made the home side lose the game. So the club had one camera installed. Doesn't run half the time, but no one else knows that.'

'Main street cameras?'

'Only the one at the front of the police station. We put that up ourselves a few months ago when we had two windows smashed. The shire council don't see the point in it yet. I've had my guys go over what we had, but it's not a great view of the street. Camera is angled more towards the door, but it does catch some of the road. They were looking for a white HiLux, with either a dog in the passenger's seat or in the back, like you asked. They couldn't see anything matching that description.'

Dave thought. 'Were there any HiLuxes?'

'A few. Couldn't see numberplates though.'

'Occupants?'

'Outlines.'

'Would you mind going back to your team and asking if they would take another look for one with a man, woman and child? I'm sure the dog will be there somewhere, too.'

Karly spoke into her radio, issuing the orders. 'They're on it.'

'Is there any camping on the grounds?'

'Only for the people running sideshow alley.'

'Let's walk,' Dave said and pointed to the boundary of the grounds. 'Tell me about your town.'

'Not much to tell. Smack bang in the middle of nowhere. Tourists come here for about six months of the year, but then, as it gets hotter, they slow down until they stop completely. There can be a bit of trouble at times. White fellas, black fellas, whoever fellas, there's no monopoly on who can cause trouble up here.'

They walked past the playground and Dave raked his eyes over the sand, looking for any sign of the gun. 'Did your guys sift this sand?' he asked, over the top of her running commentary.

Karly looked across at the swing set and the churned up sand.

'Ah, no.'

'Have you searched the rubbish bins and through the hay in the animal stalls?'

Crimson flamed around Karly's face. 'No, sorry. I didn't think.'

'Better get another team back here to do that.' Dave felt the familiar surge of frustration. If only he'd been here earlier. Still, it wasn't Karly's fault either.

Karly was speaking quickly into her phone, organising what he'd asked. She'd barely hung up when she apologised again.

'You haven't run a murder investigation before,' Dave said. 'You did a great job at shutting the scene down as quickly as you did. But let's get looking for the gun that shot Leo.'

Dave pulled into the one and only roadhouse on the main street of Meekatharra and came to a stop under the only tree in the parking lot. Red dust covered the yellow and white building, peeling advertising paint in the window telling him that the steak sangers here were the best ones until Kununurra.

He grabbed the photo of Leo and put his hat on his head, before walking to the roadhouse.

Inside a bell jangled as the door slammed shut. Warm humid air rose from the bain-marie and wrapped him in the smell of oily chips, dim sims and crabsticks. The air-conditioner was battling against the heat outside.

'Help you, love?' A lady in her mid-fifties, with her grey hair scraped up into a bun, looked at him from behind the counter. 'Chips or coffee?'

Dave fixed her with a smile. 'Neither at the moment, thanks.' He brought out the photo and held it up as he introduced himself. 'I'm wondering if you have seen this man in here lately?'

'You the cops?' Her voice was curious.

'Sure am.'

'What's this poor bugger done, then?'

'I'm trying to trace his movements over the last three days.' He stopped as he calculated how many days it had been since Leo had been seen on the video withdrawing money from the ATM. 'Four days,' he corrected himself.

The woman held out her hand and fished her glasses from a stained white apron. 'Let's have a look here.'

Dave checked for working cameras. He couldn't see any and he frowned. 'Any security here?' he asked.

'As in cameras? Nah, don't need them. I've got Cruiser here.' She nodded and Dave belatedly found himself looking at a large Alsatian dog, curled up next to the drinks fridge. He wasn't asleep but watching Dave's every move. 'Don't even try to put anything in your pocket, or he'll have your guts for garters.' She smiled fondly at the dog. 'Cheapest most reliable security system I've ever had.'

'He looks it. But what about your bowsers?'

'Everyone knows about Cruiser here. And if you're a tourist and you don't, and you drive away, I just ring the cops. Tell 'em the numberplate. Money always comes back.'

'I see.' Although Dave didn't really. Sounded pretty much like potluck to him and he was sure Bob would say the same.

Bob. That anxiety sitting in the bottom of his stomach curled its way towards his heart again. Instead, he focused on the woman.

'No, I don't reckon I've seen him,' she said. 'He's got a memorable face, you know, being so pale and red up here. Most of us are dyed brown whether we like it or not.'

'I think he might've been driving a HiLux with a dog in the back. He could have had a woman and a small child with him.'

'You don't know much about this guy then, do ya?'

Dave conceded she was right.

'Is there anywhere else he might've got fuel?'

'Pub sells it, but he's a lot more expensive than me. By three or four cents, cheeky blighters.'

'Great, thanks for your help.' He dug in his pocket and pulled out a card. 'If you do remember that he came in, could you let me know?'

'Course I can. A good-looking, young man like you.' She gave him a wink and tucked his card down between her breasts. 'If something comes to light, I'll be sure to let you know.'

CHAPTER 24

Dave cruised up and down the streets of Meekatharra looking for a HiLux ute. It wouldn't take him long. There were only seven streets running parallel to the highway and once he'd driven all of them, he could start back on the crisscrossing.

It seemed to him that every second vehicle up here was a HiLux and he wasn't sure how he could work out if there were any abandoned ones because they all had a neglected look to them. Covered in red dust, a few panels beaten in. Some were parked on road verges, others under lean-to carports. In fact, all the ones Dave had seen would fit right in with the ones back in Leo's shed.

He thought back to Sam Dooney's comment about them being a dime a dozen. Maybe that's why Leo had bought them all. Hiding in broad daylight. Nothing silly about that theory.

As he drove, he dialled the number for the local vet surgery and waited until they answered. 'I'm Detective Dave Burrows, I'm investigating the death of a man up here recently. I'm wondering if you could tell me whether or not you've got a tan kelpie that may have been brought in? Her name is Coffee.'

'Sorry, we haven't got any kelpies in here at the moment, runaways or otherwise.'

Dave thanked her, knowing it had been a long shot, and kept driving slowly down each street in a grid-like fashion.

When he'd left, the showgrounds had been a bundle of activity. Karly had pulled two teams, from where Dave didn't know, and had them scouring the grounds in the hope of finding the gun. Unless the murderer was very stupid, it was unlikely they'd find it, but still it had to be done.

Turning the corner, he found himself back at the pub. Tiredness hit him. It was only four pm, but with the drive last night and Bob's news, Dave felt as if he'd been run over by a steamroller. He pulled up in front of the hotel and took another photo of Leo out—he'd check with the publican before going back to his room to read some more witness statements and go over the photos again. The box of evidence recovered from the scene was packed and ready for Dave to transport to Perth in the morning.

Inside the pub, the front bar was full of workers looking to clear the dust from their throats. Beers lined the bar, and one fella lifted his in a cheers motion to Dave.

'How you going, copper?' he asked.

Dave nodded back. 'Good, mate, good.' He used to wonder how people pegged him as a police officer. Shannon had told him once he couldn't be anything else. His stance, his voice, the way he commanded attention. He'd never been sure whether the things she mentioned were good or not.

The publican came out from the kitchen, wiping his hands on a tea-towel. 'Beer?' he asked.

Dave nodded his thanks, then held out the photo as the man took a glass from the rack and tilted it under a tap.

'I was wondering if you've seen this bloke here at all? He might have been getting fuel. Would've had a tan kelpie with him, probably travelling by himself, but perhaps with a woman and young child.'

The publican put the beer on the bar and reached for the photo. 'Hmm, his face is familiar but I'm not sure why. Don't reckon he stayed here, though. Who is he?'

'His body was found in the showgrounds last night.'

'Ah, I heard there was a problem down there. I should have been called out, but I had me hands full here being the show.'

'Called out?' Dave asked. 'Do you volunteer?'

'Yeah, ambo. I was rostered on last night but swapped with a mate so I could be here. Us owners need to be on site when big events are on. Never know what might happen otherwise.' He nodded towards the photo. 'He doesn't look local. Where's he from?'

'Place called Yorkenup.'

Realisation spread across the publican's face. 'He's had his face flashed all over the TV, hasn't he? What's his name again?'

'Leo Perry.'

'Yeah, well, I reckon I know his face from the box, rather than him sitting at my bar. Got it going all the time over there.' He gave the photo back, nodding towards the TV hanging on the wall. 'Sorry, I can't help you.'

'Worth a shot. Okay if I check with the other lads?' Dave indicated to the guys sitting on the stools.

'They'd be offended if you didn't!' He grinned.

Dave took his beer and went to each of the men. Ten minutes later he was no better off.

'Right-oh, lads. Well, if you do remember something, can you give me a call. Number's on the card.'

They all raised their drinks to him and agreed.

Dave drained his glass and ordered another, before leaving for his room.

Yawning, he wasn't sure how much longer he could stay awake, so he sent Shannon a message.

Thanks for getting Bob through the medical system so quickly. Do you have any idea about a prognosis?'

There wasn't any answer and Dave assumed she was in the morgue.

On the table in his room, the witness statements were beginning to blur in front of his eyes, so instead he grabbed a magnifying glass and started to comb through the photos.

The banging was loud and insistent, and it took Dave a while to realise someone was at his door.

He raised himself up from the table, where his head had fallen, and wiped the dribble away from his mouth.

'Hold on, hold on,' he rasped. The room was dark, so he must have gone to asleep before the sun had set. Looking for a light switch, he ran his hands down the edge of the wall near the door and found one, bringing the room to light. He squinted, then yanked the door open.

Karly stood there, a quizzical look on her face.

'Early night?' she asked.

'Cat nap,' he responded.

Seeing a movement near her legs, he glanced down. She was holding a thick lead, and at the end of it, a tan kelpie was shaking near her knees.

'Are you kidding?' Dave dropped to a squat and held out his hand, a thrill shooting through his stomach. 'Bugger me dead! Coffee? Hey there, little girl, is that you?'

The dog's ears twitched at the sound of 'Coffee', but her shaking didn't stop. Instead, she continued to sit as instructed, her eyes darting everywhere as if she were looking for someone.

'Stay there,' Dave told Karly. 'When I call her name, drop the lead and see what happens.'

Dave walked to the end of the row of hotel rooms and turned around.

'Coffee,' he called in a commanding voice. 'Here, Coffee!'

The kelpie leaped to her feet and darted towards Dave. He caught her around the collar and rubbed her coat.

'Look at you,' he said softly. 'Where have you been hiding out?' Coffee dropped into a sitting position again and looked up at him. 'Well, little dog, I've got some bad news for you. Your owner can't come back, but don't worry,' he ran his hands over her ears, 'I'll look after you until I can get you back to Jill.'

Karly came to stand next to him, smiling. 'She's a find, isn't she?'

Dave was surprised at the bubble of joy sitting in his chest. 'Where?' was all he could ask.

'Someone picked her up running along the highway. About ten kay north of town.'

His head snapped up. 'Near the camping place you were telling me about?'

Karly nodded. 'That direction, but futher on. If you're keen, we can go for a run up there.'

Still patting Coffee, Dave nodded. 'First, let's find some food for Coffee and take her to the vet to get checked over, and then we can head out there.'

'I've organised for the vet to feed her when she looks her over.' Karly paused and looked at Dave. 'Okay to go out there in the dark? Or would you rather go first thing in the morning?'

'Nah, let's go now. If anyone is there, they'll be camped for the night, and we'll be able to ask a couple of questions.'

'No worries. My car or yours?'

'Coffee can ride shotgun to the vet, and then you can jump in with me after we've dropped her off,' Dave told her. His eyes dropped to the dog again. 'Well there, little girl, I can't tell you how pleased I am to see you.'

The dog thumped her tail and looked up at him, his gentle voice calming her.

He opened the door into the troopy and told her to 'Get up'. Coffee threw him a confused look. 'Ah, you don't ride shotgun? Today you do. Come on, get up,' he patted the seat and, finally, Coffee jumped in.

Shutting the door, he went around to the driver's side and got in, following Karly's vehicle. He picked up his phone and rang Bob. It went straight through to his message bank.

Dave's stomach dropped. Bob never turned his phone off. Ever.

He left a message. 'Yeah, it's me. Coffee has been picked up running alongside the highway. I've got her now.' Silence as Dave tried to work out what to say next.

He wanted to tell Bob he loved him, but that wasn't the done thing. In the end he just said, 'Hope tomorrow goes well.'

Was he going to have to get used to Bob not being involved with the investigations? Would his partner quit after the op? The uncertainty unhinged Dave's world in a way he didn't like. Bob was the axis that kept him steady.

When Karly pulled into the vet's, Dave jumped out and picked up Coffee, while they waited for the after-hours vet to arrive. Lights swept through the parking lot only moments after they had pulled up, and a young woman with long black hair got out, carrying a bag.

'Hey, Karly,' she said. 'How're things?'

'Hey, Georgie. This is Dave. He's a detective from down south.'

Georgie threw Dave a curious smile and waved hello, before turning back to Karly.

'This dog was handed in after being found running along the highway,' Karly told her. 'Can you please check her out for us tonight while we do a little more investigation? We'll be back later to pick her up. Dave wants to keep her with him.'

'Course. No trouble. She looks pretty happy though, doesn't she?' She bent down to run her hands over the dog whose tail was wagging slowly. She could have been patting or examining the animal, it was all done with the same tenderness. 'Hello you. Want to stay with me for a little while?'

Dave handed Georgie the lead. 'Her name is Coffee and she has a family down south that will be very happy to see her, when I can get her to them.'

'Leave her with me. If I've gone home by the time you get back, just send me a text. I only live around the corner so it's not hard to come over,' she explained to Dave.

'Appreciate that, for sure,' Dave said, wondering if he should ring Jill and let her know that Coffee had turned up.

He decided against it. She had enough to deal with.

Bob had told him that he'd explained Leo's death as gently as possible to Stephen and Jan after the ID, and that murder seemed likely. Jan hadn't spoken since before the ID and Stephen seemed to be just as shocked, still

288

exclaiming there was no way that Leo could have known anyone from up north.

Red and Robbie had relayed the news to Jill. The feedback was that Jill's initial tears and shock had been replaced with a steady stoicism.

'Tell me about this camping spot,' Dave said as he flicked his lights onto high beam and headed out to the highway. Two triple road trains passed him, going in the other direction, causing the troopy to shake under the wake of their winds. 'You've had officers out there already?'

'Not this one. I'd forgotten about this site. Popular with free campers,' she said. 'Young ones backpacking around the state. Sometimes the trucks call in, so there is room for them to get in and out, but they prefer to come into town so they can get a feed and a shower.'

Dave nodded his understanding.

'Well, Coffee has been somewhere out this side of town, hasn't she? We just need to find out where.' He looked across at Karly. 'And when we find *that*, it will be very interesting to see *who* is there.'

CHAPTER 25

Even though the night was dark, the pinpricks of light from the stars were enough for Dave and Karly to be able to see the outlines of shadows and bushes as they bumped their way down a gravel road towards a camping area eight kilometres from the highway.

Dave could see why the triple road trains wouldn't come in here that often: it was a long way from the highway and, as a driver, you wouldn't want to get halfway in and find you couldn't get out.

On the other hand, he could see why it was appealing for the free campers: it was far enough off the road to feel safe, there was a toilet block and the camping area was sitting on the edge of a waterhole.

'Through here.' Karly pointed to the right-hand side of a fork in the road.

Swinging the wheel, Dave put his lights on high beam, driving from side to side, making sure his lights picked up every corner of the camping area.

The ground was devoid of tents, or swags or any type of camping gear. The rubbish bins were overflowing and a couple of areas had rings of stones that looked empty, except for cold ash.

He pulled up and turned off the car, letting the silence overtake them. The tick of the engine, starting to cool. A low rumble, so low you had to really strain to hear the trucks on the highway. The night was silent of all animal life. 'Doesn't look like anyone is camped up here tonight, does it?' he said.

Karly opened her door and took her torch from her belt. 'Let's check around anyway.'

She wandered off towards the toilet blocks around the back of the large red boulders that seemed to rise from the ground.

Dave got out, his hand also on his torch, but instead of walking off, he stayed still and listened some more. The air was too still, too silent for there to be anyone camped here. People often thought they were quiet, but what they didn't realise was every move they made held some kind of noise or disturbance, which would cross the atmosphere in waves, letting animals and astute people who were aware know they were there.

There weren't any humans camped here.

'Dave?' Karly called out.

He turned at the sound of her voice and flicked his torch on. 'Coming,' he called back.

Rounding one of the rocks, he saw her crouched down with her hand out over an old fire.

'It's still warm,' she said. 'There's a fire ban up here at the moment, so no one should be lighting fires.'

'How'd the fireworks get the green light then?' he asked.

'There's got to be a certain amount of green grass around them, and if there had been a breath of breeze, which could have made the sparks drift, we wouldn't have been able to let the explosives off. Pure luck, which we work towards every year.'

Dave turned slowly and flashed his torch around the area. It was clean. He checked the rubbish bin close by and wrinkled his nose at the smell of rotting meat and salad, dirty nappies and cigarette butts.

'Trouble is there's no saying who has set up camp,' he told her. 'If Leo had been here, surely his ute would be in town and his camping gear would still be around, because he hasn't been able to come back.'

'Someone could have stolen it. You never leave anything for too long in these parts. Cars get stripped down and the best of everything taken in about the first hour after a breakdown. If he was staying here alone, he'd want to have taken his stuff with him.'

'You think he had someone with him?'

'Seems the obvious thing to me.'

Dave nodded. He was leaning towards that theory, too. Maybe that person was the one who killed him.

The thought made him frown. Could've the person who was with Leo killed him? That would answer the previous question he had—how did the killer know where Leo was? Was that why Coffee was running loose? A fizz of excitement hit his stomach. 'We need to find that person, then,' he told Karly.

A flash of silver caught in the light from his torch, and he walked over, toeing the ground to uncover a bottle lid. He grimaced. 'Let's get a team out here tomorrow and see if they can find anything useful. There's not much more we can do tonight. If he was with someone, they're not here now. But I'm going to put out an updated media release reflecting that.'

'No worries. I'll sort it when we get back to town.'

In the troopy, Karly spoke again. 'I guess we really need to find the vehicle, too. There should be answers there.'

'The trouble is we haven't got a rego to run or put out an alert on,' Dave said. 'I could say, let's stop every HiLux ute from the early 1980s, but I think we'd be stopping every second car on the road.' Dave put the vehicle into gear and drove back towards town.

'How do you know it's a HiLux?'

Dave briefed her on the vehicles Bob and he had found in the shed at Leo's farm. 'Seemed he loved to buy old HiLuxes and drive them. It was a HiLux we found over near Hunter Rock, so it's a fair assumption that's what he was driving when he came to Meekatharra. But not having a rego makes it difficult to track. I can't issue a "Be On the Look Out" without a numberplate. It's frustrating because usually we have more to work with. Not just a body, a dog and a few hypotheticals.'

'We have a few more things than that,' Karly said. 'The gun. I read the autopsy report and the gun was a service revolver from World War Two. Ballistics commented that it was an unusual type of weapon.'

Dave nodded. 'That's right. Shannon recovered the pill from Leo's head but we can't match it to anything unless we have a gun.'

'My grandad fought in World War Two.'

His glance slid across to her as he flicked his blinker on and turned back out onto the highway. 'And?'

'Well, I remember him telling me that service pistols or revolvers always stayed in the family. They were rarely given back to the defence force. I think they all had to be registered, I'm sure there's the exception to the rules, but they were supposed to be.'

'You want to run a report on registered World War Two handguns?'

'Might help.'

Dave thought about that. He hadn't finished reading the report that Shannon had sent through, because he'd fallen asleep. Karly Hepworth, despite her lack of detective experience, had some good points.

'Okay, you do that. Once we've picked up Coffee, I'm going back to my room to finish reading the reports and witness statements. There're a couple of things I want to check, then tomorrow morning I'm heading back to Perth with the box of evidence to get it checked in and listed, so

I can start to go through it. If you come up with anything, give me a call.'

Karly's shoulders slumped slightly as he spoke, and he frowned. He couldn't help it that Karly couldn't come to Perth with him. She was stationed here. Changing the subject, he asked about her goals. 'You want to be a dee, you said?'

'Not just a dee. I want to work with the stock squad.'

'Come from an agricultural background?'

'My parents own a station out of Carnarvon, so I've grown up around these parts.'

'Ride a motorbike and a horse?'

She grinned. 'Champion bareback rider from the Onslow rodeo,' she told him.

'I'm impressed!' Dave said. 'That's a great rodeo. I've been a couple of times and had lots of fun. Much more relaxed up here than down south. I love the way no one takes themselves too seriously.'

'I took my horse, Ebony, over to South Australia and had a go at the Barker rodeo, in the Flinders Ranges there, but I didn't do any good. Didn't give my girl enough time to recover from the trip. Rookie mistake.'

'All learning. You'll know for next time.'

'Are there any vacancies coming up in the stock squad?' she asked.

The question made Dave pause. There could be.

The horrible heavy feeling of anxiety and fear returned. Not that it had left him, but he'd been able to bat it down while he'd been working and asleep. Now, as he passed the sign telling him he was five kilometres from Meekatharra, the thought of Bob going under the knife tomorrow made him feel physically sick.

'There're certainly some changes afoot down there,' he told Karly. 'But you haven't done the detective course yet, and you need to have aced that before anything. If your goal is the stock squad, then you have to understand this will take time.'

'I told you I've got my name down for the dee's course. I said to my sarge I wanted to apply and he reckoned I was wasting my time.'

'Wasting your time applying to the stock squad or becoming a detective?'

Karly's face set, her lips in a straight line. 'Both.'

'Interesting. What was his reasoning?'

'Because I'm a woman, and I'm from up here.'

'We've got a woman on the team. Lorri. She's a great detective. And where you're from has nothing to do with it.' He slowed and flicked on the indicator to turn down the street to the vet surgery. 'Look, if you want to have a go, do it. I don't know what I'll be able to do to help, but I'll try.'

She smiled. 'Would you?'

'Course. Like I said, not sure what type of help it will be, but I'll do my best.' He brought the troopy to a stand-still and turned in his seat to face her. 'The stock squad are a special breed of detectives. We need to be able to ride horses and bikes, and know how to muster stock. Do a count of livestock and not get queasy when we set foot near an abattoir. And the weather plays a big role, too; hot, cold, rainy, whatever it is we're out in it if we need to be. So, if none of that bothers you, have a crack. I'll let you know when a vacancy comes up.'

'That'd be so awesome if you would,' she said. 'You've had a pretty cool career already.'

Dave felt the hot flush of embarrassment and his voice turned serious. 'I can promise you, Karly, you do not want to have experienced what I have.'

CHAPTER 26

When Dave opened the motel room door, he could smell bacon cooking. The sun hadn't quite broken the horizon and yet, outside, men in high-vis clothes were swarming over the parking lot.

Dave let Coffee out for a run. She wagged her tail, looking back at him as she stopped to sniff a couple of places, then squatted to pee. Dave lugged the boxes of evidence out to the troopy and stowed them in the back, clipping a couple of ties around to make sure they couldn't move.

He made himself two coffees in his travel mugs, then whistled to Coffee, holding open the door. She came running, and this time jumped in the front without hesitation.

'There we go,' he said. 'You're getting used to travel-ling in style.' He texted Karly to tell her he was on the move and to keep him updated with anything she found out. She had already messaged him last night to say that she had a team mobilised to search the camping grounds.

Their ETA had been one hour, and by the time they set up the lights and started, she was sure the search would only take a few hours. He knew she was also hoping to come up with information on the service gun that had been used to kill Leo. Privately, he thought she was dreaming, but he recognised some of himself in her personality. Grit and determination. Letting nothing stop her from finding the outcome she needed. Karly was probably like him as well in that she might push the boundaries to get the arrest. He grinned to himself. When she passed the dee's course, her partner was going to have their work cut out for them.

The team that had been searching the showgrounds hadn't found anything they could use. No gun nor any other evidence. Although there had been a couple of dolls tossed into a bin, which had caught Karly's attention, since one of the showbags found near Leo had been most likely for a girl. She'd bagged them and was having them sent down to Perth.

Dave had pored over the photos of the crowds, and marked a few to show Bob when he got back. He was sure once the op was over that Bob would be raring to get back into work, even if it was just desk duties, so he wanted to have something for him to work on.

Interestingly, the photos showed clear images of the people who were close by. He'd texted Karly asking her to give someone the task of identifying as many people as they could from the photos, then reinterviewing them. He could stay and do it, and normally he and Bob would have done just that, but the pull back to Perth was too strong. Dave had to be close by when Bob came out of surgery.

His mobile was in his hand and he couldn't decide whether to try to ring Bob one more time. He didn't want to get the message bank again. It was too much of a reminder that things weren't normal. Maybe he could text Betty. Dave gave a snort, he could hear exactly what Bob would think about that.

'*For god's sake son. What are you thinking involving the women? Just do your job. I'll be fine.*'

Out on the road, Dave switched the radio to the ABC; the station had been his constant companion when he'd been out bush camping by himself. Even if Bob had been with him, they'd always listened to the Country Hour and afternoon shows.

The news came on and Dave turned up the volume. He'd emailed off a media release to Media Relations before he left and he was hoping they'd released it already.

Five minutes later and there had been no mention of Leo. 'Bugger,' he said softly.

Coffee opened her eyes and stared up at him from where she was curled up in the passenger's footwell. She lifted her head and gave a little whine.

'I wanted it out today, Coffee,' he told her. 'We've got to find out who your boss was travelling with. I think that person holds all the keys.'

The road was straight and morphed into a shimmering illusion on the horizon as Dave drove back to Perth. Trucks appeared from within the moving mirage and came towards him with fast-moving ferocity. Sometimes he felt as if they were going to swallow him up as they went by. Or drag him backwards into the wake.

For once there were very few caravaners on the road. The heat had driven them down south a few months before, leaving only the locals to brave the dust and flies.

Glancing at the clock on the dash, Dave realised that he'd been driving for two hours and he needed to let Coffee out for a break. Searching the road for a parking bay, he found one a few more kays down the track and started to slow.

A couple of other vehicles were already there, so when he pulled to a halt, he grabbed Coffee's lead and clipped it to her collar, not wanting to take any chances the dog was going to shoot through again. She had such a beautiful nature that he'd fallen in love with her a little overnight, and giving her back to Jill was going to be hard. Having her companionship had been enough to make him consider getting a dog of his own; he'd always loved dogs.

Encouraging Coffee to jump over the driver's seat and down onto the hot earth, Dave swiped at the flies and loosened his grip on the lead, letting Coffee wander until it became tight and pulled her back slightly.

He got out a couple of bottles of water and plugged in the twelve-volt kettle to make himself another hot drink for the road and also poured some water into a bowl for the dog.

From the other vehicles, kids were running around—their parents letting them expend as much energy as possible in the hope that they'd fall asleep when they were back in the car. High-pitched squeals came from one of the kids as she fell over on the stony red dirt and the mother came running to pick her up. The child opened her mouth to howl and Dave winced, remembering how painful gravel rash could be.

'It's okay,' Dave heard the mother say, as she brushed gravel off the child's clothes and knees. 'You're fine.'

He leaned his hip against the side of the troopy, waiting for the kettle to boil.

'Coffeeeee.' Another squeal, this time from a different car that was parked behind a tree.

Dave looked for the lead and saw Coffee had walked under the troopy to the other side and was now sitting next to the tyre in the sun. Her eyes were closed in blissful warmth.

His eyes flicked to the young child who was running across the parking lot towards the dog.

'Coffeeeee! Look, Mummy, it's Coffee. We thought you were lost,' the little boy told the dog as he squatted down in front of her and put his arms around Coffee's neck. The dog's ears flicked and she moved from lying down to sitting up in seconds, then put her paw on the boy's knee and her nose to his.

'Hello, there,' Dave said. 'I'm Dave. What's your name?'

The little blue-eyed boy, whose face was ringed with red curls, stared up at him. 'Where did you find Coffee?' he asked.

'You know this dog?' Dave asked, moving closer. He squatted down and examined the child's face. One of Dave's skills, Spencer had told him a few years back, was his ability to be able to see family resemblances when no one else could.

This kid was a dead ringer for Leo.

So many pieces of the puzzle fell into place. Leo had a secret family. A love child. A woman who he loved enough to up-end his life for. But how had he managed this when he hardly ever left the farm?

From the partially hidden HiLux, a woman now came running, her long blonde hair flowing. She looked so gentle and soft and unconventional compared to the uptight and fashionable Jill.

'Charlie, you can't run away from me, I've told you before.' The woman pulled up quickly when she saw Dave, her child and the dog all squatting in the dirt.

Indecision crossed her face, until Dave saw her draw herself upright and smile. 'Sorry that Charlie is bothering you and your dog,' she said. 'He's a little over-excited after being cooped up in the car for so long.'

Dave stood up and handed the lead to Charlie. 'Would you like to take her for a walk, Charlie? Maybe over to your car and back again? You'll need to hold on tight so she doesn't run off, and stay away from the highway, okay?'

'I'm going to give her one of her treats,' Charlie said, his face alight. 'She loves mince balls.'

'Does she? Well, she's one lucky dog if you've got any of them with you.' Dave eyed the woman while he spoke.

She looked like she was about to take off at any moment. 'Off you go now, Charlie. Bring her back once you've given her the treat.'

Dave and the woman watched Charlie skip over the dirt, holding Coffee's lead. Once the boy was out of earshot, Dave turned to her. 'I'm Detective Dave Burrows,' he told her and watched her face turn white. 'I'm investigating the murder of Leo Perry. I believe you might know him?'

'I'm sorry, I don't know what you're talking about. I've never heard that name in my life.'

'Really? Could you tell me then how Charlie knows Coffee's name? This dog was owned by Leo and was found running down the highway last night. How did you come to lose her?'

Flapping her hand, the woman gave a weak laugh. 'Charlie had a dog, ages ago, called Coffee, but he died. Charlie still misses him. You'll have to ignore him. He calls every dog by that name now.'

'What's your name?' Dave asked.

Caution crossed her face. 'Pardon,' she said. 'I don't have to answer questions from a stranger on the side of the road. I need to get going. You can come and get your dog and leave us alone.' The woman, who was wearing a flowing skirt and fitted top, turned on her thongs and started to walk away.

'Leo was murdered. I suspect the person who killed him was a travelling partner. Perhaps I need to arrest you on suspicion of murder?'

Spencer had always talked about a cop's spider senses and Dave had that feeling now. The falter in her step was enough for him to know. His feet were moving before he could stop himself. His large fingers wrapped around her upper arm, and he swung her around to face him.

She let out a loud shriek. 'Get away from me! Don't touch me. I don't know you . . . Help!'

The people from the other car, parked nearby, stood up from their chairs. The mother grabbed the kids and hustled them into the car, while the man came towards Dave and the woman.

'Ah, what's going on here?' he asked. 'Can I help? Mate, you shouldn't be bothering her.'

'I'm Detective Dave Burrows,' Dave flashed his ID. 'This lady and I need to have a chat. If you're worried, I'll give you a number to call to verify that I am in fact a police officer.' He glared at the man who took a couple of steps back.

'I'll leave you to it,' the man said, before quickly climbing into the car with the rest of his family and leaving.

A fleeting thought about how easy it would be to kidnap a woman on her own out here came to Dave and he then refocused.

Dave still had hold of the woman and she was trying to extract herself from his grip. 'Stop it,' he told her. 'You'll upset your kid and you need to talk to me.' Frowning, his next words were harsh. 'Why won't you admit you were with Leo? Did you kill him?'

She spluttered. '*What?* I *loved* him.' The words were out of her mouth before she could stop them. 'Oh no,' she clamped her hand over her mouth, tears filling her eyes. 'I still love him,' she whispered.

Dave nodded. 'Are you Sophie from Hunter Rock?' he asked gently.

CHAPTER 27

The woman's eyes widened in genuine shock and she shook her head. 'No,' she muttered, not meeting his eyes. 'I don't know who you're talking about.'

'Really? I thought we were passed that now you've told me you love Leo. Come on,' Dave said, pulling her with him. He opened the passenger's door and indicated for her to get in. 'Coffee? Water?' he asked.

She shook her head.

'Well, Sophie, you and I have a lot to talk about. And I need the truth, because, on the evidence, I could arrest you for Leo's murder. I don't believe you killed him, but you're going to need to tell me who did.'

'I don't know,' she whispered. 'I don't know.' Her shoulders started to heave and fat tears ran down her cheeks. 'I took Charlie to the toilet and when we came back Leo was against the tree. He . . . he, ah, looked like he was sleeping.

But that was weird; he wouldn't have gone to sleep; there was too much noise and too many people around.

'Then I saw the blood. It was fresh and still dripping. God, I was so scared.' She cast around as if someone was going to come out of the bush and do the same thing to her. 'I didn't know what to do, and then I realised that now he was dead someone would identify him as Leo. No one could ever know about me and Charlie, so I left. The keys were in the ute, so we just got in and raced away before anyone saw us or realised that Leo was . . . dead.' Her voice faltered on the last word, while her hands ran up and down her upper arms. Moving, shifting, trying to rub the shock and pain away.

'Where did you go?' Dave asked, writing notes down.

'Back to where we'd been camped. Leo didn't want to stay in town because he was worried about being seen. And neither of us thought the show was a good idea, but Charlie had seen the posters and was desperate to go. He'd never seen fireworks or the dodgem cars before. I'd never had the money to take him, so Leo said we should go, just for a tiny bit.' Sophie started to cry again. 'And that was what happened.'

'When did you lose Coffee?'

'Oh god, that was just awful. Charlie and I, we got back to the camping area where we'd left her guarding our camping gear. A deterrent rather than ferocious. And we were never going to be long. The chain was just lying in the dust. She's the only reason I didn't leave straight-away. We tried to find her. Walked all through the bush and out on the open plains calling for her, but it was like she'd disappeared.

'And this morning, we were just about out of food, so I had to make a decision about what I was going to do. There wasn't any point in going back to Hunter Rock. We only lived there because it was easy for Leo to come over and see us. And now I wouldn't have the money Leo had been giving me to live on . . .'

Dave nodded. 'So where were you going?'

Sophie hoisted her shoulders in a shrug. 'I didn't really know. Away from Meekatharra. I haven't got any family, so I guess I was just going to drive until I found somewhere to stay. See if I could get work in a roadhouse or something. I asked a couple of stops back, but no one's hiring because it's summer and there's no work.' Her voice was despairing. 'And, of course, there's Charlie. Leo looked after us and now he's gone. I don't know what we're going to do.' This time her weeping was loud and ugly and full of grief.

Dave put a hand on her shoulder then passed her the tissue box. 'Stay here,' he told her.

Coffee was having a good time, thanks to Charlie, when Dave arrived at the HiLux. The boy had unpacked one of the folding chairs and Coffee had curled up, sleeping on the seat.

'I've given her three mince balls. Dad says she can only have that many at a time otherwise it upsets her tummy and she *farts*!' He was gleeful, using a word that he knew made adults look twice but wasn't bad enough to get him into too much trouble.

'Raw meat will do that to a dog,' Dave agreed. 'Do you like Coffee?'

'I love her. Dad said I could have her if anything ever happened to him.'

Pursing his lips at the words, Dave sat down cross-legged on the ground. 'Did your dad think something was going to happen to him?'

Charlie's eyes were wide pools of blue when he looked over at Dave, his fingers constantly stroking Coffee's fur and ears. 'Did something happen to Daddy?'

Dave suddenly felt out of his depth. 'I tell you what, how about you and I pack your car up and we'll get Mummy to drive it? You can come with Coffee and me in my troopy. I'm a police officer so I've got lots of sirens I can use, if you want to hear them?'

Charlie's eyes seemed to grow even wider. 'Really?' he asked, his tone sounding like he had entered a church. 'Oh coooool!' He shot up and Coffee jumped at his sudden action, leaping from the chair, her tail wagging and mouth open, smiling.

Dave grabbed the lead and wrapped it around the bull bar of the ute, while he helped Charlie fold up the deck chairs and the handful of biscuits Sophie had put on the table.

'Where do you live, Charlie?' Dave asked as they worked together.

'In Hunter Rock. Across the road from Mr Sam. He's nice. I like it when he tells me stories about the trains.'

'Do you go to school?'

He shook his head. 'I go to kindy. With Miss Smales.'

'Do you have to catch the bus to do that?'

'Miss Smales comes to my house,' he told Dave. 'We do all the kindy work together.'

Dave regarded the little boy. His vocabulary for such a young kid was expansive and he didn't seem to have any fear of other people. Coffee seemed to be calming for him. Dave wondered if the boy was autistic. His cousin's child had been similar. Overly bright, great vocab and no fear.

Noah was nothing like this little boy. Neither was Charlotte. Dave rubbed his chin as he thought.

'What are you doing?' Sophie walked over, looking at Dave as if she wanted him to disappear.

'Okay, here's what we're going to do. Sophie, you need to give a formal statement, so you're going to come back to Perth with me. Then we're going to work out how we can help you and this ripper of a kid, Charlie. He's such a great conversationalist, isn't he?'

Sophie smiled. 'He didn't talk until he was two and a half, and he hasn't stopped since.' She put a hand on Charlie's head and he looked at her adoringly. 'It's been Charlie and me by ourselves for so long, hasn't it, mate? Leo would come as often as he could, but farming and his other life, well, I knew I'd see him at least twice a month. Anything else was a bonus.

'When Charlie was diagnosed with autism, Leo wanted to spend more time with us. He tried. Sometimes it worked, sometimes it didn't.'

Dave nodded. 'Okay. I'm going to take Charlie with me, is that okay? He can have Coffee with him that way. You can either go in front or behind.'

'I'll go in front,' Sophie said. She got into the driver's seat while Dave whistled to Coffee. 'Be careful with Charlie,' she said. 'He's all I have of Leo now. He's all I ever had of Leo.' Her face seemed to crumple and, slamming the door shut, she started the engine and drove out of the parking lot.

'Right-oh, young man, let's follow your mum.' Dave noted the numberplate and sent a message to Karly, asking her to check who it was registered to. Not that he needed to, Dave had just about filled in all the gaps.

There was only the question now of who killed Leo, because it wasn't Sophie.

~

The streetlights had just been switched on when Dave and Sophie pulled up in the stock squad car park.

The office door was still open and Lorri's car was parked next to the shed. Dave shut the gates so both Charlie and Coffee would be able to roam the compound to their hearts' content. He looked across at the little boy, who had fallen asleep two hours into the trip. His ginger eyelashes touched his cheeks as he slept, and his skin looked so soft and babylike. Not only was his colouring Leo's, the shape of his chin and the high cheekbones had been a gift from his father as well.

Once again, Dave thought about Noah and Charlotte. He wondered how they would react once they found out they had a half-brother.

He opened the passenger's door and Coffee jumped out from where she'd been sleeping at Charlie's feet, then reached out to gently touch the boy.

'Wake up, buddy,' Dave said.

Charlie opened his eyes and saw Dave. Confusion crossed his face, then fear.

'Mummy?' he whispered. 'Mummy?' Much louder this time. He screamed so loudly, Dave took a step back in surprise.

'It's okay,' Dave said, but before he'd finished the words, Coffee came running and jumped into the seat next to Charlie. She sat on his lap and put her chin on Charlie's shoulder, giving a loud sigh.

Charlie's arms went around the dog and he hiccupped into her coat. 'Mummy,' he whimpered again, shying away from Dave.

Sophie was getting out of the HiLux and Dave waved her over quickly. 'Sorry, I upset Charlie when I tried to wake him up.'

'Don't try to wake him. Not worth it.' She watched Charlie and Coffee for a second. 'He'll be okay, just let them both be until he's ready to move.'

'Did Leo ever leave Coffee with you? She almost looks like she's a therapy dog.'

'I used to wish he would, but there wasn't a way to do that. It would've seemed strange if he went back to the farm without Coffee, but that dog is the best thing that happened to Charlie. They love each other in a way that only the two of them understand.'

'Does Charlie eat pizza?' He glanced over to the office as Lorri came out.

'Only ham and pineapple. He's hard to feed. Sensory issues.'

Dave wasn't sure what that meant but made a mental note to do some research on autism. 'Okay. We'll order some and book you both into a motel. But first we need your statement. Lorri is going to watch Charlie until he needs you, okay?'

Sophie nodded and took a breath. She wiped her hands on her skirt. 'Sorry, Leo,' she whispered, glancing at Charlie. 'I know this isn't what you wanted.'

Dave escorted her into the office and found the room where Lorri had set up a recording device and left two glasses of water.

His phone call to her earlier had sent her to the shops to find some toys and biscuits of the same brand that Dave had noted when he'd helped Charlie and Sophie pack up.

While his fingers itched to call Bob, to tell him what had happened, but there hadn't been a text from Betty to say his partner was out of surgery yet, and Dave had no idea what time it had been booked for. He didn't know if Bob was overdue or not.

'Okay, Sophie, I need you to state your full name for the tape,' he told her after he'd introduced himself.

'Ah, Sophie Jane Lancer,' she said.

'And your date of birth?'

She recited that and yawned, before wiping her hands on her skirt again.

'Let's start with how you met Leo?'

A smile spread across her face. 'So unexpected,' she said. 'I'd broken down on the side of the road. Just outside of Yorkenup. He stopped to help and then we got talking. He couldn't get my car going, so I went back with him to his farm and he lent me one of the old utes he had there.'

'Where were you living at this stage?'

'Funnily enough, I had moved to Yorkenup to work at the school. They'd been advertising for a receptionist and I had experience from when I'd worked in Perth. Leo came into town a couple of times, and popped in to say hi and see if I needed anything. He took my car to one of his mates to fix.'

'What type of car?'

'HiLux dual cab.'

Chris wouldn't have even realised it wasn't Leo's car, Dave thought. How convenient!

'The school didn't work out so I applied for a job at a machinery dealership in Northton and moved over there. Anyway, about four weeks after I had done that, he turned up with a bottle of champagne and a basket of food and took me up to a lookout just on the outskirts of Northton.

We spent hours up there, lying under the stars, talking and planning for the future.'

'Did you know he had a family?'

'Not then. About another month later, I had gone to Yorkenup to surprise him and I saw him walking down the street with a woman who was pushing a pram and clearly pregnant.' She swallowed hard. 'I left and refused to answer his phone calls, but about a week later he turned up at the office and told me he wouldn't leave until we'd talked. He told me the baby Jill was carrying wasn't his, he wasn't sure whose it was, but Leo knew it wasn't his. I believed him, and then he started making plans for us to be together.

'Leo was clever,' her voice fell into a dreamy recollection. 'And he came up with a plan to get some money. Everything was so tightly held on the farm, so he had to be very careful. I took some letterheads from work and we mocked up invoices that his dad approved.' She shrugged. 'Easy enough to do, when you have access to what you need.

'The trouble was I fell pregnant, too. When Charlie was born, it didn't take long for us to realise he was different, but it takes time and money to find out what's wrong, so for a little while we were treating the symptoms, rather than knowing what was wrong, even though the doctor had told me he was "at high risk of having autism". So, Charlie needed extra help, and Leo had to stay on the farm longer to be able to organise the money. That's why I shifted over to Hunter Rock. It's quiet and not a lot of people go there.'

Dave tapped his fingers, thinking of other questions to ask. 'Why Meekatharra?'

Sophie smiled. 'It was different. We didn't intend on staying there. We had a job lined up in Kununurra with accommodation and special help for Charlie. We couldn't wait to start a new life together.'

'Sophie, did you kill Leo Perry?'

She looked startled for a second then the word shot from her with force. 'No.'

'Do you know who did?'

'No.'

CHAPTER 28

'You want to come for a drive with me?' Dave's opening words to Shannon were brisk.

'Sure,' she said on the speaker phone, 'where are we going?'

'We're going to arrest Leo's murderer.'

Silence filled the car and Dave continued to drive away from the motel he had just dropped Sophie and Charlie at. He'd filled the fridge with as much food as he could and given them Lorri's phone number along with a bag of dog food.

'I'll be back as soon as I can,' Dave had told them both. 'And Charlie? Can you look after Coffee for me?'

'Yeah,' the boy had said, smiling. 'I love Coffee!'

Sophie had looked exhausted when he'd closed the door, leaving them to collapse with their grief. Tonight, Sophie would be telling Charlie that his dad wasn't coming home.

Another child asking where their daddy was.

'You know who the murderer is?'

'No, but I'm pretty sure they live in Yorkenup. Bob said he thought all the answers were there, and from everything Sophie has told me, I'm sure he's right.'

'I'll be waiting out the front,' Shannon told him.

He grinned. This would be fun. Although he still hadn't heard from Betty and that worried him.

Dave pulled into the state building and parked, waiting for Shannon to open the door and climb in. He didn't have to wait long.

'Hey,' she said.

He smiled and leaned over to kiss her. 'You, Shannon, are a sight for sore eyes.'

'Oh, I do like that welcome,' she told him, running her fingers down his cheek. 'You're looking good, too, Burrows.' She slammed the door and pulled on her seatbelt. 'Now, I need to be back here by tomorrow afternoon, so try not to find another case that needs investigating before you drop me off, all right?'

'I'll see what I can do.' He nodded to a file sitting on the dash. 'I've got some work for you.'

'Here I was thinking it was a social trip.'

'Once we've got the work out of the way it can be.' Dave gave her a slow smile. 'We can take all the time in the world to get back to Perth if you like.'

She swatted him. 'Great idea when I just told you I need to be back tomorrow afternoon. Let's make social plans for the weekend. What's in the file?'

'Open it and see.'

She pulled out a piece of paper that had a list of numbers, dates and times on it. 'Telephone numbers?' she asked.

Dave nodded. 'I got Leo's mobile from the evidence box when I got back to HQ. It's not his normal phone. There's only one name in the contact list and that's Sophie. My guess is he chucked his other phone.

'The outgoing calls have been cleared as have the incoming ones, so I requested the call charge register in and out. These are the numbers. I haven't had a chance to go through them properly, which is where you come in. Leo disappeared on the day the fire came through. Are there any phone calls out during that day? More towards the afternoon I believe.'

Shannon ran her finger down the list then nodded. She read out a number.

'That's Sophie's number,' Dave said. 'Can you mark that with the pink highlighter I've brought. Just run through and mark all of hers so we can cross them off the list. She's not the killer.'

Shannon nodded and did as she was asked.

'Okay, then the day he was shown on CCTV withdrawing money for Sophie and Charlie. What calls were made then?'

The car was bumping over the road, so Shannon had to turn one of the pages over and use it as a ruler. 'None. The next call was at nine o'clock in the morning, two days later, and it lasted for three minutes and twenty seconds.'

'Can you mark that with a blue highlighter?'

Again, Shannon did as she was asked, then waited expectantly.

'Are there any more of those numbers?'

'Ummm . . .' Shannon drew the word out as she looked for the last three digits from that phone number. 'No, just that one call.'

'What about the day of the show?' He told her the date.

'There are three calls that day, all to different numbers.'

Dave frowned. 'That many calls?'

'Yeah.' She recited them and Dave tapped his finger to his mouth.

'That's more than I expected. What were the times and duration?'

'First one in the morning at seven thirty for thirty seconds, second one at nine thirty for three seconds—they're from the same number—and the last one at five thirty that night. That one lasted for two minutes.' She flipped back a page. 'There's also a thirty-second call on the evening beforehand.'

'Yeah . . .' Dave's voice trailed off and he drove, concentrating, not on the road but on the information Shannon had given him. 'It's that last one,' he finally said more confidently than he felt. 'The fireworks started at seven thirty and only went for fifteen minutes. So whoever he spoke to then, I'm sure that person is the killer. Does that number match any of the others on there?'

'No, definitely not.'

'What's the bet it's a burner phone?'

Shannon held up her hands. 'I'll have to rely on your expertise to know that, Dave,' she said, but he could hear the excitement in her voice and knew she was as invested as he was.

He looked over at her. 'We're going to nail this prick,' he said with a grin and reached out to take her hand.

The road into Yorkenup was as quiet as ever. Shannon stared out of the window, taking in the old buildings and leaning verandahs. 'It's so quaint.'

'It's nice, isn't it? Not that I'd want to live here, but it's great for a visit.'

He pulled up next to the pub and switched off the engine.

Shannon frowned. 'I'm not Bob, Dave,' she told him. 'I don't want a drink before we go to work.'

'Don't worry, I just want to check something here.'

They both got out and Dave strode up the pub steps. The raucous laughter from inside hit them both, and Dave felt Shannon fall in behind him. He waved to a couple of familiar faces then made his way to the RSL room.

Standing in front of the display cabinet, Dave started to talk. 'Karly, the young constable up in Meekatharra, brought this to my attention. She told me that you think the pill that killed Leo was from a service pistol.'

Shannon nodded. 'I do.'

'And Ballistics also said how rare those guns are.'

'They really are.'

'So, if we look at these blokes here—Copple, Hunter, Mason, Mayfield and Pearce—they're all locals and I'm guessing they still have family in the area.' He broke off as the publican came in through the door.

'G'day, Dave. How are you getting on?' he asked, coming to stand next to them. 'Are you mixing business with pleasure?'

Dave grinned. 'Shannon is our forensic pathologist. She's here to give me a hand. Actually, I'm glad you're here. What can you tell us about these men?'

'Well, they're all local legends. As you can see from the medals in the cabinet, they were decorated officers when they came back from the war. I like a bit of memorabilia here, my dad was in the war, too, so honouring these blokes is important to me. This guy, Copple, he doesn't have any family here anymore, but his uniform was donated to the museum in Perth when he died. Hunter, his family is here.'

'And who are his family?'

'A daughter, a nurse and the other teacher. The grand-daughter works here for me at times. Jacinta.'

Realisation spread across Dave's face. 'Yes, I remember her,' he said dryly. He caught the look Shannon gave him, but ignored it as he was still focusing on the publican.

'Mason and Mayfield, their families are here as well, a son and daughter each. One's a shire councillor and the other runs the ambulance service in town.'

'And Pearce?' Dave asked.

'Oh, well, you've met his descendant. Andrew Pearce, farmer on the east side. Mates with Leo.'

'Married to Nicola,' Dave said, nodding. 'Yes, I know him. I noticed the similarities between Andrew and his grandfather when I was here last.'

'He's got a lot of memorabilia. I get a little annoyed that he won't bring it in so we can display it. Uniforms and the trunks the boys used to use. There's so much history there and I can't for the life of me see the point in keeping everything locked up where no one else can see it, can you?'

Dave shook his head. 'I agree with you. It would be great to get it out here on display.'

'Well, I'd better get back out the front.'

'Have Andrew and Nicola come in tonight?'

'No, my guess is they're with Jill and the little ones. I see Andrew's ute there a lot and he's the one who can take time off, working for himself and all. Easier for him than Leo's other mates.' The man hesitated. 'Is there any news?'

Dave nodded. 'Yes, we believe that Leo was murdered.'

The man's face dropped. 'You can't be serious?'

'Unfortunately, I am.'

⌒

'Okay, I need more to get a search warrant on Andrew's house,' Dave said. 'How am I going to get that?'

'You're not,' Shannon told him briskly. 'Everything you've got is circumstantial. You'll have to go and talk to him, see if you can get a confession.'

'He's got World War Two gear in his house. What's the bet that he's used his grandfather's pistol to shoot his mate? Karly was going to do a register search, but I haven't heard the outcome. I'm sure I don't need to now.'

'Why?' Shannon replied. 'Why would he do that? I'm not seeing a motive here.'

A small smile crossed Dave's face. 'I'll tell you, but you have to be prepared to hang on for the ride. I'm probably going to cross a few boundaries, which won't make the hierarchy happy. You okay with that?' He didn't give Shannon time to answer, just walked to the car and got in, waiting for her to do the same.

Shannon didn't say anything on the way to Andrew's farm. They'd driven past the motel and found Jill's room, and Jan and Stephen's room, in darkness.

Dave had smiled. 'Let's go,' he said.

When he drove into the Pearces' driveway, he was glad to see the lights still on. The element of surprise worked well, but he wanted Andrew focused.

'Here's my phone,' he said to Shannon. 'Can you program those two numbers in for me?'

Shannon took his phone and did as he asked, then slipped the pages in her pocket. 'Back-up,' she said.

'Good idea.'

Dave drew the troopy to a halt next to the fence surrounding the house and they both got out.

'Just follow my lead, okay? I might ask you for details about the gun. You're okay with that?'

'Not the ballistics side of things!' Shannon sounded panicked. 'Jesus, Dave, a little notice here would have been good.'

'I've got the utmost faith in you.' He gave a charming smile and Shannon hit his arm.

Knocking loudly, they waited. A round of high yapping started. Two dogs, Dave surmised. Jack Russells.

Andrew's face formed a surprised raised-eyebrow look when he saw Dave at the door. 'Dave,' he said. 'You've got news?'

He nodded. 'Can we come in? This is Shannon, our forensic pathologist.'

Andrew's eyebrows seemed to go even higher. But he held the door open and let them through. 'Sorry, Nicola is out. She's taken the kids to Perth for a theatre show. Jill's as well, to give her a bit of breathing space. Not due home until tomorrow.'

'That's okay, we weren't really needing to see her.'

'Come through into the lounge. I've got the air-conditioner on.'

They took the seats he offered to them. When Andrew sat, he clasped his hands in front of his knees and waited.

'Andrew, Shannon here removed the bullet that killed Leo from his skull. We've traced it back to an old service revolver. Do you own anything like that?'

'What? No. I—' He looked around. 'Why would I have a handgun from the war?'

Dave leaned back and crossed his ankle over his knee. 'Right, this is how I see it, Andrew. You know we're going to find this gun and you know we'll be able to tell that the gun has been recently fired. So, you can either be part of the problem or part of the solution. Which way would you like it?'

Andrew shot to his feet. 'What gives you the right to walk into my house and speak to me like I'm a murderer?'

'Are you?'

'*What?*'

'When did you speak to Leo Perry last?'

'Before he went missing. I can't tell you the exact date or time.'

'Are you certain?'

'Of course I'm sure. I can't talk to someone who's missing, can I?'

'Do you own a mobile?'

'Doesn't everyone?'

'What's your number?'

'I don't have to give it to you.'

'What's your number?' Dave repeated.

Andrew crossed his arms.

Dave took out his mobile and pressed a couple of buttons. He waited for what seemed like an age. Just as he thought he'd made a mistake, a chirping came from the room next door. Nodding at Shannon, he let her go through to retrieve the phone.

'Have you got two phones, Andrew?'

'No.'

Dave pressed another button. This time a phone sitting on a nearby coffee table rang.

'Interesting, two phones. And who are your contacts in this one?' Dave reached to pick the second phone up but Andrew was quicker.

'None of your fucking business,' he said as he snatched it up and put it in his pocket.

'Putting it there isn't going to make any difference, Andrew. I can get a warrant for the phone.'

'Dave!' Shannon's voice made him take his eyes off Andrew and turn.

First he saw the gun. Stupidly, he wanted to say, *That's the gun I'm looking for*, but then he registered it was pointing at Shannon's head.

And all too late, he realised Jill was there, and she was the one holding the gun.

CHAPTER 29

Ice dripped through Dave's veins as he took in Shannon's face.

'Fuck,' he whispered. He had never even considered that someone else might be in the house. What a stupid, rookie mistake. He thought about the dogs barking and realised they hadn't been at the door. They must have been with Jill when she'd hidden after the knock at the door.

Slowly he reached for his gun.

'Oh, I wouldn't,' Jill said. 'I've got this covered.'

Dave couldn't think. He had to keep Jill talking, but not one question came to him. All he could see in front of him was an image of Shannon on the floor, bleeding from her beautiful face, and then her faced morphed into Bob's. He was frozen.

Not again, not again, not again. The words kept reverberating around his head.

'Dave!' Shannon screamed at him and he blinked.

'Jill,' he stuttered. 'Ah, maybe it wasn't Andrew who killed Leo after all,' he said. 'Was it you?'

'You reckon Andrew would have the stomach for that?' There was scorn in her tone.

Dave turned to look at Andrew, who looked as frightened as Dave felt.

Jesus, he thought. *How dangerous is she?* The answer came quickly: *Incredibly.* She'd kept her act up very well over the course of the investigation.

Dave reassessed. 'Why did you need to kill Leo?' he asked. 'He was disappearing. Leaving you. He wasn't going to cause you any more trouble. Why couldn't you just let him go?'

'You really think that? How do you reckon I was going to live? Stupid prick, if he'd managed to kill himself in the fire, things would have been much easier. There would have been a body, and insurance money. I would have been fine. But he had to run off with that little floozy and weird child of theirs, and leave me here to pick up the pieces. Oh no, he wasn't going to get away with that. He owed me.'

Dave turned to Andrew. 'Leo rang you, didn't he? Told you where he was.'

'Yeah,' Andrew said, looking down. 'He wanted me to get another ute to him. Change it over from the one he'd been driving in case anyone had seen him the day of the fire. Leo trusted me. We'd been mates for ages.'

'More fool him,' Dave said, before he could stop the words coming out. Shit! He didn't need to upset them any further, especially while Jill was still holding a gun near Shannon.

'Don't tell him anything more,' Jill said. 'We have to get out of here! Now.'

'It's finished, Jill,' Andrew said. 'We're not getting away from here. What are you going to do, kill two police officers and get two life sentences? Let's just cut our losses. Sweetheart, let's tell him everything and we can still be together after all of this is over.'

'What? God, sometimes I think you're more ridiculous than Leo. This won't ever be over. Jan and Stephen will see to that.'

Dave leaned forward to Andrew. 'Noah's your son, isn't he? This is how all of this started?'

'Yeah, and the baby Jill lost before she and Leo got married—that was mine, too. We knew each other long before Jill met Leo.'

Shannon drew in a breath and Dave's eyes cut to her, then back to Andrew willing him to go on.

'I can see how Noah looks like you, Andrew,' Dave said.

Neither of them answered.

'But Charlotte is Leo's. Gee, that must have hurt, knowing that she'd been shagging your mate.'

Andrew pressed his lips together.

'Tell me,' Dave added, his tone conversational, 'did you both know about Sophie?'

Jill snorted. 'The boys told you everything you needed to know about Leo. He wore his heart on his sleeve. All of a sudden he was happy all the time. Whistling again, a spring in his step. Didn't take too long to work out what was going on, even without him saying anything.

'I followed him one afternoon. He thought I was in Perth but that time I just left the kids up there with Mum and Dad and came home early. I stopped on the road and waited until he was leaving the farm. He was turning in the other direction so he never saw me. It's pretty easy to follow someone when they're not watching for a tail.' Jill's voice lowered. 'And there she was. Such a pretty little thing. All glowing and rainbows. A smile that would light up his world. As soon as I saw her, I knew Leo was in love. I'd already suspected that anyway. She was the opposite to me in every way. And Leo didn't love me. He hadn't for a long time.'

The gun dipped slightly and Shannon took her chance. She moved quickly and elbowed Jill in the ribs, winding her. It fell to the floor and let off a shot with the impact.

Andrew screamed, covering his head and dropping onto his stomach.

'Shit, is he shot?' Dave yelled. 'Shannon, are you okay?'

Jill tried to follow the gun, but Shannon kicked her legs out from under her, then landed on top, yanking Jill's hands behind her back, waiting for Dave to come and help her.

Dave, knowing Jill was contained, lurched forward, grabbing Andrew and pulling his hands together quickly, snapping on the cuffs.

From his shorts he brought out a cable tie and moved to wrap it around Jill's wrists.

'So, you had to kill Leo to get him out of the way,' Dave puffed as he hoisted Jill to her feet and looked at her. 'What were you going to do with Nicola?'

Neither of them answered.

Dave was silent for a minute, not sure why there was a heavy feeling in his stomach. Something was wrong.

'Jesus, I'll have to ring Red and get them onto Nicola's rego, her car. Issue a "Be On the Look Out", make sure she's safe. They've probably cut the brake-line or something.'

EPILOGUE

Dave stood back and watched Charlie interact with Charlotte and Noah in the compound of the Rural Crime Squad. Sophie was standing a little way away, her arms folded. Next to her were Jan and Stephen.

None of them was speaking, only watching the children play.

Jan had her hand over her heart, tapping at her chest as if she was reminding herself that, even though Leo was gone, there were pieces of him left behind.

Lorri and Bob stood alongside Dave.

'Jeez, you did well, son,' Bob said. His arm was in a sling. Only a week out from surgery, the doc was happy with his progress, but the long-term outlook hadn't been good. The operation had taken longer than anticipated after they'd found secondary cancer in other parts of his body from other scans. Bob had known this before he'd gone into surgery, but hadn't told Dave. The toll the operation and news had taken on Bob was obvious to those who loved him. His face a horrible yellowy colour and bags underneath his eyes.

'There's no way I would have made two plus two equal four like you have. Good thing you've got that ability to see family resemblances. I mean, I can see them now that they're all lined up together, but by themselves? I wouldn't have had a hope in hell.'

'And thank god you worked out that Nicola was in danger, Dave,' Lorri said. 'She would have been killed driving home the next day and it would have looked like an accident.'

'Shannon helped with some of that,' Dave said. 'I was lucky she was there.'

'I can't believe you took her with you, son,' Bob said. 'She's not authorised. It's a wonder you haven't been given a stern talking to.'

Dave looked at his feet, knowing he'd pushed the boundaries. 'I know. But she was involved because she'd done the autopsy.'

Bob snorted. 'That won't wash with the top dogs.'

Shrugging, Dave looked up as a movement caught his eye. 'She loved being out in the field.'

Stephen walked over and held out his hand to Dave. 'We can't thank you enough,' he said.

'No thanks needed,' Dave replied. 'It's nice to see you able to enjoy each other's company.'

'We won't abandon any of these children. All three of them are our link back to Leo. And that is extremely precious.'

Dave smiled. An arrest is easy when the suspect spills the beans on everyone involved. Once Andrew had been transported to the police station and was under caution, he'd told them the rest of the story.

When the CCTV footage had come to light, Jill had flipped. Suddenly her grand plan of collecting the life insurance money had crumpled. She needed a body.

When Leo had rung to ask Andrew to help him with another vehicle, Jill and Andrew had been together and she'd left immediately to drive to Meekatharra.

'She's like a stalking cat,' Andrew said. 'She's happy to sit and wait until an opportunity comes up and it did.'

The gate slid open and an unmarked car drove in.

'Who's this?' Dave asked.

'Ah, didn't I tell you?' Bob replied. 'The divisional super-intendent wants a yarn with you.'

Dave's gaze slid from the car to Bob and back again. 'Does he?' Dave replied. 'And what if I don't want to talk to him?' He wasn't in the mood for a lecture about what procedures he hadn't followed.

'Don't be a dick, son. Just go and speak to the man.'

Dave turned to face his partner as another thought dropped in. 'You're not coming back, are you?' Dave said to Bob. The colour drained from his face. 'Tell me that's not true.'

'Who knows?' Bob said. 'I'd like to think so, but I can't be sure. Got no idea what the future is going to hold with the chemo I gotta have.' He stood tall and straight but Dave saw his jaw working.

'Bob?' Dave's voice cracked a little.

'For fuck's sake, son, go and speak to the boss, okay? We can do this shit later.' Bob turned away from Dave and walked over to the kids.

Lorri put her hand on Dave's arm, then she left, too.

'Burrows,' the divisional superintendent said, stepping out of the car.

'Sir.' Dave's gaze went to Bob, where he was squatting down talking to Noah and patting Coffee.

'Burrows, you've heard about Holden. Needs some time off.'

'Yes, sir.'

'So, the Rural Crime Squad needs someone to step into the commanding role. A person with knowledge and skills; someone who knows what's going on.'

Dave was barely listening.

Bob now had Charlotte riding a small bike and was wheeling her around with his good hand.

'The force is very pleased with all you've brought to the squad. Although you don't always follow rules.' He fixed Dave with a hard stare. 'Anyway, despite that, and due to your good work, we're going to promote you to Acting Detective Sergeant as Officer in Charge.'

Dave didn't want to take his eyes off Bob in case he disappeared, but he knew what he was being offered was a massive promotion and the end goal he'd been working towards. Although it was only due to his friend's ill health. He felt hollow.

'Thank you, sir. I'd be very honoured.' Dave held out his hand mechanically, and the two men shook.

'One thing I do know, Burrows, life is never boring when you're around.'

'I wish it was, sir.'

'We're going to be a couple of good men down. You up to the job?'

Dave thought back to his father and the words he'd thrown at him as he'd left Wind Valley Farm: '*The quicker I'm rid of you the better off we'll all be.*'

He thought of Spencer and he watched Bob. He owed this job to his mentors, the ones who had been a father figure to him, unlike his real dad.

'Yes, sir,' Dave answered, feeling a heavy hand on his shoulder. He looked around, thinking someone was behind him, but the space was empty.

And just then, somehow, Dave knew that Spencer had heard every word of the conversation.

ACKNOWLEDGEMENTS

I want to start off by thanking the readers. I've said it before and I'll say it again, without you, I don't have a career, so a huge thanks to all those who read these books, give them as presents, recommend them, and who love Detective Dave Burrows as much as I do. (No, you can't have him, I created him and I have first dibs!)

Thanks to the booksellers and librarians who recommend these books, I can't thank you enough. I appreciate your generosity.

All the Guns on Team Fleur, I love working with you all and thank you, thank you for all your efforts. Together we're stronger! Can't wait to get writing so we can do this all again!

Christa and Deonie for whipping a pretty raw piece of work into something readable in a matter of a few months. What legends you are.

Gaby, heartfelt thanks for everything including your friendship and care.

DB—what can I say? You're awesome. Thanks for your friendship.

Rochelle and Hayden, love you both.

My forever friend, Cal. And Aaron. You're both the best.

All the girls and the guys. You know who you are. Thanks for being there even when I'm in the midst of deadlines, a bit distracted and tired (or sick as I've been for so much of the last year!). Love you all.

Last but not least, Jack-the-kelpie. My friend, secret keeper, companion.

With love,

Fleur x